The Old Arbutus Tree

Leigh Matthews

For Tom, with love and gratitude for all those cups of tea, hours to write, and painstaking reading.

"The arbutus is an elegant and powerful tree, with its layered bark shimmering like copper and its vibrant leaves reaching out from craggy cliffs along the coast. The arbutus is a tree of storms, and of courage, and of the implacable spirit of endurance."
Kwantlen University

Endings

The thirty year old man was the first to die. His finely tailored suit, shiny city shoes and air of authority did him no favours with the gunman and Rose knew this as she turned away.

"Look, I'm a lawyer, I can help you, why don't you put down the gun and we can talk?" Robert MacGowan spread out his arms towards the ominous figure in the black balaclava who was currently pointing a rifle at the clerk of the West Shore Credit Union on Main Street. The gunman turned towards him and Robert MacGowan, LLP, would no longer be defending any of Pitcher Creek's residents, rich or poor.

Rose closed her eyes as the baby's cries pierced the air. She slumped further down behind the desk. Then the real mayhem started.

Fifteen out of twenty people left the credit union alive later that day. Along with the luckless lawyer, the casualties included Cassidy Winlaw, a stay-at-home-mom waiting to discuss a loan extension to help her husband's ailing truck repair shop. She was hoping to call in a favour from her old boyfriend who was now, rather fortuitously, the manager at the union. Bill Tether was another local in the bank and the paper had, initially, reported that he had tried to shield Cassidy as the rifle swung towards the huddled customers caught in the ropes demarcating the waiting line. Afterwards, as the confusion subsided, the police determined that the bullet that killed Tether was also the one that nicked Cassidy's femoral artery. It was as her blood spread thickly across the spruce green linoleum tiles of the bank's main foyer that the local RCMP gathered outside assessing the situation.

McReedy was the fourth to die, blood forming an auburn stain on the breast of his yellow Hollywood Theatre uniform. The small cone of popcorn, his usual late lunch, had spilled across those same spruce green tiles and swelled grotesquely, fat with blood from Cassidy Winlaw.

Cassidy's little girl, Rebecca, was red-faced and exhausted from screaming, still strapped into her stroller when the police arrived. Small crumbs of sticky sweet popcorn were scattered over the blanket that had been tucked around her to keep out the last of the spring cold. The warm caramel aroma of McReedy's popcorn had made Rose's stomach growl involuntarily at the time, it had been a long drive, but the memories attached to that smell would stick with her now.

As the RCMP entered the Union they stepped cautiously over the fifth prone body, the small frame barely blocking the door. This last victim, not named as such in the town's paper, was the one everyone wanted to forget, particularly Rose.

Part One

CHAPTER ONE

Outside, the slow creep and scrape of the plough announced that the first real snowfall had finally arrived and, one by one, most of the hundred-and-five heads of sleeping Pitcher Creek high school students hunkered back down into comforters and blankets. In the early light the muffle of textile felt a strong enough barrier for the inevitable ire of their parents, ready with mittens, gumboots and the hand-me-down toques, keen to get the kids packaged up and off to school, regardless of inclement weather.

Rose was just shifting into wakefulness, initially overcome by the strange brilliance of light shining through her bedroom curtains. Another winter day, but this time masquerading for a brief moment as mid-summer. The chill morning air in the room brought Rose back to reality and she heard the plough heading up their street, carving a path through the latest, and heaviest inundation. It wouldn't take long for the grumbling machine to push aside the snow on their five house row, forming banks, like trench walls, ready to be used as battlements during the inevitable snowball fights on the way to school.

Through the thin wall of the adjoining bedroom Rose heard her sister, Sara, spring into action. As the older girl's footsteps pounded down the hallway Rose pulled the covers over her head and groaned. Sara flung open the door, leapt onto the bed and started banging her fists onto the form she assumed was her little sister underneath the thick blankets.

"Snow Day! Snow Day!"

"I know, let me sleep."

"C'mon, get up Rose, there's stuff to do. We can make a giant snowman and dress him in dad's clothes - he can have his pipe - and you have to help me make a bunch of snowballs ready to launch at that bloody Darren Tether." Sara's voice lingered over the profanity, wrapping her tongue around the strange sound. She had been trying out swear words all term, mostly just to annoy her mother but also to fill the spaces left in conversation, to punctuate the disappearance of her father who was away somewhere back in England. Sara was also hoping to push her mother into swearing herself, then she figured she'd have a free pass and could say whatever the hell she liked. Her current favourites were bloody and bugger, said in an alarmingly male middle-aged cockney accent which earned her a strange kind of respect amongst her classmates.

Rose had wondered if the adoption of her father's accent and vocabulary was also intended by Sara as a peculiar punishment for her mother, reminding Jane of the empty space at the dinner table and the uncharacteristic shouting that had preceded her husband's sudden departure. Although Sara could be cruel sometimes, Rose had decided that her older sister just wasn't capable of that kind of malice. Sara must also have failed to realise that her dad had taken his pipe and tobacco when he left. Rose had looked for the pipe in the drawer in her father's study, hoping to fold herself into the familiar warm musty smoke smell. When she saw that the pipe was gone, along with his manuscript, but that the engraved lighter had been left behind, she had sunk into the tattered old armchair and sobbed as silently as she could. Rose knew her mother wouldn't tell her why her father had left but she had given up thinking he would come back. Sara, it seemed, was steps ahead in letting him go, already gifting his shirts to hypothetical snowmen.

The pummelling carried on and Rose burrowed her head into her pillow; she pulled the duvet closer around her. "Sara, let me sleep, I'm tired... someone kept me up half the night talking about Darren Bloody Tether."

"What? What'd you say? That's not true!" Rose emerged properly from the duvet and saw a flush of red rising into her sister's neck and cheeks as she realised the meaning of the mumbling. Rose was sick of hearing Sara talking about this object of hate at school, especially now that the boy kept hanging around their place when his dad came to work on the garden for her mom.

Bill would show up in his pickup, with Darren riding alongside him in the front, elbow propped on the window, regardless of the weather. In his red checked shirt and muddy jeans, barely held up with a thick leather belt, he looked like a miniature version of Mr Tether. The boy never seemed to smile, just lurked around, his head bowed, sneaking glances at the girls from underneath his greasy unkempt hair. Days when Darren showed up with his father meant twice the anxiety for Rose and she had spent half the summer and now almost all of fall trying to avoid running into either of the gloomy duo.

A few days after Mr Tether first showed up to do the landscaping work, Rose's mother, Jane, had made a point of casually inviting the 'boys' onto the porch for lemonade. To have a chance to cool off during the late summer heat, she had said. After that, if Mr Tether was there alone and had stayed into the evening, Jane would offer him a beer, nonchalantly raiding the fridge on the back deck. Her mom barely drank and, when she did, it was always some cheap wine in a garishly labelled bottle. Rose eventually realised that the fridge was being restocked with Bill in mind and she didn't understand why her mom would want to keep the guy around for any longer than it took for him to dig out the old diseased apple tree, reinforce the back fence, or finish whatever task she'd set for that day.

After a while Rose's curiosity meant that she made sure to keep the window open in her room when she went to bed. Her mom and Bill would sit on the front porch just below and so she could eavesdrop on their conversation. She discovered that Mr Tether was very different with Jane than he was with Rose and Sara, and even with Darren. Instead of barely audible grunts and sighs he spoke more softly in a considered, almost lilting, voice. They talked about things that needed doing around the garden, and then, after a while, household tasks too, like fixing the loose panels in the bathroom and redoing the floor in her parents' bedroom. They talked about the people in Pitcher Creek, their school days, and old movies they liked; Rose heard her mom laugh for the first time in months.

Bill began to bring little things for Jane, at first it was just a cutting from his own garden to put in the front planter. Later he brought her a watering can in the shape of a pig, saying that he couldn't resist it and just thought it would make Jane smile. Rose hadn't really worried about the shift in the relationship until she saw that smile and felt the heavy silence afterward. Over the three months Bill had been coming to help out with the garden his visits had changed from once a week to almost every day. Some days he turned up with the same old tools in the truck, a packet of fertiliser or a new shrub but these were just excuses and Rose knew he wasn't really there to work.

When Darren came along for the ride he'd work with his dad for a while and then be dismissed to play with Sara and Rose. Usually, this meant that they should take their bikes across the field at the back of the house and head down to the tree house at the creek, or ride into town to see what the Hollywood Theatre was playing. Jane would absent-mindedly shove five dollars into Sara's hand and tell her to look after her sister, and not to go in the water. She didn't even glance at Rose as she headed back into the house to offer Bill some coffee.

Rose hated those days. She wished she could just stay home and read in her dad's study, curled up in his chair, surrounded by the papers and books he'd not bothered to pack up before leaving for England. It was all too obvious that her mom wanted to get her and Sara out of the way. She might be young but she was certainly not stupid and she wondered if Sara and Darren were making out in the tree house and in the back row at the theatre just because they knew their parents were doing something similar back at the house.

If only her dad would come home, Rose thought, then he'd get rid of Darren and Bill. He had been gone so long now though that Rose figured he must know about her mom and Bill and that it was this that was stopping her dad coming home. She tried not to hate her mom, especially as Jane had been so miserable when her dad had first left, but the way she was acting with Bill was pretty sickening.

Her dad had gone back to England in spring when Rose's grandma died and she knew he'd talked about staying on to get the house sold and catch up with friends he hadn't seen since his schooldays. That was in May though, and these last five months without him had been hard, even the study was starting to lose its sense of him and Rose tried to keep things messy as he'd left them, fighting the urge to tidy. Still, the void created by her dad's absence didn't excuse her mom's behaviour.

How could her mom possibly like Bill, a dirty landscaper, after being married to a writer, an academic, an educated man for all those years. Rose just didn't get it. Bill was horrible, even if he did bring her mom gifts and, when he smiled at her Rose had to try hard not to wince. Bill's smile was all shiny teeth but his eyes never met hers, just hovered over her body like he couldn't quite work out what to do with her. When he had first started coming to the house Rose had told her mom that she thought Bill was weird and that he creeped her out but her mom had just brushed her off saying "Some men are just like that Rose, not everyone's loud and boisterous and uses highfalutin talk like your father." She had given her daughter that 'one day you'll understand' look that Rose hated so much. The look served as punctuation some weeks, especially when Rose complained about Sara talking all night about Darren.

What Rose didn't understand was why Sara pretended to hate Darren so much when she chose to hang out with him. If anything, Rose was the one with the reason to despise him. Darren and his buddy, Matt McReedy, seemed to think it funny to throw stuff at her from the back row at the Hollywood, and they would elbow her really hard sometimes in school as they ran past her in the hall. Like father like son she guessed, wondering what it would have been like to have a brother. Would he have been like her dad or as stupid and irritating as the other boys at school?

Rose knew her dad had won some award along with his degree and his first book had a prominent quote on the front of it from Canadian Geographic, calling it the 'singular guide to the flora of the Canadian Rockies.' The dust jacket also had a picture of him as he always dressed; a clean white shirt, partially hidden underneath his trademark sweater with the green diamonds. In the image, the diamonds were grey, his hair jet black, and his eyes bright white. Rose loved this picture and wished that all the photos of her could be in black and white, ironing out the blotchiness of her complexion.

When Rose had grown old enough to realise that not everyone's dad worked at home she had thought it odd that he dressed so well every day. He had said that if he just sat in his study in his dressing gown and slippers he'd not feel like he was working, just loafing around. Every year Rose's mom would buy her husband a new Christmas sweater to add to his collection but his favourite was still the one with the green diamonds. Rose knew her dad had taken this with him because she'd looked for it after he'd left, hoping to crawl inside it and pretend he was still home.

Rose remembered when she was smaller, curling up in his lap in the armchair in his study, studying the pages of this book as he pointed out the different specimens he'd photographed and hand-drawn. These plants were like friends to him, all with their own quirks and patterns, and she had grown familiar with them in these pages but they were still just a jumble of green in the forest unless her dad was there to push the other leaves aside to show her some wild garlic or the Gentiana calycosa he'd been so excited about on one of their hikes. This flower, the mountain bog gentian, was disappearing from Alberta he told her in a whisper, reverent almost. He had talked about the gentian's tubular flowers and how some would close up rapidly as a cloud passed then reopen with the sun's reappearance. Her dad knew all kinds of weird things like this, and Rose felt blind as she walked through the woods with him, like he was seeing a million little lives all happening around them and all she saw was a wild tangle of weeds.

Her mother shook her out of her reverie as she fell onto Rose's bed next to Sara, the two of them looking strangely alike as they grinned at her. "C'mon Rose, help your sister build a snowman out front! You should be all bundled up in your boots and mittens and be building ice fortresses outside, where's your sense of fun?"

Rose tried to pull the duvet back over her head, groaning. Recently, her mom had begun acting in this gratingly girlish way and, as she helped

Sara snatch the duvet away, the pair of them were giggling like fourth-graders.

"When can we go to London to visit dad?" Rose stared at her mother as the laughter stopped. The two thick lines appeared between her mother's eyebrows and Sara pursed her lips like her mother, the two of them staring down at her lying in her pyjamas on the bed.

"Your dad is too busy to have us go there and bother him right now Rose, we've been through this. He'll be back soon once he's sorted out the house."

"But that's what you've been saying for months. He's not coming back is he? Does that mean I can go and live with him in England instead?"

The frown lines on her mother's face smoothed out for just a second and her mouth gaped a little in surprise, then she recovered herself, quietly told Rose that that was not an option and that she should get dressed and come down for breakfast. Sara glared at her little sister and grabbed her mom's hand as they turned and left the room, flouncing downstairs to make pancakes which would be cold and soggy by the time Rose sat down at the kitchen table.

After breakfast the phone rang and Rose ran to the hall to answer it before Sara got the chance.

"Rose? It's dad! How are you my little chicken? How's school, and Sara, and... your mum? Is she doing OK? Are you looking after her for me like I asked?"

"Dad! When are you coming home?"

"Soon sweetheart, I've just got to sort some things out. I miss you pumpkin. I hope you're being good for your mum. How did the history test go? 'A' plus plus I bet!"

"I got 93%. Ms Kininskis said that I didn't answer the question on Napoleon fully but the question was badly written so how was I supposed to know that she wanted us to talk about both battles?"

"That's my Rose, always fighting your own Waterloo. Just consider that a 7% donation to the others in the class who didn't try, eh? Now, is your mother there? I need to talk to her about something." Rose noted the tiredness in his voice, and she wondered what he was doing in England, if he even knew anybody there any more after he'd been here for so many years.

After Rose had been born they had not had enough money to go to England and so she'd never met her dad's side of the family. They had taken Sara to see her grandmother once, but she had been too small to remember anything about the trip. Now the royalties from her dad's book had slowed and his new one was still a pile of sketches and photographs lying around in his study, waiting to be joined by the stories he had told Rose on their many hikes.

Her dad had talked about going back every Christmas but her mother had said that travelling with two small children was just too much. When it came to practical parenting, Jim had always been a little lacklustre, preferring to defer to his wife and simply picking them up from school when told to and taking them to piano practice and volleyball games according to the schedule she'd laid out on the refrigerator. His thoughts were off in the woods, rifling through shrubbery for a sighting of a round-leaved orchid with its burgundy spots. Or coming home with tales of majestic Indian Pipe, describing how they stretched their ghostly white heads up out of a mass of dead and rotting mulch, sucking life from their neighbours before turning black and collapsing in on themselves. Rose would gape in awe at him across the kitchen table as he talked in between slurps of coffee, her mom apparently failing to see the sparkle in his eyes and asking him if he'd pick Sara up from volleyball at five. Now he never told her those kinds of tales, all their conversations being necessarily short or on a bad line. Perhaps England had no interesting plants to entertain him like here.

Rose held the phone away from her ear and yelled to her mother in the kitchen, wishing she could talk to her dad for longer. It was late in London though and she imagined that he would be eating dinner soon, a book propped up in one hand, his fork hovering above his plate for minutes at a time as he became engrossed in some lengthy paragraph.

Leaving the phone for her mom, Rose went upstairs and took the bundle of photos out of her dresser drawer. Along with the pictures she'd taken with her own camera, a gift for her birthday last August, was her favourite picture, one her mom had taken. In the photograph, her father stood against the backdrop of the Pacific, staring out across the ocean and not even realising the camera was pointed at him. This was on their trip to Vancouver Island where he had wanted to study the Garry Oaks. Her mom and Sara had gone with him, Rose too, but only as a silent passenger yet to be born. Her dad had said that in the photo he was peering out across the ocean hoping he could see China and Rose had told him not to be daft as China was more than 9000 kilometres away. He'd tickled her sides and asked "and how many miles is that Rosie?" Rose had cut the edge of the picture off as Sara had spoiled it by pulling a face. She'd kept it separately of course, as proof that her sister was not always as mature as she liked to believe she was at nearly fifteen.

Sara rarely talked to her dad when he called; she was often out with Darren or her friends or just made up some excuse. It seemed strange to Rose that Sara was angry with her dad for leaving and didn't see that he'd come back if her mom hadn't got Bill round all the time. Sara was only ten months older than Rose but she liked to make out that she was so much smarter and more sophisticated. Sara was too selfish to be smart, though, never thinking much about what other people felt or how her impulsive behaviour affected anyone else. There was a chance that Sara might have to stay back a grade as she was already falling behind in Math and English. Rose was secretly hoping she could convince her teachers to let her skip a grade as the thought of being in tenth grade with her sister was simply terrifying. Maybe it wouldn't come to that as their mom had talked about hiring a tutor for Sara, if her marks hadn't improved by Christmas.

Sara
December 8th

Rose is such a brat. This morning she asked Mom when Dad's coming home just to upset her. What a bitch. As if mom's not pissed enough at dad having taken off. At least she has Bill though, he's really nice to her and like a grown up version of Darren so so much sexier. Anyway, mom pretty much started crying when Rose asked about dad but then she made me pancakes (the good ones with tonnes of blueberry maple syrup!) and I got a lift to Heather's to walk to school with her.

Heather said that she made out with Greg yesterday after art class and she kept going on about how romantic it was as the snow started falling as they kissed. I know Greg's an awful kisser though (Tammy and I called him the washing machine!) so it can't have been that romantic. I guess Heather's not kissed that many boys! Anyway, kissing in the snow sounds pretty dumb, I know they do it in the movies and everything but you'd just get cold and your nose would run or get stuffy and then it'd be really gross.

I think I'm getting a cold anyway, and I reckon it's Darren's fault. He ran up behind me today and shoved snow down the back of my coat. I tried to get him back but he'd already gone in for Math so I just glared at him and thought about how to get revenge. He's so weird. Like, he'll be all sweet and hold my hand at the Hollywood but then make fun of my hair in front of everyone. Why can't he just be charming and suave and mysterious like his dad? Bill bought mom a red Chrysanthemum and she blushed when she saw me looking. I think it's because we were looking through the florists' dictionary at the store last week and Chrysanthemum means sex or something, I'll have to look it up again. I bet Bill didn't even know, or maybe he did. See? He's so smooth!

It's so obvious dad's not coming home. I don't know why they don't just tell us and get it over with. All his crap is still here anyway, and Rose spends all her time hiding out in the study like she's pretending he's still here or something. It really smells in there, like wet books and nasty smoke from dad's pipe. At least it's not full of skunk cabbage or whatever. God! When they used to stink out the kitchen with one of their 'experiments' - so gross. No wonder mom chucked him out. Rose probably thinks they'll get back together, I mean she's too little to get it but clearly mom just doesn't love him anymore and I don't blame her, dad just sat around writing and drawing all day. Or he was off in the forest or at the lake and then he'd bring mom a bouquet of some nasty looking grass. I don't think he ever just bought some roses like a normal guy. I guess he wouldn't though, with the store and all, mom's got enough roses of her own!

Mom said I had to get better at math before she'll let me work in the store but I don't see what the problem is when the till does everything. Ms Kininskis threatened to keep me back a year so mom's hiring some older boy to tutor me. I bet he's going to be such a nerd. It sucks that I'll have to spend time with some spotty math geek when I could be out with Heather and Tam.

CHAPTER TWO

Jane had moved the fruit bowl from the centre of the dining table and back twice already, walking around pointlessly it seemed and then placing it back on the cotton doily. Rose sat on the middle of the stairs watching her, unnoticed. Her mom kept muttering about brain food and teenage boys being hungry and then she saw her bring a plate of cookies from the kitchen which almost made it to the table but hovered an inch above it and were then whipped back into the kitchen. There were Oreos on that plate so Rose would keep an eye out for when they were left unattended.

Her mom was fussing because Sara's new tutor was arriving, imminently. Sara, of course, was nowhere to be seen but her mom seemed to have missed this key fact in light of her obsessiveness over presenting a good image. Presenting a daughter to tutor would also be a good idea Rose thought. Maybe she could take the lesson instead, she needed some help with simultaneous equations and now her dad wasn't around she was a little stuck.

Jason, the boy that was soon to be served all of the snack food in the house, was an eleventh grader but he didn't go to Pitcher Creek anymore because of some incident a few years ago that no one really spoke about now. From what Rose could piece together from her mom's conversations and the things Darren and his buddies said at school, Jason had been beaten up pretty badly and had spent a while in hospital. After that, his parents had decided to send him to a bigger high school the next town over where he might just slip by unnoticed. Rose was a little envious as she imagined that the school in Silver Lake had a proper computer teacher. Her mom had said he was heading off to college soon to study some new computing course. She had sounded impressed but Rose knew she had no idea what she was really talking about.

As much as Rose loved all the books and plants and sketches she had pored over with her dad she knew she had no real affinity for it. She had always enjoyed fiddling around with the camera more but now she didn't go hiking with her dad she had started playing around with the computer at school instead, trying to teach herself some programming stuff. It made sense to her, and no one else at school understood it so they could only mock her to a degree for staying behind when everyone else was off at volleyball practice or at the Hollywood.

There had been another kid at school for a while that had hung out with her in the library after class but his dad was just working on the new road north so he headed back to Edmonton sometime during Easter break. Rose didn't much see the point of making friends when she intended to leave Pitcher Creek as soon as she could. Sara had already planned her entire life in the town and so had Tammy and Heather and her other volleyball friends. Maybe they were better off that way Rose thought, at least they knew what they wanted; she just had the plan to leave and was hoping things would work themselves out from there. She thought about talking to her mom but Jane was so busy these days, taking Sara to practice, running the store, seeing Bill. It was nice that her mom wasn't so sad any more but Rose missed her dad and it seemed like her mom and Sara were just determined to forget he ever existed.

Rose wondered if the reason her mom liked Bill was because he was simple. He didn't mumble his responses into a book and wave goodbye without even looking at her. He didn't really say much at all. Content, instead, to let Jane ramble about nothing much and smile while he glugged down beer after beer.

Rose was right that Jane had liked Bill right from the start. He was such a straightforward kind of man, not saying much but meaning what little he did say. He reminded Jane of the boys she had dated back in Calgary in her brief college days, before Jim had arrived in the town and impressed her with his accent and knowledge of the Beatles. He had taken her out on long hikes where they didn't really get far because he'd stop to inspect a flower and then kiss her shyly. She had liked how gentle he was with her, checking it was OK to kiss her, to hold her hand, to stay in the same room on that first weekend away. Funnily, it was Bill's forthrightness that drew her in now. He was so assured; she could just lose herself in him and not care for a while.

People at the store had started making sly comments about Bill, how it was so nice that he was helping her out like he was, that he must have been so lonely after his wife had died and that that poor boy obviously needed a mother figure... someone like Jane to put him back on the right path. Jane wrapped up their flowers and nodded and smiled, knowing that it made sense for her to be with Bill and that, with time, she would start getting dinner invites and be back in church with him by her side. She had forgotten about these little things, being stuck out at the house watching Jim frown over his books, unwilling to go anywhere and never realising how she couldn't turn up at dinner alone. When they were younger the girls had play dates and Jane had an excuse to spend time alone with her friends but once they were older, especially after Jim had left, she wasn't quite sure how to meet people's curious stares at the store or in line at the bank. They knew she was alone. Jane would spend hours in front of her dresser mirror, trying to decide if she should dress deliberately plain and frumpy or to show off what was left of her youthful figure. Her old school friends would catch her eye as she walked down the cereal aisle at the grocery store and would suddenly remember to laugh at their husband's jokes and clutch at his arm. She had despaired at the idea that everyone was off limits, that she couldn't have that easy conversation with anyone's husband any more, even laugh at a foolish message someone would write in a card for their wife at her store in case someone saw her through the window and thought she was overstepping. Then Bill had simply presented himself at her door one day and she wondered at how she had forgotten him.

Bill had rapidly become part of their household, mending Sara's headboard, replacing the light bulbs Jane couldn't reach and even fixing the faucet in the store's prep. room when she asked. It was becoming difficult for Jane to think about how the house would run without him and Jane knew that she needed to talk to the girls about their dad staying in England and the possibility of Bill moving in. She was angry though, Jim had just removed himself from parenting duties it seemed, a phone call a week to ask about their grades, a long-distance pat on the head for Rose, and a hasty never mind for Sara. It wasn't fair that she had to talk to the girls about things on her own. She saw how Rose was when she hid in the study and she knew that Sara missed him even if she pretended not to.

Only yesterday, Bill had said exactly what she was thinking when Sara had come downstairs in a new silver dress Jane had not seen before. Jim wouldn't have even noticed but Bill had been so angry and told Sara she wasn't going out like that, that boys would get the wrong idea and that Sara wasn't that kind of girl. It was exactly what her father would have said to her and so she kept quiet. She hadn't even needed to say anything, it was so obvious that he really cared about the girls and it was scary how grown up Sara had looked in the silver dress. It was nice to have someone back her up for once, although she had noticed Sara's lip quiver as she looked wide-eyed at Bill for a moment before turning to go upstairs.

Jane snuck an Oreo off the plate and bit off the top, ready to grab another and do the same so she could sandwich them back together. Instead, she heard the sound of a car scraping across the gravel at the front of the house and Jane shoved the half cookie into her mouth and crunched hastily, the cream sticking to her teeth as she tried shouting to Sara with a mouthful of crumbs.

Sara crashed down the stairs as her mom opened the front door to see a battered old Lada parked in the drive, the green paint rusted over the wheel arches from the salty roads. Jason trotted up the steps, his head down to avert her gaze. As the young man entered the house he shuffled his feet a little and tentatively offered Jane, and then Sara, his hand as he'd been told to do by his mother over breakfast.

Jason Forrest had just turned sixteen, and, like Rose, was already planning his escape from Pitcher Creek. After his exams next year he was hoping to head off to college in Calgary, his place looking pretty assured for the new Computing Science course they were teaching there. His parents were the owners of Forrests' Grocery store on Main Street, two doors down from Jane's store, Floral and Hardy. Jason was not happy that they seemed intent on following him to college, selling the store and moving the two hours or so south just so that they were close by for support.

Jason had skipped ahead a grade and, although he was smart, they were doubtful of his ability to cope on his own, especially after the business with the boys at Pitcher Creek High. They could probably get a fair bit for the store, there was goodwill after all and it wasn't like the people in Pitcher Creek had many other options for their groceries. The prices of some of the places in Calgary were quite high though, lots of new money around it seemed, money that hadn't made it to Pitcher Creek yet. They were hopeful of working things out before Jason's course started next year, otherwise he might have to go alone and that was a terrifying prospect for his mother.

Once the awkward handshakes were over, Jane escorted Jason and Sara into the dining room and asked what Sara's first lesson would be about. Jason pulled a familiar-looking math textbook out of his messenger bag and opened it up to a chapter on probability.

"I'll go and get you both some cookies," Jane said, eyeing the long-forgotten symbols spidering across the page. As she left the room she heard Sara sigh and felt a pang of sympathy for her older daughter, she had never been much for math herself but the thought of Sara just marrying Darren straight out of school, starting a family and being stuck in the same old town forever was too much to bear. She wanted Sara and Rose to see something of the world before they came back and settled down, perhaps probability would help somehow.

Rose stayed seated on the stairs, having been bashed over the head with a copy of Marie Claire by Sara on her way to the door a few moments ago. She gripped the railings and peered through, listening to the mumbles from the dining room, waiting for her mother to come back with cookies. She sat there with her own copy of the math textbook, racing through question after question, feeding off the atmosphere of austere learning that it seemed Jason had brought into the house. Occasionally there was a squeak as the boy's half-formed voice snuck out from under his control. Sara's sighs became more melodramatic as the hour went on and then, finally, Jane poked her head back round the door and a second or two later Sara ran past, barely pausing to grab her coat on the way out of the back door.

A few minutes after Sara's hasty departure Jason emerged from the dining room, clutching books and notepads, a pencil behind his ear. Jane was still apologising for her daughter's rudeness as she shyly handed him an envelope, his name carefully written on the front in the lavish florist's handwriting that adorned all the cards sent out with orders from the store.

Jason nodded and smiled, "Thanks Mrs Hollister, same time Thursday?"

"That'd be great Jason, thank you so much. Hopefully Sara will be a little more focused then. It must be frustrating when it all comes so easily to you!" Jason just smiled a thin little smile and said nothing. "Ms Kininskis says you're off to college in Calgary soon, some computer thing I hear. That's exciting. You'll enjoy Calgary! So much to do and see, not like Pitcher Creek that's for sure." As she spoke she wondered just how ready Jason was for the big city, she couldn't imagine him in any of her old haunts and thought back to how her teenage self probably would have teased someone like Jason mercilessly. She paused for a second, reflecting on how strangely fitting it was that she now wanted her own daughter to be a little more like him than like her.

Jane closed the door as Jason said goodbye and descended the porch steps. She turned and almost jumped backwards as she saw Rose right behind her, ready with questions.

"Can I have a tutor? Can Jason teach me?" Rose smiled what she thought was a winning smile but which actually contorted the natural childish beauty of her face in repose and made her look slightly ghoulish as it strived for an older coquetry.

"Rose, sweetheart, you don't need a tutor, you're already clever enough and can get on fine by yourself. You certainly don't need to spend more time poring over books like your dad, now why don't you put on your gumboots and join your sister outside, I think Darren's coming over soon and you can all head out to the movies or something?" Jane kissed Rose's forehead, furrowed as it now was, and went into the kitchen to finish arranging a wreath.

Funeral wreaths always took her a long time to do as she worried about making them perfect. They meant so much to those giving them. A last act of kindness in many cases. This time, however, she knew that the customer who had ordered it was all ready to spend money on his dead mother but might not even make the funeral itself as he was caught up in some career-making corporate fraud trial in Edmonton, too important to miss for the sake of family.

Judy MacGowan had worked for years at the town library and had, night after night, given piano lessons to the local kids so she could save enough to send Robert to a good school in Red Deer. Judy's husband, Arthur, had died from emphysema when Robert was five, allegedly brought on by some industrial chemical exposure. The company he worked for had never admitted any liability, though, and the MacGowans had scraped together every last cent to cover the medical bills and the funeral costs.

Jane thought it was awful that Rob MacGowan could not even be bothered to show up at his mother's funeral when she'd done so much for him over the years. Judy had poured everything into raising her son on her own and given him this chance at a good career. It almost made Jane happy that Sara had no apparent aspirations to leave Pitcher Creek. Talking to herself in the kitchen, Jane said "I hope my children at least have the decency to come to my funeral!"

"Mum! Are you dying?" Rose had snuck in behind her and the sound of her voice nearly made Jane cut her finger rather than the stem of the carnation she planned to feed through the outer edge of the wreath.

"Of course not Rose! Don't be silly. I was just thinking about Judy and how sad her funeral will be tomorrow."

"We should go, to Judy's funeral I mean. She was a really wonderful piano teacher and made great lemon ginger cookies every time I went for a lesson, with these little bits of orange peel in the frosting that made your tongue tingle. I liked her. Of course, we're all dying." The words had just poured out of her as she played with the discarded stems on the kitchen worktop, and she felt her mother's eyes studying her closely.

"Sometimes Rose, you astound me. One second morose, the next beautiful and sensitive and kind." Jane put her arm around Rose's shoulders and gave her daughter a little squeeze. "Would you really like to go? We can if you like, I'll ask Noreen to watch the store, but she did request an open casket so it might be a little upsetting. We can always sit at the back and not actually go up to say goodbye. You would have to miss the morning of school though and don't you have that English test tomorrow?"

"That's only for those who failed the last one. I'll just be sitting reading and being quiet so can we go to say goodbye to Judy instead?" Rose was thinking about seeing the old lady lying down in the coffin, her mother's flowers nearby, and suddenly she wasn't quite so sure she really wanted to go, but she had liked Judy. The old lady had always been kind to Rose even if her piano playing had been rather clunky and mechanical. She'd never met her grandma in England and now the old lady had died she never would. To Rose this was almost like saying goodbye to two people: one she'd sat next to every Wednesday for an hour and one whose picture hung in the hallway but whose strange flat voice she'd only heard over the telephone.

"OK, but Sara won't be happy that you're skipping school and she has to go so promise not to tease, right? Right Rose? You know I rely on you to be the sensible one."

"Sara wouldn't really want to go anyway mom, she was always horrible to Judy behind her back, making faces at the cookies and the funny way her house smelt." It had bugged Rose that Sara was actually better than her at the piano, despite not really caring much and forgetting to do homework. Sara couldn't even read the music but when she followed the old lady's instructions there was something beautiful about the grace of her fingers on the keys, especially in contrast to Rose's methodical plunking of note after note. Rose had all the theory but just couldn't seem to get her fingers to move where she wanted them to across the keys. At least Judy had been patient with them both, even if it appeared that Rose would never be very accomplished.

"Oh, look, I cut it too short." Jane threw a carnation into the sink and put her hands together, turning to face Rose. "Sorry, sweetheart, I need to concentrate on getting this wreath finished right away, before Bill, Mr Tether, arrives. Why don't you go and find your sister and have some fun instead of talking to me about death and funerals, eh." She spun Rose around and gave her a little nudge towards the back door just as she heard the sound of Bill's truck on the gravel out front. Rose saw her mother blush a little as she looked into the front hall and smoothed down her hair.

Sara
January 15th

I had another lesson with Jason tonight. Mom has him coming round all the time now as she obviously thinks I'm an idiot who needs all the help I can get. He's nice and all but it's not like I'd ever hang out with him. Tammy was teasing me that Jason's like my boyfriend now, but she laughed when I did an impression of him. Anyway, she's just jealous because she fancies Darren.

Jason's so pathetic, like he's scared of me, which just makes it so much easier to make fun of him. I know I shouldn't and I think Rose saw me so she'll probably tell mom and I'll get a lecture on being nice to those less fortunate. He wears his pants really high though, so I did the same with mine and made my voice kind of squeaky. It's no wonder his parents moved him to Silver Lake. I bet there are other geeks like him there that he can hang out with. He got beaten up real bad after school a while back, something to do with gym class, I don't know what. Darren said he was in hospital for a while and that he had some kind of amnesia. His parents were worried that he wasn't a genius any more but maybe he was just pretending not to remember who beat him up as no one got charged with anything. Anyway, they sent him to the bigger school, instead of making him sit next to the guys that did it. It's good that Darren's tough and strong, like his dad, no one would even think about beating him up.

Jason was really sweet earlier though. He seems to really care if I get algebra! I actually felt like I was disappointing him every time I got something wrong so I stopped saying anything but then he just made me try and said that he used to make loads of mistakes when he was first learning algebra. I bet that's not true but it was nice of him to pretend. He's like some genius or something and mom said he's going to Calgary and that he'll become some millionaire computer whiz kid. Maybe I should marry him and be filthy rich! Darren would probably beat him up if I even joked about that though, he's pretty protective.

Darren and Matt were disgusting today in history, when Mr Day wasn't looking they threw these drawings at me of sex positions. Darren and me haven't done it yet but I think he wants to and I think he's told Matt that we have so Matt had written 'Sara' and 'Darren' above the figures in the drawings. They're so gross. Why can't Darren be nice all the time, maybe a little more like Jason, quiet and sweet? I know Darren's smart too but he acts so dumb. At least he teases Rose more than me these days, and she deserves it for being so damn smart and sweet and nice.

Ha! Just imagine if Rose and Jason had babies, they'd be super smart and take over the world! Who'd want to have babies with Rose though, they wouldn't be able to look at her ugly face long enough to even kiss her, let alone do any of the other stuff. I wonder when me and Darren will do more than just make out. I wish he'd brush his teeth more, he always smells of cigarettes and like something just rotted in his mouth but at least I have a steady boyfriend, not like Tammy and Heather.

CHAPTER THREE

Rose was waiting outside the school gates when Tammy and Sara turned up, arm in arm. Heather trailed behind, her glasses half covered with the bangs that made her face look square and crowded. Rose felt sorry for the girl, she knew that Sara and Tammy laughed about Heather behind her back and she wondered why she put up with it.

Compared to her friends, Sara looked older, a little taller, more like her mom now. Their hair was the same length and the same colour too, and Rose thought about her own dull dark hair, and the baby fat she still had around her thighs and her belly. She knew some of the other girls in her class were dieting and some even throwing up after lunch. She had heard them in the bathroom and it had made her feel sick too, but for a different reason. Sara's blonde hair flicked out behind her as she flounced up to Rose and elbowed her in the ribs. "Hey little sis, waiting for someone special? Why aren't you first in line for the bus Rosie, then you can sit up front with all the other little kids who might throw up."

Sara always showed off in front of her friends, making sure to be particularly mean to Rose and make her feel very much the younger sister. Rose used to think that growing up just meant being nasty to people as that seemed to be what Sara and Darren, and all the other kids at school did. Now she just knew that it was done in desperation, but that didn't really make her feel any better when Sara ridiculed her in front of everyone.

Rose sighed and moved away from Sara's prodding fingers.

"Bill's picking us up today. Mom said she was going to be busy at the store so she asked him to bring the truck. I don't see why we can't just get the bus like everyone else." Rose rolled her eyes as she saw Sara wink at Tammy and turn to face her. Sighing dramatically, Sara put a hand on Rose's shoulders, preparing to be condescending.

"Rose, Rose, Rose, mom is just worried. The school bus is dangerous see. One of your many many admirers might try to kiss you and chase you all the way home." Sara started laughing before she even finished speaking and Tammy fell into fits of giggles at the thought of little Rose having any admirers. A couple of seconds later Heather made a squeaking noise, a half laugh, perhaps in sympathy or confusion. Sara went on, "So she sends Bill, ahem... Mr Tether, to come and make sure you're safe. He's so big and strong and will make sure nothing bad happens you see, because he's a gentleman." She paused for a second, looking thoughtful and Rose wondered what else she was going to throw at her to make her feel stupid. "Now, if you were really grown up you would have just gotten the bus already wouldn't you?" Sara gestured to the crowd of kids bustling onto the bus across the yard.

Fine, Rose thought. She'd rather squeeze into a seat on there than sit in the rattling, cold cab of Bill's pickup. Let Sara sit there and freeze. She'd only have to witness her sister twirling her hair and giggling anyway, like Bill would think she was older and worth looking at. Rose started towards the queue for the school bus and she heard Sara laughing wickedly behind her for a few seconds. Then Sara called her name and Rose thought, with a certain satisfaction that it would really be her sister that was in trouble if Rose headed home on the bus instead of waiting for Bill.

She wondered what story Sara would tell Bill to explain why Rose had caught the bus. He'd probably be on her side anyway; the two of them were always conspiring these days, sharing little in-jokes and even making fun at her mom's expense. Although Rose didn't really feel jealous it did seem that Sara had pretty much replaced her dad and Rose wasn't part of the family any more. They were all supposed to be going to one of Sara's volleyball games next week and Rose felt sick at the idea of people seeing them as a family now. She couldn't wait to leave Pitcher Creek, at least then she wouldn't have to watch Sara playing 'daddy's girl.'

CHAPTER FOUR

"So Jason, how's my Sara coming along? Have you transferred your mathematical genius to her yet?" Jane was showing Jason out after his lesson when Rose came running up the porch steps.

"Jason, can you teach me BASIC?" Rose looked up at the young man and her mother standing side by side on her front porch and adopted a pleading expression, resisting the urge to scream 'pleeeease.'

"Basic what Rose? What are you talking about now sweetheart? You know Jason's here to help your sister. You don't need tutoring and I'm sure Jason would rather be out with his friends than teaching you whatever fanciful idea's entered your head this time." She put her hand gently onto Jason's shoulder and started down the stairs but Jason turned at the touch and Jane saw a strange glimmer of excitement in his face. She couldn't recall seeing him that animated before and it was a little alarming.

"I wouldn't mind, Mrs Hollister, programming's fun so I can help Rose if she wants to learn. Or at least she can borrow..." he started pulling a copy of PC Magazine out of his backpack and then presented it to Rose in an oddly reverent fashion "...this! It's the latest issue and there's a whole interview with Bill Gates. It's really inspiring for people like, well, me." He was about to say 'like you and me' but thought better of it, not everyone, or their mothers, were happy to be called geeks. He blushed at the thought that Rose might be a little like him.

"Well," Jane was wavering, she already had Jason at her house three times a week now as Sara still didn't seem to be improving at school, despite Jason reporting that she understood things much better than when they'd started the lessons. He'd nervously suggested that, perhaps, Sara might just be too distracted at school and that she thought getting good marks might lose her some friends. She'd been really preoccupied recently, in a daydream, twirling her hair and only paying attention when Jason coughed pointedly but still quietly. Then she'd turn to face him and give him a wide but clearly false smile, apologising and giggling. This faux flirtation made Jason blush and then Sara would feel the blood rising up her own neck as she felt bad for manipulating him, however easy it seemed to be.

Jane liked Jason, finding his nervous little smile endearing when he appeared on the front porch on Mondays, Wednesdays, and Fridays. She wanted to ask him to stay for dinner or to tell her about school, but figured it would make him feel awkward. He was a painful reminder of how she had hoped for a son when Rose was born and how she had tried to convince Jim that they could afford three children. They had decided to wait until money was not so tight and then all of a sudden it seemed she was forty and tired and most nights Jim slept in the study, somehow forgetting to come to bed and just falling asleep at his desk over the pages of a book she knew he'd never finish.

Jane had thought that a son would be easier, less worry than the girls, more resilient. Looking at Jason she could see now that this was not the case at all, the way his mother worried over him incessantly, and how everyone heard about it in the store when they went in just to buy a bottle of milk or some bread. Jane knew that Jason had been in and out of hospital since he was beaten up that time, that he had had blackouts for a while. His mother had said that he was fine now, he'd been cleared to drive after all, but she still looked worried of course.

Jason didn't seem to have made any friends in town and Jane figured he was probably bullied at the new school too. He was smart but there was also something a little off about the boy, something other, something Jane couldn't quite place but which lent him a certain sadness that made her want to mother him even more. Although it was common knowledge that he had been beaten up pretty badly no one seemed to really know why. The kids clearly knew but wouldn't tell, dealing with it in their own way.

Moving the boy to a different school was probably the best thing for everyone in town. He could just disappear, out of harm's way perhaps, just another strange boy who had never quite fit in Pitcher Creek. He certainly was not like Darren, or Matt McReedy, and even Bill had said that the kid freaked him out a bit and that she should watch him with the girls. Jane just thought he was shy though and she was a little wary of saying no to Rose's request in case Jason felt it was because of him and his strangeness.

"The thing is, Jason, all this tutoring, I'm not sure our funds can really stretch to having you teach Rose as well, especially when she's doing well enough already at school. And, well, I don't even know what you're talking about!"

"Computer programming, Mrs Hollister! I don't mind, I wouldn't charge or anything, it'd be fun to have someone to work with on stuff. Maybe I can just stay a little longer after my lessons with Sara and talk to Rose about QDos and things?" He was still holding the magazine but made as if to offer it to Rose and said, almost conspiratorially, "You'll love it."

Rose clutched the magazine to her, happy to have an ally again. She looked up plaintively at her mom. "Please? See, Jason said it won't cost you anything, and it will help me get through school because I won't be so bored if I have a project to think about." Rose moved up the steps to stand next to Jason and be on a level with her mother, figuring it would be harder for her mother to patronise her then. She saw the two frown-lines flatten out on her mother's face.

"OK, but I don't like the fact that this will mean even more time at your dad's computer and cooped up inside. I'll have to sign you up for field hockey or volleyball or something so you see sunlight occasionally!"

"But, it's winter!" Rose trembled with the cold but also the thought of the hockey team, and, even worse, the girls' volleyball team, many of whom were Sara's friends and who teased her relentlessly.

"Well, curling then. Now, thank Jason for the magazine and go inside." Rose threw a big smile at Jason and shouted her thanks as she scurried off to her dad's study to pore over the Bill Gates interview. When she'd gone, Jane turned to Jason, "Are you sure you don't want compensating for the tuition, it hardly seems fair to have you teach both my daughters and have no time to yourself! And, I warn you, Rose is very... demanding and impatient when she's learning things." Jane was now a little suspicious, as much as she liked the boy it seemed odd that he'd rather spend time with her girls instead of boys his own age. Bill had muttered something about him being a fruit but Jane had not paid much attention as any guy who didn't drink beer and watch hockey pretty much fell into that category for Bill. Anyway, wouldn't that make him harmless to the girls? Bill didn't make much sense sometimes but at least he meant well by Sara and Rose.

Jane realised that Jason was still smiling at her, she smiled back. "Honestly, I don't mind at all, it's actually quite fun working with someone else on these things, and..." Jason was about to say he liked Rose and he thought she'd probably be easier to teach than Sara but he stopped himself and then said he'd better go but he'd see them all on Monday. He couldn't help wonder why Rose was so keen to spend time with him, she must be shy too he figured, she certainly wasn't as pretty as Sara who was so relaxed and confident and who had even started painting her nails during their lesson earlier. The smell of the varnish had made him sneeze violently. Jason knew Sara was going steady with Darren, and the thought of them sitting in the back row at the Hollywood made the blood rush back to his face as he drove home carefully in the snow.

Sara
February 13th

Rose and Jason are such nerds. He stays behind now after my lesson so that they can hang out in the study and do this weird shit on the computer dad bought last year. I don't get why mom lets her have him as a tutor too, it's not like she needs it. She should have to have dance lessons or something instead, that'd teach her. Jason's all happy and friendly and relaxed with her. I guess she's too young for him to really fancy so he's not nervous like he is with me. He thinks I don't notice when he blushes but I do and there's no way he likes Rose more than me, how could he?

Anyway, hopefully they aren't laughing at me in there. I just couldn't get what Jason was saying today about quadratic equations. I know I need to for the make-up exam but it's not really my fault I failed. Darren kept jabbing me with his pencil. He pretends he's so cool and couldn't care less about school but I saw him get his test back and he got a B! I don't get it. He acts so dumb but he's actually talking about college. Tammy saw too and then she was teasing me that there's no way he'd stick around in Pitcher Creek if he was smart and that either I'd have to marry him straight after school or get myself pregnant so he'd have a reason to stick around. Maybe I'd marry him but I don't want to just have a baby.

Mom keeps trying to talk to me about 'being careful' but I can't listen to her, it's just too embarrassing, especially as I hear her and Bill sometimes now. Anyway, so Darren and me still haven't actually done it. He put his hand under my shirt today, behind the art studio. He took his glove off first and his hands were so cold! I think he was a bit surprised that he'd actually done it and it didn't even really seem like he knew what to do once his hand was there. He didn't even move his hand or anything, just left it there while we were kissing! I didn't really like it and I couldn't stop thinking about how the split in my gumboots mean that the snow was soaking my socks through...

Of course, I told Tammy and Heather that we'd got to second base and that his touch made me tingle all over though, just like it's supposed to. Tammy was super cool about it as she has already slept with Matt (so gross), but Heather went the brightest shade of red I've ever seen and had to head to the library really quickly. Her mom doesn't let her have boys over to the house and she's really never done anything with any of the boys at school. She's so childish about these things and has to rely on me to explain stuff to her. She even gets changed in the washroom in gym class, maybe there's something really wrong with her body or something. Tammy thinks Heather has a crush on her as she caught her staring at her boobs once when she was getting changed at her house.

Maybe I'll have sex with Darren soon. I mean, Bill stays over at ours and so Darren's alone in his house and I could totally sneak out without anyone noticing. Tammy said that it's ridiculous that I'm fifteen and haven't even slept with a guy yet. Maybe she's right and he'll go off with some other girl if I don't do it soon. Tammy said that Matt was constantly trying to get her to have sex with him but Darren hasn't really been like that.

Bill already thinks that me and Darren are doing it. He practically called me a whore in front of mom when I wore my silver dress the first time and she just stood there and bit her lip. He's always telling me not to grow up too soon, that people will get the wrong idea if my dress is too short or cut too low. He gets really angry about it sometimes, but he says he's just worried because he knows I'm not like that and that he doesn't want anyone to see me like that. I guess he's right, I don't want to look like a slut but it's not like I'm a kid anymore and I don't just want to dress like mom does in those random old cardigans and work pants covered in stains. Everyone thinks she's such a frump! She started dressing nice for Bill at first but I guess the honeymoon period is over as she's back in her crappy work gear.

Bill's probably getting sick of her because she's been really dopey lately, going to bed early after a glass of wine and being all groggy in the morning. Menopause or a hangover or something I guess, she's so old now! Bill's up on his own in the kitchen then and sometimes I sneak down to talk to him as he always wants to hear about my day and school and volleyball and things. I know he's not dad but he clearly cares more. Maybe Darren will end up being more like Bill when he's older but it would be nice if he was a bit more suave and sexy now. The silent broody thing is getting a little old and I'm not even sure he cares that it's Valentine's Day tomorrow.

Dad obviously won't send mom anything from England. I bet he won't even realise it's Valentine's Day. I know Bill has bought her this gorgeous necklace, with a little studded heart pendant. The box was in the glove compartment of the truck when I was looking for gum the other day and it's so beautiful. Mom has no idea, she's so lucky!

CHAPTER FIVE

"Why do you laugh at that shit? It's not funny Rose. I never understood why dad thinks it's so hilarious." Sara was standing in the doorway of the study watching Rose as her face contorted, tears streaming down her cheeks as a man explained something about a parrot being shagged out. "You're so weird."

Rose recovered herself and turned away from the TV to look at Sara. "Just because you don't get it doesn't mean it's not funny." She turned back to the programme and was about to turn the volume back up when Sara walked over and perched on the edge of her dad's desk.

"He's not coming back you know. It's like he's totally forgotten we even exist."

"That's not true. He called... last week." Rose knew that was a lie. She hadn't spoken to her dad for a while now and she was taking solace in the form of Monty Python. Sadness crept through her; having been quashed briefly, Sara had let it escape again. The tears clouding her eyes were not happy ones now.

"He doesn't give a shit Rose. About us, about mom, about any of it. We're better off without him. We're better off with Bill. He's dependable at least." Sara said this whilst pouting slightly, wrapping her blonde plait around and around her index finger, glancing up to assess Rose's reaction.

"Bill's an idiot. Compared to dad he's just some stupid guy who's nice to mom and makes her feel better about being alone."

Sara stopped twirling her hair and stared hard at Rose. She paused a second and then clutched at the pendant at her neck, holding it tight in her fist.

"Bill's not stupid. He just doesn't bother with all that unnecessary stuff that dad does. He lives in the real world Rose. Maybe you should try doing that for once. Maybe someone will notice you then and you won't be such a dork." Sara ducked out of the way as Rose threw the remote control at her, hitting the bookshelf instead. "Doofus."

"Shut up Sara! Why don't you just go and spend some time with your precious Bill if you love him so much. Go and ask him to help with your math homework and watch his brain explode into his beer."

"You're just jealous because you fancy Jason and he only has eyes for me! You should see how much he blushed when I touched his hand the other day!" Sara smiled as Rose's eyes widened and her jaw fell slack. For once, her little sister had nothing to say.

Satisfied in winning the fight, Sara jumped up and flounced out of the room, flipping Rose off as she went. Sara really was insufferable Rose thought. As if Jason would fancy her, she was so stupid. Rose thought for a second about what boys liked though and realised that it probably didn't make a difference. Sara was a lot prettier than she was and Jason never blushed when they were practically touching as they worked at the computer together. She guessed it didn't matter how smart she was, even to someone like Jason, not when Sara had actual boobs and not just socks rolled up in her bra. She was right about Bill though, he was certainly not smart but she guessed he wasn't totally dumb either, after all he seemed to have charmed Sara and that was a great way to win over her mom.

Rose knew her dad wasn't coming back but she wasn't ready to have some new guy try to take his place, especially one who burped after dinner and left water all over the bathroom floor every morning. She missed her dad. He might have been lost in his own thoughts a lot of the time but at least he had them. Bill was an idiot in comparison. Someone stupid for her mom to dress up for Cass's wedding, someone to go to dinner parties with, parties her dad would have described as 'unbearably tedious' years ago, doing impressions of the guests until Rose cried with laughter and her mother vowed never to take him out in public again.

She went over to the bookshelf and retrieved the remote control, placing it back on the desk. Opening the cupboard under the shelves, Rose retrieved her camera and checked how many frames were left. She needed to take five more pictures before she could rewind the film and get it developed. It had been ages since she had been out to photograph anything. It was mainly when she went hiking with her dad that she had taken her camera out. He would get her to take pictures of random plants that she never recognised, or he would take a picture of her as she climbed a tree or jumped the stones to get across a creek. He had said that he wanted to capture these moments, so he would remember them when she was all grown up and didn't visit her old pa any more. Rose had laughed when he said that but now she wondered if he had taken any of those pictures with him, or if he'd started to forget what she looked like.

Sara
March 15th

I had my fitting today for my dress for Aunt Cass's wedding! I can't believe it's only a month away! It's beautiful, like really lovely and not at all blancmangey like mom said it would probably be. All the bridesmaids' dresses are this pale purple colour with these tiny green lace flowers at the neck. They're really sweet and I think Rose is regretting saying she didn't want to be a bridesmaid now she's seen me in my dress. She'd make the pictures look stupid though as she's so much shorter than me, mom, and Ruth, and she'd fall over in the heels and make a big scene. Ruth looks really good in the dress, she's so tall and supermodel thin and I think Cass would like to say she can't be her bridesmaid now even though she's her best friend. When I get married I'll have to make sure I only choose my ugliest friends to be bridesmaids! Like Heather and Rose, not Tammy as she's really pretty these days and has huge boobs now.

Aunt Cass's dress is even more beautiful than mine, of course. Mom said she thinks it's kind of silly as it's pretty big and the train is really long. On the way home she said in this snide voice that subtlety was not Cass's strong point but she's probably just jealous too as her wedding dress is really boring and was dead cheap as her and dad were so young and poor and blah blah blah. God, how she loves telling that story to make us grateful for everything we have, like I care.

When we got home Bill asked what the dresses looked like and my mom just said they were fine but after mom had gone into the kitchen I told him how pretty our bridesmaid dresses were and he said he was sure I'd look beautiful in it, very elegant. Just to wind him up I said that I'd seen a wedding dress that I really liked and his face went all weird. He told me to stop being silly and I tried to say sorry but he just went and sat on the back porch and drank his beer. He's so easy to fool but I probably shouldn't as I think I made him mad and he hasn't really talked to me the rest of the evening, just looked at me and seemed quite sad. I think Bill talked to Darren about me as he's been avoiding me and been dead quiet at dinner the last few nights. I can't really work out what's going on with them but they're both kind of mad at me I think.

Tammy said she saw Matt giving Darren some condoms and that I'd better watch out but she must have forgotten that I'm taking the pill now anyway. She can't take it as it made her really fat and a bit weird so she gets really bad cramps and stays off school when she has her period. My mom's stopped reminding me to take mine every morning, I think because Bill's at the breakfast table most days and it embarrasses her. I wonder if her and Bill are even still having sex. I hope not as it's too gross to think about when my room's so close. Bill said that mom was taking some sleeping pills as she was super stressed out about the wedding so she's in bed really early most nights anyway. The house is kind of quiet then as Rose just hides out in her room, or in dad's study with her books and things. I think she avoids Bill; I guess she just doesn't want to see how nice he can be as she still thinks dad's coming back.

CHAPTER SIX

The calm silence of the Hollister house was broken by the peal of the phone, followed by Jane's exclamations and then the adoption of the calming tone she always took with her younger sister Cassidy.

"Cass, shh, c'mon, it can't be that bad. What? No, it's really not a good idea to change the whole colour scheme now. I mean, well, the dress is only a slightly different shade of white, it's not like it's green or anything. Cass, no, Cass, be sensible now, ivory and pale ivory? Really? No, the flowers absolutely do not have to change, it will be perfect as it is and besides I've already figured out the central arrangements. It'll take me days to do more and there just isn't time or the need for it, really."

Having run from the study at the sound of the phone, hoping it was her dad, Rose stood at the top of the stairs, but then gave up listening and turned to go back in, knowing that almost all of her mother's conversations with her younger sister started like this and finished in the same way, with her mother giving in. If her mom had to do a whole new load of flowers then she wouldn't be here in the evenings this week and that meant Sara might not get her lessons. Even though Jason had been tutoring Sara for months now, Bill had suddenly decided that the two of them shouldn't be left unsupervised, not when Jason would obviously be attracted to the girl, her being so pretty and all. Rose heard her sister screeching at her mom downstairs and realised that her suspicions were right, Sara wouldn't be getting her lessons this week.

"But, mum! I'm sixteen soon, that's just stupid!" Rose couldn't help but feel a little vindicated. Sara had been making a big fuss recently about planning her party for her sixteenth birthday in October and acting like she was so much better than her kid sister. Rose had heard Darren

36

talking with Matt McReedy outside the library earlier in the week, and although she hadn't really fully understood their conversation, which seemed to be largely about Darren sleeping with Sara, she had gotten the general idea from the ugly smile on Matt's face. Darren looked like he might be about to punch his friend in the mouth at first but, after a moment, he had just sniggered too. She wondered at how Sara would feel, knowing that she was being talked about like this. It also upset her to think that Darren was as bad as Matt McReedy, who everyone knew was doing his best to sleep with all the girls in school by getting them into the Hollywood for free. Darren was actually quite nice to her sometimes these days, or at least didn't tease her as much as before. She had caught him looking thoughtfully at Sara, and then at her on occasion and wondered what he was thinking. It unnerved her a little and almost made her feel thankful that boys didn't usually take much notice of her, particularly when she stood next to Sara.

Running up the stairs, Sara stormed past Rose, not even pausing to hit her over the head like usual. She slammed shut the door to her bedroom, causing the 'Sara's Room' sign to swing sadly from side to side. The sign was haphazardly painted in lime green and pink, little garish daisies smiling out, inviting but sickly. It struck Rose as odd that Sara had not replaced this sign or thrown it out as her older sister had become so particular about her room in the last couple of weeks, throwing out loads of her old toys, although her favourite, Stumpy Dog, remained. Sara had even got her mom to buy her these new, plain bed covers to replace the pink and purple ones and she'd ripped down the posters from her walls, leaving these horrible dark patches. Bill had said that it looked a mess and that he'd be happy to paint Sara's room but after he left Rose heard Sara quietly ask her mom if they could maybe paint it together.

Sara spent a lot of time hiding in her room these days, even asking for her mom to put a lock on the door. Jane had spoken to Bill about it but he just said that it was the kind of thing that teenagers did. That they needed their privacy and that he had no idea what Darren was up to half the time. Her mom said that it was different for girls and that if Sara wouldn't talk to her then she was going to take her to see Dr. Collins as maybe she was anaemic. Sara was so listless and broody, no longer jumping out of bed first thing in the morning, and skipping volleyball practice this week. Jane worried but Bill had just laughed and kissed her wrinkled forehead and said that Sara was fine but that the lock probably wasn't a good idea, just in case.

Rose went down into the kitchen to talk to her mother, finding her leaning against the sink, staring at the plans for Aunt Cass's wedding. She was toying with her necklace, twirling the silver daisy round and round, tightening the chain against her neck. She looked up as Rose walked in and let the necklace, her Valentine's Day present from Bill, drop back to her chest. Jane set her face into the now familiar expression of exasperation and fatigue.

"Honey, look, I really don't want to talk about your sister and her tantrums right now, I've got too much work to do on these new arrangements for your Aunt Cassidy." She picked up the stem of an amaryllis and rummaged through a box of tools for some twine. "I'm busy, Rose, can you just go and finish your homework or watch some bloody telly or something."

Clearly her mom was stressed if she was using her dad's profanities. Sara didn't even really say such things any more, having pretty much decided to be angry at her dad and, it seemed to Rose, replacing him with Bill. Acutely aware of his absence suddenly, Rose was tempted to ask her mom if he ever planned on coming back but, instead, said "I could sit in with them, while they have their lesson, if that makes you feel better? I wouldn't say anything but I can check that Sara's paying attention and being nice to Jason and concentrating and everything." Her mother stopped trimming the ends of the amaryllis stems and turned to her daughter, Rose saw that her eyes were wet, not quite crying but close to dropping that first, all-important tear that presages a flood. Rose thought about slipping her hand into her mother's hand but she was still clutching the flowers and the scissors and so Rose held back.

Her mother seemed to have collapsed in on herself, her bones barely supporting her thin flesh that looked pale and papery in the harsh fluorescent light above the kitchen counter. It was not just Sara that had become listless and moody recently, Jane also looked exhausted, waking without feeling rested. Perhaps things would be different once the paperwork had gone through and the wedding was done. There was just so much to do and Jane felt a fleeting desire for a glass of wine, which alarmed her as it was still early. She just wanted to lie down on the couch, put on a record and drain the glass of merlot, or the bottle perhaps, until she swam down into sleep and could leave the damn amaryllis to arrange themselves.

Putting down the scissors and wiping quickly at her eyes Jane said "That's very sweet of you Rose, but I still don't think it's a good idea for you girls to have your lessons with Jason while I'm not here. Just in case." She didn't say just in case of what but Rose had heard Bill's pronouncements on the matter and knew her mom would just defer to him, as she had begun doing more and more recently. Bill had said that there were things that it was better for women not to know about the thoughts of a teenage boy, especially when it came to their daughters. Thinking back to the conversation she overheard between Matt and Darren earlier, Rose was beginning to see his point. It seemed to her that it didn't really stop after you were a teenager either.

It seemed strange to Rose that Bill had all but moved in and yet Darren was still living in their old house in the middle of town. If they were going to be a proper family then he should just move in with them but Rose saw that Sara and Darren dating made that pretty complicated if Bill's ideas of propriety were to be maintained. Maybe the rules just didn't apply where his son was concerned.

Sara
April 10th

The wedding's next week and mom's stressed out. Bill told mom not to let Jason come over because he didn't trust him, so I don't get my lessons this week. It's not like I'm ever going to do any good at school anyway, I'll probably just end up married in a couple of years and be like Aunt Cass. Mom's amazed Cass's dress still fits as she's really starting to show. She had to have her dress let out so everyone's going to know now as Agnes might be great at making dresses but she sure as hell can't keep a secret. She asked about my necklace when Rose and I went to her house to pick up our dresses last week. Rose looked at me kind of funny. I wonder if she knows. Maybe I should get rid of it.

My cocoa's gone cold but I should drink it anyway, I guess. Mom and Rose already drank theirs downstairs and Bill will want the cup back before I go to bed.

CHAPTER SEVEN

Rose was watching a Fawlty Towers episode from her dad's video collection, trying to work out why it was funny when Basil whacked Manuel over the head for the seventeenth time. Her dad always snorted beer out of his nose it seemed when he watched this stuff but it had taken Rose a while to see why it was funny, at first she had always just laughed along in sympathy, trying to remember that her dad was really clever and she must just be missing the joke. Perhaps this is what everyone in England was like. Rose wasn't too sure she wanted to visit if so, but he'd been gone nearly a whole year now and didn't seem to have made any progress on coming back.

The programme's credits were interrupted by a door slamming downstairs and the angry stomp of her sister through the hallway. Rose stayed in the study, but turned the sound down to listen in as another load of footsteps crashed through downstairs. Jason wasn't due to arrive for another half hour or so and, besides, he didn't crash so much as slide into a room without anyone noticing. She opened the door to the study as quietly as she could and tried to peek out just as Sara appeared at the top of the stairs, red-faced and breathless.

"Just go away Darren! Leave me alone!" Sara's voice broke mid-sentence and she turned to push Darren away but he held her arms and pulled her into him trying to kiss her or hug her or something. Rose turned back to the television and fast-forwarded to the next episode, she did not want to witness her sister making out with her boyfriend or having a fight with him, it was all so juvenile. She turned the sound back up, but then decided to put the headphones on instead. Her dad's headphones were great, if a little too big for her. They completely covered her ears and were padded so they kept her ears all warm, like she was just surrounded by the sound of the programme or the music and not part of the real world at all. She played the next episode, the one where Basil tries to turn Fawlty Towers into an upmarket hotel but gets the wrong kind of clientele. Her dad had said this was very British and that one day, when they could all afford to go, they would visit the town in Dorset where he'd been born.. Then she'd see what he meant and how different things were to Canada.

It was hard for Rose to imagine living anywhere that strange though, having spent her entire life cooped up in Pitcher Creek. She had only ever visited Calgary twice for a school trip and Edmonton once with Sara and her mother where they seemed to spend the whole weekend at the mall rifling through racks of clothes. Calgary had just seemed to be one big building site, so dirty and noisy and she'd wanted to be back home, walking next to Alder Creek looking for lotuses in the quiet swimming holes between their house and the town, or taking long exposure shots of the creek when it was swollen and raging.

Rose had asked if she could just stay in the bookstore, which was huge and like a library as it had chairs and even tables that you could sit at to read the books before you decided if you wanted to buy them. Mr Banyen didn't let you do that in the bookstore in town, but then he didn't really have room for chairs as he'd turned half the store over to selling random hardware recently. Rose wasn't quite sure what hacksaws had to do with books but maybe people needed that kind of thing more than Tolstoy in Pitcher Creek.

Rose was halfway through the next episode when she heard another bang. This time it was just down the hallway, probably Sara's bedroom door slamming again. Then there were raised voices and so Rose turned the sound up a bit more to drown it out. Sara was probably throwing things at Darren. She didn't understand why Sara still said she was dating Darren when they barely ever saw each other and just seemed to fight when they did. Rose figured it was probably just because he smoked pot and stole liquor from his dad's stash and had access to the fishing cabin which he'd hotbox with his friends sometimes. Rose knew he was quite a stoner and she'd even seen him in the woods one time when she'd been on a hike with her dad. They'd been looking at some mushrooms growing underneath an old oak, with Rose trying to take a half-decent picture with her new camera and her dad rifling through some dog-eared wild plant guide muttering about buying a separate mushroom identifier. Darren, Matt McReedy, and a couple of other boys from school had stumbled out of the trees nearby, startled to see Rose and her dad, they had stood staring like moose in the road, wide-eyed and unblinking, until Rose's dad had asked Darren if he was alright and was he on a fishing trip with Bill. The weird look in his eyes and the slow creep of his laugh had made Rose promise herself she'd never do drugs. Her dad had sighed sadly as Darren ran off into the trees.

"Strange boy, eh Rose? I don't think he'll be catching any fish today, what do you think? Shame his mother's not around to pay him some attention." He bent down to look more closely at the mushrooms and then cried "Aha! Here's an orchid Rose, look." He gently brushed aside a couple of fallen oak leaves to reveal the tiniest of flowers and Rose wished she could take it home for her mother to show her what she'd missed. Maybe Sara wouldn't have started going steady with Darren if her dad had stayed, and Bill certainly wouldn't be living with them, changing their routine and leaving his things lying around everywhere.

There was another crashing sound from next door and this time it was followed by someone running down the stairs. Rose took off the headphones and heard another door slam downstairs. She craned to see out of the study window, expecting to see Darren cycling across the back field, but she guessed he'd gone round to the front instead. She could hear Sara crying in her room and thought it must have been a pretty bad fight this time, maybe they'd even broken up for good. As she moved from the study to Sara's door she thought she heard someone walking on the gravel in the driveway. It must be Darren; maybe he'd borrowed Bill's truck. It was too early for Jason to arrive and so Rose gingerly went into Sara's room to see if she wanted a cup of tea or something.

Sara was curled up on the bed on her side with the comforter pulled close around her. Rose saw that she still had her shoes on, which was odd. They were the red ones with the big silver buckles that Rose secretly coveted. They were a startling splash of colour against the tangle of the plain white sheets.

At first, Sara didn't notice that her little sister had walked in and she let the comforter fall away a little as she turned away from the wall. Rose gasped and covered her mouth with her hands as she saw the blistering red marks across her sister's collarbone and the grotesque clown-like grimace transforming Sara's usual smile. The noise of Rose's surprised reaction alerted Sara to her presence and she screamed at her sister to get out of her room. Instead, Rose ran over to her and put her arms around her sister as she sobbed and shook. She didn't ask what had happened as she figured it must be pretty bad with all the marks and she felt the skin on Sara's back as she held her, realising that her dress had been ripped at the back. A silver necklace was lying broken on the pillow, a shimmering heart.

Rose knew that this was more serious than just a regular fight so she wrapped the comforter around her sister and ran downstairs to ring her mother at the store. She saw that the front door was unlocked and so she twisted the latch and hurried to the phone. There was someone on the porch steps, the sound of shoes scuffing the boards, then her mother's voice broke in and Rose tried to breathe and let her know what had happened. She could see Jason outside now and she crouched down behind the telephone table so he wouldn't see her. He knocked and tried the door handle and she was glad that she had locked it. He couldn't come in now, not with Sara like she was. Rose just wanted to tell her mother to come home to look after Sara because she didn't know what to do.

"Mom, Sara's hurt, Jason just came by and I don't know what happened. Can you come home mum? I don't know what to do. There are all these marks on her. I think he hit her, and she won't stop crying and she still has her shoes on in bed and Jason's still at the door. Mom, I have to go. Please come home now!" Rose hung up the phone and leant against the wall for a few seconds, trying to figure out the chaos in her head. She remembered that Jason was still outside and so she crept to the door and saw through the glass that he was already back in his car. She was glad he was leaving as she didn't know what she'd say to him, what he'd seen. Rose went up to Sara with the box of Kleenex from the hall table and waited for her mother.

"Sara? Rose?" Jane sprinted up the stairs to her daughter's room. The door was slightly ajar, unusual for her older daughter's room as Sara gad been so insistent on her privacy in recent months. "I just passed Jason in his car heading home, what's going on?" she fell silent as she saw Sara wrapped in the white comforter she'd bought last Christmas. Rose was beside her looking pale and crying too but not seeming to have noticed her own tears just yet as she tried to pat dry her sister's face which was a mask of grief. "Oh god, what happened, where's Jason?"

"He just left mum, and I found Sara crying and she has all these marks on her and she won't say anything and..." Rose's voice dropped to a whisper, "...there's blood mom and her dress is ripped." As she said the words she realised what she was saying and what it meant, and she looked at her sister, and she saw that she was broken. Rose felt the wetness on her own face then and she clutched at her mom and buried her face into the warmth of her coat.

"Sara, honey, let me look at you... oh god, what did he do. My Sara, I'm so sorry. I have to call Andy, we need to get you looked at, and make sure you're... just stay here honey I'll be back in a minute." Jane ran back downstairs to call the station, wiping her coat sleeves across her eyes and trying to force the image of her daughter's face, cold, empty, from her mind. "Andy? It's Jane Hollister. You need to come over, now. Jason Forrest just raped my daughter."

CHAPTER EIGHT

Rose wasn't sure what Andy was asking her, his expression was so serious that she had to fight an urge to laugh. He looked like a different man to the one who always waved at her from his car whenever he passed her in town. He had done her parents' taxes every year since she could remember and Andy and her dad would drink beer together on the back porch sometimes, even heading out for a fishing trip or a weekend hike to the lake once or twice a year. Now Andy was sitting in a plastic chair across the table from her and he was asking if Jason had ever touched her, had ever said anything about Sara, if she'd ever thought he was strange or if he made her feel afraid or threatened. All these questions that just made her worry she wasn't remembering things right, that she was failing a test they had set without telling her what to study.

Sure, Jason had sat next to her and talked to her and they had fun together, he was nice and they shared some interests but why weren't they asking about Darren? Wasn't he the one who had hurt Sara? Her mother kept talking about Jason being at the house and him driving away as she'd arrived home. No one seemed to be talking about Darren and they had been here for hours now. Why hadn't Sara said they'd had a fight? Why was everyone staring at her but nobody actually listening to what she was saying?

"Did Jason ever touch you Rose?" Andy repeated the question softly, like this made it more normal somehow, less embarrassing. "I know this is difficult but we're trying to help your sister so you need to tell us what you know. Staying quiet and hiding things doesn't help anyone." There was a woman sitting next to Andy, she had arrived half an hour before and spoken only to introduce herself as a community victim support services worker, but Rose had never seen her in town before and figured she'd come in from Red Deer. Rose wondered why she was a victim. It was Sara whose dress had been ripped, whose neck was all red, and who had bruises on her arms. It was her sister who was hurt, who had been raped. Why did this lady think she was a victim too? Why was she acting like Rose had been hurt and needed help? This lady wasn't dressed like a policeman, more like a lawyer or something, and so Rose was afraid of saying the wrong thing and getting someone in trouble. Rose felt weak and a little faint and the lady seemed to smile as she asked for some water. Perhaps she was happier when Rose played her role, like there was a reason for the lady to be there to defend her.

"We just talked about computers and stuff and he showed me how to do things on the computer. Jason's nice, I like him!"

Andy smiled at Rose again, and she knew he was just trying to help but his smile was indulgent, like he thought if he grinned at her and told her she was doing well she'd tell him what he wanted to hear. "We know you want to help your friend Rose and that's understandable, but we need you to help your sister now too, OK?" Rose didn't know what to say. Jason wouldn't hurt her, he couldn't have hurt Sara, it just wasn't what he was like but Andy was so convinced. Maybe Bill was right all along, and Rose guessed that they were asking her about Jason because Sara had told them that he was the one that had hurt her. But she'd only seen Darren in the house; Jason had been trying to get in, hadn't he?

"But Darren was in the house, he was fighting with Sara!" Rose looked at Andy, expectantly, and he smiled. They knew all about that, he said. Darren had already come in with his dad to talk to them. Rose relaxed in the cold plastic chair and felt relieved. They must know that it was Darren then, not Jason who had hurt Sara. "Can I see Sara now?"

"She's talking to a counsellor at the moment Rose, just to make sure she's alright. She's going to need everyone's help, yours too, to get through this... this difficult time." Rose wondered why Andy was talking like it was somebody's funeral; no one had died today, she thought, not really. "How about I take you back to the front desk so you can wait with your mom?" Andy looked over at the support lady who smiled almost as if Andy's glance had flipped a sympathy switch somewhere.

"Let's go get a hot chocolate Rosie, and I'll take you to your mom, you'll want your mom now, eh?" Rose found her voice irritating, she sounded like she was reading a Dr Seuss book to first graders, but she gave in, knowing there wasn't really a choice. The lady smiled at Rose, a thick lipsticked smile that just made her think about Sara and how sad her lopsided mouth had looked.

Rose was taken back into the station foyer, past the interview rooms. She looked into each one as she walked by, hoping to see Sara. Finally she spotted her, sitting on a doctor's bench, her coat wrapped round her and her head bowed. Her legs were dangling over the edge of the bench, too short to reach the floor. Rose saw that her sister's feet were bare and she wondered about the red shoes, where they had gone, and why. Rose continued to stare in at her sister as she went by but then she saw Darren in the room too, leaning against the far wall of the room, his hands tucked into his jeans pockets. She lunged at the door handle, jumping across Andy who caught her and held her back.

"Why does he get to see her?" Rose screamed, and the lipsticked lady took hold of her arm and tried to pull her away down the corridor telling her that Sara and Darren needed some time to talk. That couples do that when something bad happens to one of them. Rose stood her ground and yelled "But it's his fault! Why can't I see her?" Her shouting caused Sara to turn her face to the door and she stared out, then dropped her gaze to the floor, her hair falling across her face, covering the mask of grief and sadness. Rose felt lost. Her sister, who teased her mercilessly, who shouted at her, punched her, who led the way, could now not even look at her.

Rose saw Darren move towards Sara and she shouted at him to leave her sister alone. He put his arm tightly around Sara, pushing her face into his chest. He had heard Rose shouting and he turned toward the door, staring at her in surprise and then shaking his head like he was warning her to be quiet.

Rose was hauled down the corridor back to her mother, who was sitting next to Bill, his hand on Jane's arm. Rose desperately wanted her dad but for now all she had were the cool sympathetic smiles and a seemingly endless river of hot chocolate that burnt the roof of her mouth and tasted like the polystyrene cups it came in. She wanted to talk to her mother alone but Bill didn't move and just kept looking at Rose across her mother, occasionally asking her if she was OK.

"Jane?" Andy crouched down in front of Rose's mother and put one hand on her knee. "You can take Sara home now. The doc's checked her over and, well, we've done everything that can be done. If you just come with me I need to go over a couple of things with you." He glanced at Rose and the said "It might be best if it's just the two of us. I'll need to talk to Jim too, if you can give me a number I can reach him at." Her mother stood up and followed Andy, leaving Rose and Bill sitting on the blue plastic chairs that were bolted to the floor of the police station lobby. Rose knew Darren's dad was looking at her but she didn't want to talk to him or see his face.

"Rose, it's very... serious, what Jason did to your sister." Bill emphasised Jason's name, making it sound harsh, abrasive even, and Rose felt the word become venomous in Bill's mouth. The way he spat it out gave the name a physical presence that ran through his body, attaching the crime to the boy by pure force. Bill's whole body was tense, angry, and Rose saw that he kept cracking his fingers in towards his clenched fists, over and over, like he was preparing for a fight. "The boy's clearly deranged and you girls need looking after, just like your mom needs someone to look after her too. I'm going to take you all home and keep an eye on things, so your mom doesn't need to worry about you getting yourself into trouble or getting confused about what happened today. Do you understand?" Bill was quiet for a second or two and Rose kept her head down, trying to process everything. Bill cracked his knuckles again and Rose couldn't help looking over. "I'm angry, Rose, just like... well, just like your father would be if he were still here. Darren should have behaved better to your sister." Rose was surprised, was Bill saying that he knew that Jason hadn't hurt Sara, that Darren had? "He should've protected her better from that boy."

Rose's body shook a little, starting at the base of her skull and worming down her spine like somebody had dropped a handful of snow down the back of her coat. She didn't say anything. She couldn't say anything to this man who seemed to think he had replaced her father, who was playing the role with so little skill but with such apparent satisfaction.

Bill moved to the seat next to her that Jane had just vacated. He spoke slowly, carefully. "But it wasn't Darren's fault, Rose. Do we understand each other? It wasn't his fault, and it wasn't mine or yours either, right?" She still couldn't look at him and kept her gaze directed instead at the cracks in the grey floor tiles. His voice grew a little deeper "Rose, this is important. You're not going to make any more trouble for your mother now are you? You're not going to change your story or make up any lies about what you heard or saw. Do we understand each other?" This time the man placed his hand on Rose's shoulder. It was heavy and he dug his fingers into her skin as Rose glanced at the ragged yellow fingernails, wide-eyed. Bill had green stains on his fingers from tying up the tomato plants in her mom's greenhouse. He rarely wore gloves when he was working and so there were also scratches and scars across his hands. He saw her looking and he pulled his hand away, shoving it roughly into the pocket of his sheepskin jacket.

He's scared, she thought. He's afraid that someone else will blame Darren for what happened and that they'll think he's protecting his son. Maybe he's scared her mother will leave him because of this. But how could they all live together now, after what had happened. The terror and the anger all tied up in Bill made Rose worry for a second about what he'd do to his son when he saw him but whatever it was, Rose thought, Darren deserved it. He'd hurt Sara, she just wasn't quite sure any more how much he'd hurt her.

Bill suddenly sighed and shook himself like a dog waking from a nap. He smiled at her, his teeth looking more yellow than his fingers in the reflected glow of the vending machine and he whispered to her "I know you'll be a good girl." Rose looked up at the sound of footsteps and saw her mother and Sara approaching arm in arm. Darren trailed behind, hands in his pockets.

Mr Tether drove them all home in silence, the whites of his knuckles showing as he gripped the wheel of Jane's station wagon. Rose's mother sat quietly between her two daughters in the back, her eyes boring a hole in the windscreen, tears wetting her cheeks silently. Rose tried to find her mom's hand but Jane was already gripping Sara's, the two women locked together but unable to look at each other. Rose turned to stare out of the window towards the foothills where the snow was still lying thick on the ground. She tried not to make a noise as the tears came again.

Part Two

CHAPTER ONE

Arbutus Lodge is not a bad place, not really, it's just quite full of bad people so there is an air of tragedy and sadness, and the constant feeling that something awful is about to happen and there's absolutely nothing you can do to stop it. My first few days here I was quite out of it, not realising where I was or why I was here and thrashing about so much that I had to have restraints to keep me safe. I had been transferred from the hospital, but I didn't remember much, just a vague memory of screams and a jumble of faces above me as I was pinned down. They gave me some Valium or something to just knock me out because I kept screaming at my mother, who I now knew hadn't even been there. She had signed the papers back in Edmonton to get me on this programme, promising then that it would fix me, that I'd get back to school soon. I don't think she believed it, even all those weeks ago.

I've accepted, though, that I must have done something so awful that it just broke my mind and I had to come here to get it fixed. It's not like the blackouts from when I was younger as I don't remember not remembering anything. I guess that doesn't make much sense but maybe the tests they did just didn't find what was wrong back then and now they know.

Dr Laurence, the therapist who runs the programme here, seems happy that I'm doing better and even talked about having visitors soon, saying that it's normal to get the family involved as soon as possible in situations like this. He hasn't said what the situation is, though, and I'm sure that my parents aren't going to come all the way out here to see me. After all, they sent me away in the first place. I could have just stayed in the prison hospital. My mother's too nervous and economical to fly anyway and there's no way they could afford the time to take the Greyhound across the Rockies and all the way across BC.

Some of the other boys here have said that I should count myself lucky as a few years ago I'd have just ended up in prison until I was eighteen and probably get hooked on something or be an alcoholic or whatever. So, although I'm not quite sure what Dr Laurence's programme's all about, it's probably good that I'm here if I'm that messed up.

He has me on clozapine, which made my heart race at first but they tried a lower dose and now I just have some anxiety, but Dr Laurence says that's understandable, considering all I've been through. Still, I've never felt quite like this before, even when I was too scared to go to school in case I got cornered in phys. ed. again. I wish I didn't have to take the medication but Dr Laurence said I won't get better without it and that it'd be worse if I tried to refuse it.

I talked about the dreams again in the group therapy session today, how they'd become more vivid, coloured in where they were black and white and grey before. Dr Feinberg said that this was a sign of progress, that I was getting closer to accepting what I'd done and that this was good. She was really enthusiastic about telling Dr Laurence so that we could talk about it in the private therapy sessions. Even if it was scarier, she said, it meant that my mind thought it was getting strong enough to heal itself. All I know is that I've been waking in the night for weeks now, the bed sheets sticking to me with cold sweat and that I'm unable to move because it still feels like I'm strapped down. I just lay there, on my back, arms outstretched, wondering how I could do something so terrible that I'd end up here with all these other boys. I guess you can't even really know yourself all that well and all this time I've been worrying so much about working out how everyone else is feeling and why they do what they do. What hope have I got if I can't even figure out what I'm thinking, or remember what I've done?

We're not all allowed to walk around the lodge's gardens freely but this week I got privileges so I get some time outside now. I spent most of the summer indoors but today I went out to the fountain behind the art studio. As I sat down on the edge of the pool one of the new nurses came running over, flicking gravel everywhere, and I was hauled back inside, back to my room. No one told me why but I guess they thought I'd try to drown myself in the two inches of water in the ornamental fountain. Perhaps they shouldn't have put such a thing in psychiatric centre; it's probably so it looks good for when our parents and probation officers visit.

I guess the fountain's out of bounds for me now. That's the thing about Arbutus Lodge, there are all these rules that you need to follow but they're not written down anywhere and no one tells you what they are so it's just easier to do nothing and talk to nobody than make a wrong move.

I look over at the clock, 2.37am. The boy in the bed next to me is whistling every time he exhales, softly, but he sounds like a broken kettle trying again and again to announce itself ready. The sheets are sticking to my thighs and my back and I'm cold but the blankets we have are pretty thin and I don't have a comforter like some of the boys whose parents bring them things.

When I was moved to the dorm after being in isolation I knew it wasn't dry and cold enough to be near home. The rain was incessant and so you could barely see out of the windows of the lodge. I had no idea where I was or how long I'd been here but I saw that some of the boys were keeping a tally carved on their nightstand. I figured I'd do the same once I knew where to start and could find something sharp with which to carve into the wood.

I had asked the boy in the next bed if we were near the coast and he pulled out map with a big ring around the lodge. I'd never been this far away from home before and I could see the Pacific opening out at the edge of the map. It seems unreal that I'm at the edge of the country, that there is so much space here and that I'm trapped inside. Arbutus Lodge is nestled like some Englishman's abandoned country mansion in the undeveloped area northwest of Vancouver. It was about a mile to the cliffs at the edge of the inlet, and a mile or so to the nearest gas station that sat on the one road through this place, back to Vancouver or north to the reservation. Most of the boys here had said that res. kids had been with them in the prison but that this kind of programme didn't work for them so it was mainly city boys whose parents had pulled some strings. I wondered at how my parents had got me here as they didn't know anyone important, having barely left Pitcher Creek in the seventeen years since I was born. It was about a fifteen hour drive from home and no one was going to visit me here. I'll admit that I'm kind of glad about that.

The lodge is named after the four arbutus out front, each about eighty feet tall and covered at the moment with red berries. I watch the birds from the dorm window, waxwings I think, flitting about most of the day now. The other trees around the lodge's entrance have just started losing their leaves and a few of the boys have been given the job of collecting them for mulch in the gardens. Dr Laurence signed me up for the job last week so I'm working with the other boys now, raking up the mess of browns and reds and golds to fill the huge paper sacks. I guess it's therapeutic, working in silence most of the time, except for the shrill 'seeeeee seeeee' of the waxwings hiding in the arbutus and the crack and snap of the desiccated leaves. There are a few maples here too, but not the right kind for making syrup. They look diseased anyway, their broad leaves falling early and thick purple scars all along the veins of the leaves. It's funny that even the trees are sick.

Like the other boys, I keep my head down while I work, stooped to the task at hand and nothing else. Nurse Statton is always close by, usually reading but looking up occasionally to check we haven't used the rakes to kill each other I guess, or sliced our wrists open with a piece of sharp gravel. Everything is a weapon here, things I'd never even considered before, like the pointed edges of tables, the nails holding the back onto a bookshelf, the snapped off end of a paintbrush in art therapy. One thing I do remember about arriving here is that the orderlies took my lace-ups and my feet were freezing as I walked in just my socks to the isolation ward. Desperation and ingenuity are clearly good friends in a place like this. Although I hope I'm well enough soon to leave I have developed a strange fondness for the lodge, for its peace and stillness; when I'm left alone of course. It's reassuring that all the others here are as crazy as me, that none of us fit elsewhere. I know, though, that we're all others in different ways but here, at least, I don't have to worry about what everyone else thinks of me or be afraid that I've misread someone's intentions. I'm not the odd boy any more.

I should get back to sleep, I have art therapy in the morning with Janice and she always notices when I have dark circles under my eyes. Last week she said I looked 'positively vampiric' and that I needed more sun, so she painted a whole canvas yellow just for the hell of it and then told me to stand and stare at it as you can't help but be happy seeing the glow of sunshine. It felt pretty silly but I think that was the point as I just started laughing after a few minutes and that made her happy too. I wish I had more art therapy and less of the group sessions where I have to sit and listen to some really horrible stuff that the other boys have done.

I never really liked art before, it seemed vague, imprecise, so easy to fail and not even know why. At least there were rules with math and coding, syntax to fall back on. You could tell when you'd done something wrong and find out how to fix it, even if that was hard sometimes. Janice says it's a form of creativity, that it's part of who I am but that I need more creative outlets to nurture that part of myself. She thinks that I get too wrapped up in myself, and that that means I can pretend other people don't exist, that their feelings don't matter. She said I need to realise that I can, and do affect others, even if I feel insignificant.

I'm not sure what Dr Laurence and Janice talk about, whether they even work together really. He's definitely in charge, and I know Janice has to tell him what I'm drawing and painting, that he uses her to find things out about me, things I might not tell him in our sessions.

CHAPTER TWO

My canvas was already on the easel and I was laying out the acrylics, red, green, blue, when Janice walked into the art studio. I should really say crashed in as I heard her running down the corridor before she threw open the door and dropped her bag on the desk at the front of the room. I stood staring at her, paintbrush in my left hand and was a little afraid to move as her eyes were a bit wilder even than usual. We were supposed to be having a private therapy session but now I was suddenly missing the hubbub of the other boys in the usual class.

"Put down the brush mister, we're going for an adventure!" Janice plucked the thin-tipped brush from my fingers, plonked it down next to the paints and grabbed my hand in hers to drag me from the room. I heard the paintbrush roll across the table and plink onto the floor as we crossed to the door. I fought the urge to go back and pick it up, concentrating on following Janice as she headed out of the room and back down the corridor.

Outside, we passed the fountain at quite a pace, continued down to the hedge at the end of the back lawn of the lodge and Janice opened the gate, holding it open for me to go through. I hesitated, we weren't allowed out of the grounds and now here Janice, one of the therapists, was holding the door for me. "Shhheeeesh! It's no trick mister, just get your ass through that gate and let's have some fun!" She shoved me through and then followed quickly, closing the gate behind her before skipping across to a green Ford pickup with considerable rust on the wheel arches. Looking at Janice's truck I suddenly felt sad at the thought of my own car. What had happened to it when I left Pitcher Creek? Did mom and dad sell it or was it still there in the driveway waiting for me to come home?

The thought of the house made the acid rise from my stomach and I tried to swallow it back down to stop the burning which often meant that I was going to be sick. It was funny, I rarely thought about the town now. Every day here seemed to leave me exhausted so I hadn't space or time or energy to think about Pitcher Creek, about my family. I realised I'd just fallen into a routine, that this was life now. I was struck suddenly by the image of my car quietly rusting away in front of my parents' place. It seemed laughable, not quite real somehow.

Janice was getting something out of the passenger side of the truck and then she handed it to me. A shoebox, a large shoebox so probably not hers as she's pretty tiny. Maybe her husband's, although I'd never noticed a wedding ring, or any jewellery come to think of it. Maybe lodge regulations meant she couldn't wear any. An earring could be lethal in the wrong fingers in this place and I'd heard a number of the boys complain that they'd had to take their studs out. Strangely, I felt proud of this newly acquired knowledge about the menace of everyday objects, as if I might have a use for it later in life. That was, until I remembered how I'd ended up here, and how so many of the other boys had the same story of stealing their father's liquor to wash down their mom's Valium.

I opened the box Janice had given me and something tried to jump out. Janice snorted and covered her mouth with her hand, whilst quickly pushing the lid back down with her other hand. She told me to follow her and I tried to ignore the shaking of the shoebox as we walked away from the truck. I asked Janice where we were going. "On a release mission, to free the frogs, poor critters."

"Where are they from? And, well, where are we taking them?" Art therapy was always a little strange but at least it was usually in the classroom, with paints or pencils and some sense of structure. This was downright weird, but kind of exciting too, especially being out of hospital grounds. I wondered if Janice had had to ask for permission for me to come with her on this escapade.

We got down to a set of steps in the woods behind the car park. The edges of the steps were set in with split stumps, now quite slippery as the tree cover was keeping the forest floor from drying out much during the day. As we went down the steps I saw that Janice's skirt was trailing and picking up mud. I had to try hard not to step on it as I followed her through the woods. My mother would think it pretty disgraceful to be so reckless with your clothes and I could picture her scrubbing out the mud by hand before the skirt went into the wash with everything else. If I'd had a sister like Janice my mom would've had a fit, it was bad enough when I came home with grass stains and mud down my back or rubbed into the front of my shirt by some of the kids at school. I'd try to hide the clothes as I'd gotten older so my mom wouldn't get so upset but she always found them before I had a chance to wash them myself.

The ground suddenly got really spongy and Janice slowed down. "Mike said that it's somewhere round here." She peered through the trees to the right and then veered off through them as she cried out triumphantly, "Follow me frogman, I found the release site!" She pushed the salmonberry leaves and branches aside, holding them for me for a second or two and exclaiming as she got branch after branch caught in the mess of her hair. I could hear water, just a slow murmur and after we pushed through a little more shrubbery we stepped out onto a stony bank on the edge of a little bubbling creek. Janice breathed in deeply and looked over at me. "More invigorating than the classroom right? Now, we have to follow it down a little ways to find the pool that these fellas will be calling home." She glanced at her watch, "Oh, and we'd better hurry before they notice we've gone!"

So we didn't have permission to do this, to leave the grounds. Janice was going to get in trouble. I was going to get in trouble. What was she playing at? As I was thinking about this the brush opened up and Janice stopped dead so that I nearly fell straight into her. I put out a hand, just a reflex, and accidentally touched the middle of her back. I pulled my hand back straight away and started apologising. "I didn't mean to, I'm sorry, it was a mistake, please don't tell Dr Laurence, I didn't mean it. Please." Janice had turned around as I'd fallen into her but she was smiling at me, she wasn't angry or upset.

"Jason, it's fine. You just fell because I stopped so quickly! I don't need to tell Doc Laurence because nothing happened. I probably shouldn't say this but, if you ask me, all your therapy with him isn't worth a jot if it's got you this wound up about even accidentally touching another human being." Janice took her hand and placed it on top of mine which was safely back clutching the shoebox full of hopping frogs.

"So, you're not upset with me?"

"Why would I be frogman? It was a mistake, you didn't mean anything by it. No one got hurt." She paused and gave me a weak smile, "It's nothing like what happened to get you sent here in the first place, you know that right?" Janice didn't wait for an answer but as she turned away and bent down to the bank of the pond she muttered something else that I didn't quite catch.

Everyone knew what I'd done and that there was something wrong with me, everyone except Janice it seemed. She wasn't afraid of me and actually seemed to like me, but I could feel that something about me wasn't right, that I needed fixing. Otherwise, why would I have such dreams, and why would I think such things about the other boys here? I hadn't told anyone about those thoughts. Not about the feeling I got when I looked over at Henry in the dining room, or when I saw Denny working in the lodge's library, reaching up to shelve books so that his shirt popped out of his waistband and gave me a little glimpse of cool, smooth skin that had made me feel like my head would burst so I had to rush outside and gulp down some cold air. It was safer, for everyone, if I just didn't let myself think like that, about anyone. The girls at my old school, the boys here, and definitely not Janice who was now crouching down to my left and poking around in the mud at the side of the pond.

"Jason, stop faffing and help me make them a little swamp. Here, take a skunk cabbage leaf and get scraping, down this side. Then we can use them as little swamp liners and back fill it from the pond to make it easier for them to get in and out at first until they figure out where they're going to set up home. Mike said we shouldn't just tip them in as it'd shock them."

I put the shoebox down and ripped a leaf off one of the stinky skunk cabbage poking out of the edge of the pond. It was littered with them all the way across and I thought how the frogs would probably be able to hop along the whole thing without even touching the water, like Jesus walking on water.

"What's going on in your head Jason, what are you thinking about?" Janice hadn't looked up, asking the question quietly, almost to the water itself. Could I answer her honestly? Would she just think me stranger than she already did?

"Jesus frogs" I muttered, and then startled myself by laughing. Janice laughed too and shook her head as she smiled at me.

"Well, aren't you a surprise."

"I guess."

"Are your parents religious Jason?" Janice looked up at me and I knew that really she was asking if I was religious, if I had just blasphemed by comparing frogs to Our Saviour. I hesitated, but I trusted Janice more than anyone else.

"My mom goes to church every week and my dad finds an excuse most weeks, but he helps out with raffles and maintenance and things. My mom stopped taking me after a while as I wouldn't go and play with the other kids afterwards and I think she just wanted to be left alone to talk with the other women over coffee."

"Did you like the services though?"

I thought about the few sermons I remembered and found I could only really recollect the singing, how I'd thought it would be nice to join the choir, maybe even have a go at playing the church organ.

"I liked the hymns." I said. "Until I realised what they were about."

Janice was silent for a second or two, looking down at the ground, and I felt like an idiot. Why had I said that? Maybe Janice was really religious, how did I know. She brushed her muddy hands on her skirt and looked straight at me. I waited for her to say something, expecting a lecture of some kind. Instead, she surprised me with a question I couldn't answer.

"Because they're about love for all, except for people like you and..." she paused, "and some of the other boys here?"

CHAPTER THREE

Dr Laurence wanted to talk about our little 'excursion' but the way he said it just made me feel all twisted up and all my words were tied tight into a knot, unable to come out.

"Janice took you on an 'excursion' in the woods, outside the grounds I hear?" I didn't answer as it was clear he already knew. I wondered if Janice had told him about me touching her back when I shouldn't have or about our discussing church and hymns and things. "Did the freedom, ah, excite you Jason? Would you like to leave the lodge grounds again?"

This had to be a trick question. To Dr Laurence excitement was a bad thing. Excitement meant that your brain had been taken over by something bad, bad thoughts and feelings and urges and so you had to just stop and lock that back away before someone got hurt. Going outside the grounds wasn't allowed so it had to be a trick to catch me out so I'd have to stay longer until I was properly fixed. I shook my head. "No, it was just a strange art class."

"Do you think you learnt anything in that class Jason?"

"I, well, I learnt there was a pond nearby that I didn't know about, and a river, and that Janice knows lots about frogs, I think." I knew Dr Laurence meant had I learnt anything about myself in the class, that was the whole point of these sessions after all, but I never knew how to answer such things. I didn't see how you could learn things about yourself when you were yourself and could never stop being yourself to watch how you did things or thought about things. The whole idea was just too weird and made it feel like his questions were little pieces of glass inside my head that were transparent so I couldn't find them after the sessions but they were still there poking into my brain when I thought about the wrong things. I know that some of our sessions are supposed to help put a barrier inside your head to stop your mind racing towards bad thoughts. I hated those sessions as the audiotapes were disgusting, about kids and things, and they would sometimes put these sensors on me to see if I got excited. How could anyone get excited about little kids like that? Some of the boys said that they had been forced to watch videos and that sometimes those images came back to them while they were sleeping. I sometimes heard the sounds of little kids in my head, and the things the guy in the tapes would say to them. It was confusing when I woke up in the wet sheets and could only half remember the bad dreams with the good.

Dr Laurence was still staring at me and I remembered something from a psych class back in school about the ego and the id and your parents being your superego I think. Maybe Dr Laurence thought I hadn't got the right bits of my parents in me and that was why I did bad things and, I suppose, why I thought about the other boys the way I did.

I had been having these therapy sessions with Dr Laurence for about three months now, since I'd been lucid enough to talk to him. In the first few days I just didn't know why I was here, but he had reminded me of my tutoring Sara and her assault and how I needed to start remembering it so as to take responsibility. I was confused and had asked why I wasn't just in jail and he said I was lucky that I was at the lodge, that lots of other boys with disorders like me would just end up offending again because they weren't getting this new therapy I was. He said that my suicide attempt showed that, somewhere inside me, I felt remorse, that it meant there was hope for my rehabilitation.

Dr Laurence said I was trying to avoid admitting to everyone what I'd done and, most of all, that I was avoiding admitting it to myself. He said that the mind couldn't hold onto the idea of being a good person having done a bad thing and so parts of me had tried to shut down instead. Now he said I was getting to the point, finally, where I could face what I had done and start to make amends.

According to Dr Laurence my brain's blocking out what I did to Sara until I'm strong enough to admit it. He said he wouldn't push me, that I should remember at my own pace as he didn't want to risk another breakdown. But every week the questions were pretty much the same. Did I remember tutoring Sara for math, and Rose being in the study? How about passing Mrs Hollister in the car as I drove home? And, anything between arriving at their house and getting back in the car. I kept telling Dr Laurence that I just remembered not being able to get into the house, but that I'd seen Rose crying in the hallway and so I'd left. I guess it was me she was scared of, me that had made Sara sick, but I really don't remember.

I can remember my mother saying we would have to move now, that no one would shop at their store any more. I knew it was all my fault, and that she'd never forgive me. Despite all her religious fervour, to my mother a bad act made a bad person and I had always been a difficult child. I remember her saying over and over as they arrested me at the house that she had tried, she had done all she could with what God had given her. My dad just walked away, into the sitting room at the back, like he had given up on me. When I was allowed a few days at home before being sent to the detention centre in Edmonton neither of them would look me in the eye, and I wasn't really surprised that they hadn't come to visit me here. I guess my dad thinks I'm weak for stealing mom's pills and hiding. I guess real men shoot themselves or do something a little braver at least.

I don't know who found me in the crawl space, whether it was my parents or a paramedic who lifted me down and took me to hospital, I just remember curling up in there and wanting everything to stop. Then the burning in my chest and my throat, and the feeling that I'd failed even in this as I woke to the bright lights in the hospital bed. I had tried to escape from the tiredness, from the endless feeling of having let everyone down, from the sense that not only was I evil for having done something so awful to Sara, but that I was so much of a coward that I couldn't even remember doing it.

As it was, I don't remember even having a trial. I guess I was in the hospital and then Dr Laurence picked me for his programme and so I was only in jail while I was in the hospital and I came straight here after I was found guilty. Everything's so patchy and no one has ever explained what was going on, even the probation officer that comes here to see me and half a dozen other boys once a month. I'm too scared to ask because what if they tell Dr Laurence and he thinks that I'm trying to cheat somehow?

Sometimes I think I remember my mom screaming at me, asking what I'd done, over and over but maybe I made that up. Maybe that's actually me screaming at myself. Janice says I'm in my own head too much and I think she's right but when I'm told I need to sort my head out it's pretty hard not to spend every second wondering about what I'm thinking and what I've done. I'd once heard my mother talking to one of the other ladies at the church, saying that it would have been easier to have a daughter, at least she'd know where she stood then. She said that at least Mrs Scott knew what Heather was thinking because she'd been a girl herself but that she had no idea what was swirling around my head. Of course, she never said this to me and she just pretended there was nothing wrong with me most of the time, blaming herself now for not getting me fixed earlier.

Dr Laurence was waiting for an answer, his pen poised over the pad of paper in his lap. I watched him run the thumb and index finger of his left hand over his moustache, back and forth, in and out from the centre. "Jason, look, we've been going over this for a number of weeks now and I know you say you don't remember anything but I think it's time we tried a little harder to get you to pull down that screen. Distancing yourself from your actions does not help you in the long run, as comfortable as it might feel right now, so why don't we start with you arriving at Sara's house on the Thursday night."

The doctor uncrossed and recrossed his legs, left to right then right to left, adjusting the writing pad on his knee and leaning forward slightly. He licked his upper lip, leaving a little sheen of spittle on the tips of his moustache, highlighted by the glow of his desk lamp. "Rose was in the study and so Sara let you in, yes?"

"I don't remember, well, no, Rose didn't let me in, she was upset. The door was locked."

"Jason, you and I both know why Rose was upset but that was when you left, not when you arrived. So, let's start again. Sara must have let you in, or you let yourself in, and you went into her room for her math lesson. Was that normal to have her lesson in her room?"

"No, we always studied in the dining room, and Mrs Hollister brought us lemonade and hot chocolate all the time. I've never seen Sara's room, or Rose's, except for..."

"Yes?" Dr Laurence leaned forward a little more, and bit the side of his upper lip. His pen shook slightly just above the writing pad. This was the first time I'd confessed to being in Rose's room and I think Dr Laurence thought I was about to have an epiphany and remember the whole thing, but as much as I wanted to get better I just couldn't recall anything differently to what I'd already told everyone.

"Well, once I did go into Rose's room by mistake when I was looking for the washroom. Sara's room has a sign on the door but Rose's doesn't and so I didn't know which one it was and her room's right next to the washroom so I got confused. I didn't go in, I didn't touch anything."

"You never went into Sara's room, not to just have a peek before going back downstairs to the dining room? A teenage girl's bedroom is an exciting place Jason. You wouldn't be the first boy to be a little tempted."

"No." I felt slightly repulsed by Dr Laurence's idea of what I might have been doing in Sara's bedroom, what other boys might have done. All these weekly therapy sessions and he still has no real idea of who I am.

"OK, OK, Jason, tell me about your lessons with Sara. Did you enjoy them?" The doctor seemed to have deflated slightly, slumped into his chair. He barely looked at me now as he asked the question.

"I, well, yes, it's fun to teach someone something and she seemed to start understanding algebra and even some of the trig stuff."

"And, Sara, you liked her? You got on well?"

"Well, she didn't like me at first."

"That's not what I asked Jason. Did you like her, did you get on?"

"Yes, I liked her. She didn't really understand math or care at first but then she seemed to want to learn and was happy when she got something right."

"So you liked it when she got something right, you rewarded her?"

"Well, yeah, I guess I tried to make her feel like she was getting better at stuff. I tried to help her understand."

"What about when she didn't understand? Did that frustrate you, that she's a pretty girl who didn't really care about the things you care about, like school?"

I didn't like how Dr Laurence was making Sara out to be really dumb but it was true, I had been frustrated that Sara was able to be so popular, that she was pretty and had so many friends and that nothing bad ever happened to her, until, well, I guess until what happened happened. I shook my head, my eyes lowered to my clammy hands in my lap. I felt my underarms damp and sticky and I just wanted to go and sit in the shower, let the water pound down on me, drowning out the noise of Dr Laurence's questions which just kept coming.

"Isn't it true that you told Sara's mom that Sara would do better in class if she just concentrated more, if she wasn't so distracted by her boyfriend?"

"Well, yes, that's true."

"And how did you feel about Sara's boyfriend?"

I thought about Darren Tether and I had to shove my hands between my thighs to stop them shaking. I fought against the inevitable images of him kissing Sara, images I had often tried to stop myself thinking about, of her putting her hands around his back, the feel of his jacket and the taste of his mouth. I clenched my fists tight. I didn't want to give the doctor the satisfaction of seeing me shake. He knew though, he must know.

"Did you think that you might be a better boyfriend than Darren?" I looked up at him, surprised, maybe he didn't know. He skipped the question.

"Did you talk about anything other than math? Did she ever ask about your friends or your school?"

"No, I don't think so."

"Even though you were at a different school, outside the town? Some girls might find that interesting, an older boy, more grown up with a car and friends in the city and heading off to college soon." As he mentioned college I felt a pressure in my chest. My course would have started by now and I would be missing the introductory classes. I hadn't even got my dorm room sorted out.

"Where will I stay when I go to Calgary?"

"I'm sorry?"

"When I get to college I'll need somewhere to stay. And, I need the reading list for my classes. I'll have already missed some so I need to start catching up." Dr Laurence looked puzzled, his mouth drooped slightly and he blinked nervously. I almost felt bad for throwing him off guard but I needed to know about college. I should be there already. I was behind in classes and would have to catch up. I'd have missed all the introductions, perhaps I wouldn't be able to find everything I needed now and I'd feel stupid to ask the others how to get to the library, where we should register for ID cards, how to sign up at the health centre. I'd not even sorted out a dorm. That was all supposed to be arranged in summer, but my summer had just disappeared in a flurry of accusation, confusion, and anger. I tried to think back to exams in spring, had I even completed those still outstanding before all this happened.

"OK, Jason, I think this was a bad idea, my questions obviously upset you so let's just talk next week instead when you're feeling better. OK?" Dr Laurence folded his writing pad over and clipped the pen to it before standing up and gesturing to the door.

"But, Dr Laurence, when am I going to college?" I stood and looked squarely at him, and realised that we were actually about the same height, maybe I was even a little taller than him. He was bigger though, like he had played football or something when he was younger.

"Jason, we've been over this." Dr Laurence walked over to the door. "You won't be going to college this semester, not until we can be sure you're better and that you'll be able to cope with the pressures that environment brings. The change is difficult enough for most teenagers, and even more so for someone like yourself who is..." he stopped himself saying something and cleared his throat, "who has been unwell. I can see about getting you some access to textbooks if you like so you can keep yourself busy with studying and then you might feel a little better, but I'm afraid it will probably still be quite a while before you're well enough to go to college, if they even save the place for you." I started to protest but he just drowned me out. "Now, I think you might find some of the boys are going on a nature walk of the grounds this morning so you can join them if you find Nurse Statton quickly enough. I'll see you next week after group therapy."

I walked out of the therapy room and Dr Laurence shut the door behind me. I think the idea of me being at college had scared him. What if I did it again, what if I hurt another girl like I'd hurt Sara? What if I did something worse, or what if I took another overdose? I didn't want to go on a nature walk or sweep leaves or paint pictures of sunshine. I wanted to get away. I wanted to have my car back, and to just drive to Calgary, get my computer set up in my new dorm and head to class. I wanted to be normal, not sick, not here. I wanted to talk to the professor I met at my interview about his research. Instead, I had to go on another nature walk, with Nurse Statton who would report any tardiness to Dr Laurence.

CHAPTER FOUR

Henry was waiting in the foyer of the older boys' dorm, rubber boots bulging at the top with his scrunched up jeans. He was trying to smooth out the folds of denim at his knees but was clearly on the verge of giving up when I arrived. He looked up at me and smiled, asking if I'd also been sent on the walk, for 'good behaviour'? Straightening up, Henry was just a little taller than me, with a little more to him in terms of muscle. He had broad shoulders but slender hips, giving the impression that he either erupted from the ground haphazardly or tapered into it. Either way he looked like he was in danger of toppling over, top-heavy like a superhero.

Henry also had a bit of a tan, having been on garden duty for most of the summer. The colour was mostly on the back of his neck though, and on his hands and arms. I knew he played the piano and I had found myself staring at his hands more than once. They looked like they had been perfectly made for such a thing, for dancing across the keys as I had seen them flutter over a patch of weeds, picking out the undesirable plants from in-between the rows of carefully arranged ornamentals.

At dinner last week we had been seated at the same table and Henry had told me he'd been here for six months, at his parents' expense. This was the first time I'd really had a chance to talk to him. He was in Dr Laurence's group therapy sessions and had Feinberg as his main therapist and I'd never heard him say why he was at Arbutus Lodge. Henry didn't seem sick to me, he felt strong, powerful, like he was confident of who he was and why he shouldn't be here. I knew that such impressions could be deceptive though. He'd just been transferred into my dorm this week and there had been a couple of nights where he'd woken screaming and crying. I'd watched from the edge of the covers as the nurse would leave her office to administer a sedative after which he snored that dead-sleep snore, waking up groggy the next day.

"Haven't got a smoke have you?" Henry leaned into me and whispered in my ear. I felt the warmth of his breath in the quiet swish of his words. At that moment Nurse Statton came out of the staff office at the bottom of the stairs and Henry almost jumped away from me. It was as if he'd felt the sudden fire roaring through my blood, the intense heat rising in me at the lingering sensation of his breath on my skin.

There was a strange look on Nurse Statton's face as she approached.

"Not harassing Jason here are we, Henry, nothing I need to know before we go and get the others?"

"No. Nothing." Henry was looking at the floor and had stepped even further away from me.

"Good, now let's go." She started turning and then glanced at me, "Are you supposed to be coming too Jason?"

"Yes. Dr Laurence said I was to find you."

"Right," she looked me up and down, "and do you have hiking boots or gumboots or anything this time?"

"Ah, well, no not really, just these." I looked down at my battered old sneakers; one had a hole in the top of the leather that had been letting the rain in this past week. I felt ashamed, especially as Henry had glanced down at my shoes along with Nurse Statton. I should write to my parents and ask for them to send some decent shoes. I don't think they really knew what they were doing when they packed my stuff to send with me here. There had been some lace-ups and these sneakers with the Velcro fastenings. The lace-ups had been confiscated when I first arrived so I'd been wearing my running shoes for months now, in all weathers and they were almost falling off my feet.

Nurse Statton clicked her tongue against the roof of her mouth and looked up at me after letting her eyes linger again on my shoes. "They'll do for now but make sure to let your feet dry out when we get back, we don't want to add trench foot to your list of woes now do we?" Nurse Statton always seemed to think every boy at Arbutus Lodge was terminally ill, perhaps some were and I just didn't know. She looked at us all like we were likely to drop down dead at her feet from sheer exhaustion at the slightest bit of stress. Perhaps, I thought, that could happen, after all I had collapsed once in the dining hall and had to be carried back to my dorm. That was only when I'd been put on some new medication though and the dose was all off for a few days until they gave me something else to work out the side-effects. I had been so dizzy and sick and I remember feeling like I had gauze across my eyes and cotton stuffed in my ears, ready for my head to explode with the pressure.

We arrived at the younger boy's dorm and there was a gumbooted huddle of twelve and thirteen year olds waiting for us. Nurse Statton did a quick roll call and then we started marching off to the gardens. Henry hung back and I did the same as the younger kids all vied to take the lead of the group.

"Statton's a bit much, right? That comment about your shoes, what does she expect if we just get packed off here and aren't allowed visitors. I've been wearing the same crappy sweatshirt for about four months now, I swear the smell of this place, the illness of it will never wash out. I'll burn the damn thing when I leave." Henry had pulled the neck of his sweater up to his nose and sniffed dramatically. I was close enough to him now, almost knocking elbows as we walked. I could detect a faint tea-tree aroma, and coconut oil perhaps, but I wasn't sure. It was nice whatever it was, clean not sick like he was saying.

"I think you smell nice." I hadn't meant to say anything and I blushed as the words tumbled out. Henry snorted in surprise and turned to look at me, his eyebrows raised. I noticed that they were both perfectly arched, no meeting of unruly hairs in the centre of his brow or strays heading off up his forehead. Did he pluck his eyebrows? I put my hand up to my own forehead without thinking and had to pretend to sweep something away from my eyes but felt the downy hair of my monobrow instead. What must Henry think of me, holes in my shoes, spotty face, monobrow? Why was he even talking to me?

"That's the nicest things anyone's said to me for months. Thanks." Henry glanced ahead at Nurse Statton who was fielding questions from the gaggle of boys surrounding her, and then he quickly patted my back before putting his hands back in his jacket pockets. He was blushing but I didn't know why. The colouring of his cheeks made him look younger and I fought an urge to reach out and touch the cool skin of my hands to the heat of his face.

"So, Jason, what are you doing here anyway? I've heard the rumours of course but it's always best to ask the horse, right?" He saw my look of confusion and added "from the horse's mouth, you know?" He realised what he'd said and exclaimed "Not that I think you look like a horse! Dr Laurence however, well, there's some ass in there alright." Henry had coloured again and he cleared his throat a little then asked again why I was here.

"I, well, I guess I hurt someone and then I got really upset about it and hurt myself and so now I have to be here to get fixed before I get to go to college." It sounded so juvenile as I said it and I worried that Henry would think I should be up ahead with the younger kids.

"What did you do to, ah, hurt this person?" Henry didn't look at me as he asked and I was reluctant to say anything about Sara as I really wanted him to like me.

"I don't remember. Dr Laurence is trying to help me remember. But it was bad, which is, I guess, why I got so upset with myself and..." I stopped; I didn't want Henry to think I was weak. He seemed so together and so solid and I just felt small and foolish walking along beside him, the moisture from the grass seeping into my shoes.

"But, you tried to kill yourself right?" I gaped at him and he actually laughed at my expression, forcing me to shut my mouth and turn away. I was so stupid to think Henry would like me, that he was different, that he might actually care but he quickly said "I'm sorry, I shouldn't have laughed, it wasn't at you Jason, I promise. It's just that your face, well, you looked... What I'm saying is that it's alright Jason, it's why we're all here really. A whole bunch of crazy boys driven crazy by other people, other boys in some cases. Not that they'll admit it." Henry's eyes darted around as he said this. "So you and I are no different really, you're just a little earlier in your 'process' of self-discovery, perhaps." The last sentence had sounded almost like a question and I saw that Henry was smiling shyly. I felt calmer, like I had an ally at last. His lips thinned out to reveal a flash of perfectly white teeth no doubt from expensive orthodontistry, or perhaps just good genes. The flushing of his face was all down to the bracing air now, no embarrassment, as we had fallen into a comfortable camaraderie. I noticed the freckles across the bridge of his nose and a light peppering underneath both eyes. I guess I hadn't really looked at his face for very long before, afraid he might see me staring.

I had become familiar with the back of his head as we sat at different tables in the dining hall, Henry just visible between the rows of other boys. I knew how the triangle of hair at the base of his skull grew in all different directions and that there were these little curls of hair behind his ears that he seemed to forget in his careful grooming regime. I wondered if the backs of his ears smelt like coconut too, and the sides of his neck, and down between his shoulders where the shampoo would run. I felt queasy and realised I hadn't answered Henry's questions. He was staring at me, almost stumbling on a loose paving slab at the greenhouse entrance, but I was sure it wasn't because he was thinking about reaching out to touch my face, or the soap on my body in the shower. I would have to stop letting myself imagine Henry liking me, it was already taking over my mind at night, and now I was daydreaming too.

Nurse Statton was holding the door for us, all the other boys already inside. She tutted as we went past and told us to keep up and stop nattering like old ladies, which made everyone else laugh. Strangely I didn't mind the offence as it made me think that Henry and I were somehow separate from them, together against them all.

CHAPTER FIVE

"Jason? You awake? Here's your coat, carry your shoes though and be quiet, Statton might be gone but she's got supersonic hearing." Henry had pushed my coat under the blanket, and had my slippers in his other hands, the whites of his eyes glowing in the moonlight coming through the slats of the dorm blind. Half asleep I forced my arms through my coat sleeves and took hold of the soft shoes. Henry picked his own trainers up from the floor next to my bed and I followed him to the back wall of the dorm, as quietly as I could. He peered round into the corridor and the hallway beyond that led to the therapy rooms and our patient files.

We had been planning this all week, once we knew that Statton was on holiday and the evening rounds would be cut to just two for each dorm. Henry had overheard one of the new nurses talking to Statton as they'd passed by his current smoking spot. This little recess between the art therapy studio and the groundskeepers' shed stank of rotting leaf mulch but it had become one of my favourite places in recent weeks. We had no choice but to stand hip to hip in there, squeezed in beside each other in the semi-darkness, while I tried not to cough as Henry blew smoke rings up into the air above us.

"Check the latch is off, we don't want to get stuck in there." We'd already passed through the first door out of the dorm and were now crouched behind the door to the therapy corridor, just below the glass panel. I reached up to flip the catch and then slowly pushed the handle down and turned on my heels, socks sliding round as I pulled the door open just enough to sneak through. I held it open for Henry and he crept through, crablike. We crawled on all fours down to Dr Laurence's room, where all the files were stored for every boy on his programme, even those like Henry who had their private therapy sessions with Dr Feinberg. Dr Laurence oversaw everything, and he was the one that made all the final decisions about who had been rehabilitated and who was a danger to society still.

We kept looking behind us to make sure no surprise dorm checks were being carried out. The sound of our trousers scuffing the floor seemed so loud in the stillness of the night, the cold corridor amplifying the noise somehow.

Henry went into Dr Laurence's room first, turning on the little torch he'd brought and holding it between his teeth as he moved towards the filing cabinets behind the doctor's desk. We knew the filing cabinets would be locked, but were relieved that we hadn't had to stand outside the room picking that lock too. I guess Dr Laurence had forgotten to lock his door for once. Henry was sure we would get in somehow, maybe even find the key in the doctor's desk drawer.

I moved behind the desk, nearer to Henry, and we both started looking through the papers and stationery in there, hoping for a secret drawer divide to reveal the much-prized key. I thought we had it when Henry whooped suddenly and said "Well, lookie here..." but when I looked over he was holding a half empty bottle of gin, not the key. He unscrewed the bottle top and took a swig then passed it to me. "God, it's been a long time, and I don't even like gin, you think the old drunk would have something better. Academics and their cheap booze, eh. C'mon Jason drink up." I just held the bottle and looked at it.

The last time I had drunk alcohol was when I had used it to wash down a handful of Tylenol and mom's Valium. The thought of the gin had brought a familiar sensation of sharp heat to my throat and I thought I might be sick. Henry saw my hand shaking and he took the bottle back and had another mouthful. "Looks like you've had enough already, eh?" Henry spoke softly and he put his hand under my elbow and took me over to one of the therapy couches. I couldn't look at him, he seemed to just radiate light in the darkness of the room and it stung my eyes, making me worry I was about to cry. I imagined that all he saw in me now was weakness, having to help me over to the couch like a frail old lady. Why could I not be strong for him? Henry had gone back over to the desk, the bottle of gin still in his hand.

He rummaged through another drawer, then stopped and looked up at me. Slowly, he raised his hand and opened his palm. A little glimmer of silver hung from his ring finger and suddenly I was terrified of the filing cabinet in the corner. This inconspicuous lump of metal seemed as if it had eaten all my secrets and knew more about me than even I did.

It was nearly the end of November and Henry had been here for almost seven months; I'd been here for nearly five, after those two months or so in the hospital. In his time here Henry had become quite hardened to Dr Laurence's group sessions and the work that he did in therapy with Dr Feinberg. I still thought the doctor was trying to help me and that the lack of progress was all my fault.

Henry had said many times that he didn't think he'd ever leave because to do so he would have to agree with them that the feelings he had had for Gregg were bad. He knew that they couldn't be, that all he had felt was love and that to agree that was wrong was to agree that he was a bad person and that could not be right. I had nodded along, silently agreeing but too scared to say anything in case the wrong words poured out. Henry said he would not let them stop him living his life and I felt stronger with him because of his bravery.

Henry had not gone straight over to the filing cabinet with the key. Instead, he walked back over to me and sat down. "Jason, I'm going to look at my file but I know you might not want to see yours, and that's cool. I can look if you want or we can just leave it and then do this again when you feel ready." Henry put his hand on my left knee and I turned to face him in the semi darkness. The weight of his hand on my leg felt strange. No one had touched me like this, with kindness, with warmth rather than restraint, for as long as I could remember, but maybe it was more than that. I could smell the juniper on his breath and, suddenly, I wanted that taste in my mouth but Henry had left the bottle of gin on the desk.

Henry had not turned away when he had found out what I'd done. He was just silent for a moment and then said that he had a similar story, although he had seemed angrier about it than I was. He was adamant that he was only at Arbutus Lodge because of the small-mindedness of others, I still felt that I was here because I was not safe to be outside, around people. I felt safe with Henry though.

I took his hand and stood up, surprising him. I led Henry over to the filing cabinet next to the patients' couch. He turned the key in the lock at the top of the cabinet and then pulled open the top-drawer. There were dozens of files, all boys at Arbutus Lodge, now or in the past year since Dr Laurence got the funding for the programme. These notes, the sum total of their lives so far, stretched the neatly labelled brown files and I felt sick.

My fingers scurried over the tops of the files, all these boys, all their problems forced into scribbled black ink on a few pages in a locked cabinet. These files held dozens of boys in limbo, not able to go on with real life, constantly watched to see if they made another mistake or tried to escape like I had tried. I got to 'Forrest', right at the back, and just plucked the file from the hanger without question. Henry closed the top drawer and opened the one below, rifling through for 'Hadley'. His initials looked like football posts, with an 'O' for Oswald forming the ball in the middle on the monogrammed dress shirt he had in his dresser. Henry's parents seemed to think it was still important for him to be well dressed here, but their son had taken to wearing his best suit for art class, deliberately burning holes in some of his clothes with cigarettes. This made me angry at first as I would have loved to have such nice things but I understood how Henry felt in them, like wearing everyone else's idea of who you are, not even being safe in your own skin.

Henry took his file and leant against the back of the patients' couch, I walked around it and sat down, my head resting against the small of Henry's back unexpectedly. Neither of us moved. I turned the cover page but then skipped through the admittance papers, stamped with 'suicide watch' and bearing the crest of the Edmonton court. I went to the back of the file; my most recent sessions with Dr Laurence.

"Still does not accept the rape. Resistant to remembering attack on girl/mother." The notes were handwritten in spidery black ink under the neatly typed summary of our session last week. Dr Laurence was right, of course, I still did not remember having attacked Sara, but he was wrong about me not wanting to. He had told me that by remembering it I could start to forgive myself and would be on the way to getting well but as much as I tried there was just a memory of Rose at her front door and then seeing Mrs Hollister racing past me in her car. Why did Dr Laurence say 'girl/mother' though? I had not attacked my mother. My eyes wandered from the page into the darkness of the rest of the room, searching through my memory for something about my mother being hurt, but there was nothing there. Dr Laurence must be talking in code, my mother represented something, or maybe he thought I wanted to hurt her. What had I said? If only I could remember things more clearly.

I read on, and my hands shook at the sight of the next page. I dropped the file into my lap and the noise made Henry turn. "Jason? What is it? What's he put?" The file included a recent letter from Sara's doctor, confirming her pregnancy. I had raped Sara and now she was pregnant. Soon, I could be a father, in just over a month and no one had told me. Instead, Dr Laurence had written on the bottom of the page "Do not disclose."

Henry had moved to sit beside me and I saw trails of tears down his face which he brushed away as I looked up at him, my head in my hands, elbows resting on the file still. He slowly pulled the file out from my lap, took in the details of the notice and just whispered 'Jeez," under his breath. "This was, the girl, right? The one they say you, well, the girl?"

"Yes." I couldn't bear it, Sara, "and... she's pregnant, she's going to have my baby." I looked up at him and whispered through my sobs, "Henry, I can't be a father, I can't be."

"And you won't be!" Henry shouted the words angrily and he took hold of my wrists, pulling me upright. "No," he spoke more quietly but fiercely, "none of this is your fault, none of it."

"But, she must be eight months pregnant now, Sara's going to have a baby, my baby next month. I raped her, I got her pregnant, this is my fault Henry, it's because of what I did to her. Why can't I remember?"

Henry whispered something, but he had looked down and away from me as he said it and so I stared at Henry, wide-eyed, questioning. "I said, you can't remember because it wasn't you Jason. Sara's baby is not your baby, someone else raped her, don't you see?"

"What? What do you mean?"

"What I said Jason. You have absolutely no recollection of raping this girl, as far as I can tell you had no reason to, or.... or inclination to, and the only reason everyone seems to think you did is because of what she said and because no one really knows who you really are, or how to fit you into their image of their stupid suburban, well, I guess, provincial town." He took a breath and pressed his eyes shut, as if gathering his strength. I knew he was talking about himself too, that his anger was not just for me, but what did he mean, it had to have been me, otherwise why would I feel so full of guilt and shame. No one could feel as dark and rotten inside as I did unless they had done something so awful. Henry went on, "The fact is Jason, I don't think you had any interest in that girl, or any other. Not... sexually."

I felt my face flushing, but it was a pleasurable heat, and what Henry had said felt right somehow, even if this was the first time I'd really let myself think about it consciously. I had tried to convince myself that I just wasn't interested in all that stuff, that I was asexual and that I just didn't care about all those things that seemed to run everyone else's lives like getting together, breaking up, marriage, divorce, children, compromise, sacrifices. I had felt lucky sometimes that I just had no interest in the girls in class, but they still made me nervous because I could feel the weight of their expectations. I'd been so scared of them, and the boys too, and I think my mother had assumed that I'd grow out of my anxiety and be normal like everyone else, find a girl at college maybe, get married, give her grandkids. Now Sara was pregnant, though, and my mother would be a grandma and she wouldn't even be able to see the baby.

Would they take it away, perhaps into foster care? Or maybe Sara's mom and dad would take care of it, raise my child as their own? I had never thought I would want children but now I felt responsible for a life and somehow that thought thrilled me. How could I ever be a father to my child though when he only existed because of something awful I had done? I thought about Sara in the hospital, who was going with her to have all the scans and stuff they do? Who was holding her hand, who had felt the baby, my baby, kick? I couldn't stop, the thought of that life, a life I had created, was intoxicating. I felt wild, my mind firing with thoughts, my body seemed to grow more solid, more real, full of a new kind of love that had a focus, an intensity and purpose.

Henry still had hold of my hands but the grip on them now was softer, his fingers slipped in between mine for a second or two, our palms touching and hands raised to frame our faces. His fingers were cool, and as they played through mine the image of his hands spread across the piano keys changed to the thought, instead, of his hands playing along the ridges of my spine, to the small of my back. He unentwined his right hand from mine and stroked my cheek, then without a word he wrapped his fingers around the back of my head, pulling me into him. I felt his tears as he kissed me and I kissed him back, the quick play of his tongue parting my lips and our mouths sliding over one another, soft and then fierce as we drew further out of ourselves and into each other. How could I have done this with anyone else, this was all there was, all there could be.

Henry's hands were in my hair and he had climbed over me, his knees squeezing against my thighs. I ran my hands over his curved back and tried to pull him closer but instead my touch had made him arch his torso away from me and now he lifted his shirt and I helped him, sliding my fingers over his chest and using my grip on his shoulders to pull myself back up to kiss him, our bodies pressed together.

I felt myself growing hard and erect and I knew that Henry was feeling the same thing, we were pushing against each other but now I moved my hands to his waist, fumbled with the zip on his jeans and slid my fingers into the folds of cotton beneath, desperately searching for a way to feel through to his skin. I undid the buttons on his briefs and slipped my hand inside, surprised at how something so familiar could feel so strange, so new, and exciting. His skin was soft and warm but underneath I felt the coursing, pulsing push of blood just as it was in me and I ran my fingers up the tip, freeing him from the tangled cotton and felt him pause for a second and moan softly at the side of my mouth. "Faster, faster, and…" but he didn't need to tell me and I splayed out my fingers to tease his release, over and over from base to tip, riding the contractions of warm skin and muscle and delighting in Henry writhing over me. Suddenly his whole body froze, his thighs clamped around mine, his head buried in my neck breathing hard and I felt those final slow waves rushing through him and then he softened into me, and I held him, and I held him, and for a second or two we were all there was.

When we left the therapy room it had been hard to stay quiet, full of whispers and laughter, holding onto each other and feeling so free and energised that even the cold reality of the lodge's hallways took a while to affect us. Back in the dorm, thankfully without event, Henry saw me to my bed and looked around in the darkness before stroking my hair and kissing me softly on the top of my head. Our hands entangled again for a moment and then our fingers slipped away from the other as Henry crossed to the other end of the dorm.

I could not sleep, the sounds of the other boys snoring was like a backing melody to mine and Henry's song which played over and over in my mind. I thought of his lips on mine, the soft skin on his shoulders, the ridges of his spine and how it felt holding him and feeling him, having him trust me so lovingly. My body would not calm and the scratch of the sheets and the quiet creaks of the bed as I tried to move without sound distracted me at first but then I had my own release, thinking of Henry on top of me, how he had run his fingers down the back of my ear so softly and then gripped me so hard when it was time.

It was not long though until the thought of those medical files simmered back up to the front of my mind. Sara was pregnant and as much as Henry seemed to think the baby was not mine, I could not stop turning over and over the idea of being a father. What he had said about none of it being true had scared me and I had just dismissed the idea as it would mean that everyone had lied to me for months, that I was here for no reason. It would mean that this baby, who suddenly seemed so important to me, was not mine. Darren was her boyfriend after all, maybe they had been sleeping together and the baby was his.

The whole town thought I'd raped Sara. Everyone would think the baby was mine, but what if it wasn't? My own mother believed it and, what's more, believed I was still a danger and had to stay here indefinitely. But if I hadn't raped Sara, if what I remembered was the truth and not some sort of attempt at protecting my fractured mind then someone else had hurt Sara, someone else had made her pregnant, and I was not to be a father. Perhaps I never would be.

What could I do? At first I had denied everything, I was so lost, being accused of things I didn't understand, but as the questions went on and on I had just agreed with them, signed anything for them to leave me alone. I had just wanted to escape, but now I was considered a danger to myself and everyone else, probably to my own child even. The thought occurred to me that I would never be allowed to hold him, to watch him sleep, to take his hand and walk to the store. Where had these feelings come from? I felt like some great darkness had been lifted and I was starting my life all over again, but I was still here and the realisation made me feel so tired of it all. I tried to think back to Henry and his kisses but the cold hard knot of guilt in my gut had returned and I could not get back to the safety of his arms.

I slept, but for the first time in a week I woke with drenched sheets stuck to me and the same fearful sense of restraint. It felt different this time though. I felt different. Sara was pregnant, but not with my baby. In the dream it had always been me looking down onto the prone body tied to the bed but this time I was staring up into a blank face. I imagined Sara having these nightmares too, looking up at the face of her attacker, but it was not me. Suddenly, I was free, free to realise that I too was under attack, that we were both victims here and that, maybe, we could help each other.

In the cold of the early morning light I dragged my fingers across the sheets and clenched my fists. This time I was going to fight back. Whatever Dr Laurence and my mother might think, I am not broken. I had sunk into the depths of myself, past the darkness, past the fear, the terror, the despair of difference and I had found something else. I had found my capacity to love and I had come back stronger.

CHAPTER SIX

"Jason! Why you look positively luminescent! What have you been doing?" Janice whirled around me and laughed softly, a genuine smile of warmth on her face. She looked at the canvas I was working on and paused, taking a breath and then exhaling slowly through pursed lips. "Now this is interesting... have we found our voice Mr Forrest?"

I had been aiming to paint a simple figure, a self-portrait as we'd been asked but as I had sketched in the lines of the limbs they had branched and twisted and soon I had a canvas covered in the dense canopy of an old arbutus. The red peeling and twisting bark stood out in thick ridges of paint and the smooth creamy grey-green beneath had shone through, cold, firm, but radiant. I had spread myself across the paper. I had painted my metamorphosis and I felt that transformation like a hot spring fuming and steaming inside.

Janice whispered in my ear, "This is great Jason, it's a huge step forward and it's really quite beautiful. You should be proud." She lingered a second or two more, then looked out of the art room window, across the fountain and at the tall hedge that bordered the lodge's grounds. Behind that hedge there was the tree that Henry and I met under on warmer days and nights, although these were disappearing fast. The old arbutus was out of the reach of the landscapers working at the lodge and its branches grew twisted and haphazardly, surrendering parts in poor seasons and reaching toward the sun when it came. When I had arrived here in early July this old tree had still had some of the tiny waxy white flowers adorning its crooked branches and the smell of honey had lingered around it. There were few berries showing now, though, and it seemed the birds had forsaken our tree for those at the front entrance of the Lodge, doing their part to keep the hospital grounds looking and sounding friendly and peaceful.

Janice looked back at me and winked, which had me wondering what she knew about the arbutus, but she just smiled and then wandered around the rest of the group to check on their progress. I stared at my painting, aware that some of the others were looking over at me, some even craning to see what had been so interesting that it had managed to make Janice stand still for a second or two. Despite the attention I did not blush and my hands did not become cold and clammy. I stood firm, proud. I felt strong.

Taking the fine-tipped paintbrush from my case I dipped it in a smear of black paint left on the palette then quickly swirled "J.Forrest" onto the bottom right corner of the canvas before I lost my nerve. I would have to show Henry the picture. Tonight, perhaps, after dinner I could sneak him in here on the way back to the dorm. Henry would understand the painting, he would understand why this tree and I were entwined, inseparable. Henry, who knew how that cool silver felt and how to peel back those strips of bright red bark slowly and carefully.

We had had to be careful this week as Henry's parents were visiting from Ottawa. There had been no question of sneaking out late at night to make love in the groundskeeper's shed that we had discovered was never locked. All week we had pretended not to look at each other, pretended that we were not clenching our fists, our thighs, our teeth until we could touch each other again. His mother spent hours in the therapy room with Dr Laurence and, sometimes, Henry. His dad, meanwhile, seemed to be off playing day-long games of golf at the private course nearby, arranged by the lodge's director. A full case review with family present was supposed to be every two months or so but my parents still hadn't visited and Henry's parents seemed to see their visits as more of a holiday than anything intended to help their son.

Henry had slipped me a note at dinner on Tuesday and I prayed it was a summons to meet him that night but instead he had just asked me to wait and to stay calm. They wanted him to lie and now that lie felt like a betrayal of not only himself but of what was happening between us. I had told him that it was worth it if it gave him back his freedom, at least for another year until he was old enough that his parents could not have him committed again. His sentence was already served so he was really only here because his parents wanted him to be and because they could afford it. This time though, he had another reason to stay and we both knew that if he left Arbutus Lodge there was no way he could visit and no way I'd be out anytime soon.

I had not read Henry's file as he had read mine on the frequent sorties we now made to the therapy room. Instead he had told me about the reasons he was entombed here. At first, when he talked about Gregg I had felt like I had been punched in the ribs, knocking the breath out of me. I could see in his eyes that this had been more than just some fumbling teenage crush and that he was not quite healed from the wounds inflicted by this boy. After a particularly bitter row about something Henry couldn't even now recall, Gregg had told his parents that Henry had molested him. They, in turn had told the school and Henry had been suspended. When he had then tried to see Gregg to ask why he had betrayed him he was caught by Gregg's mother as he climbed through the boy's bedroom window. She had called the police and, as the older boy at sixteen, Henry had been found guilty of assaulting a minor and was effectively treated as a paedophile in need of rehabilitation.

His parents had been tipped off by a psychiatrist friend about the new programme going on at Arbutus Lodge, noting that they could holiday on the Island when they visited. Henry also thought that the decision had been helped by the fact that the lodge was far enough away from their home in Ottawa that they had no call to visit their black sheep of a son. The distance convenient too in that it meant none of Henry's friends could visit him and so the Oswald-Hadleys' friends could simply forget that this wayward boy had ever disrupted their dinner party conversation. The donation they gave to the initiative at the lodge was also appropriately expensive, allowing the Hadleys the comfort of thinking that their money was being well spent on getting Henry into shape, ready for his return as their golden child. Lavishing money on his treatment felt to Henry like they were trying to buy a new son, one that would slot right back into life by marrying a nice girl from college and buying a place near theirs in the suburbs.

Henry had not seen Gregg since the night he had tried to sneak into the younger boy's room and it was clear to me that things remained unfinished between the two of them. Things that needed saying but could not be said for reasons of distance, time, and fear. It was this that caused the stoop in Henry's posture, the slight trudge to his walk on some days. I wanted to tell him that I was fine with him having felt like this before, and having done these things with someone else before me, even if it wasn't quite true just yet. The thought of someone else feeling Henry inside them, seeing the flush of pleasure rise in his face and the sharp breath of ecstasy against their neck not mine made my skin feel two sizes too small and my fingers and toes tighten up and into my body.

Henry's parents would be gone tomorrow and if he confessed his sins and admitted his deviancy it would not be long before he was also leaving. Dr Laurence had been trying to get Henry to explore his feelings for women, even mentioning Janice on occasion to try to provoke a response. Although Henry was wise to many of the therapist's tricks he was not sure how to use this latest development to his advantage. If he falsely confessed to a crush on Janice, or even Nurse Statton as we had joked one night last week, would that mark him out as a danger to them or would that be proof in Dr Laurence's mind that Henry was making progress away from his sick taste for younger boys. If Henry had told the good doctor what was really going on almost every night in the groundskeeping shed, again with a younger boy, he would be at Arbutus Lodge until he turned eighteen next year and would be marked out as deviant forever.

We had planned a midnight run to the therapy room to read the latest additions to our files after Henry's parents left. Perhaps there would be some clue to help Henry decide how to approach the subject of sex with women when questioned by Dr Laurence. Meanwhile, my own sessions had become extremely pained as there was still no mention of the baby and so I felt on the edge of being caught out for the whole of each hour-long marathon of lies.

Dr Laurence was still focusing on my mother, how I felt about her, how other women made me feel in contrast to her. I knew that he had a theory that I was obsessed with my mother and that my obsession and desire made me angry with the other women I met, especially those I felt attracted to. It was hard to keep a straight face as he hinted at such ludicrous things and I wondered when he'd decided this about me and how little he'd heard of what I'd actually said over the past few months. Had he just selectively ignored anything that didn't fit his diagnosis? Even if I did blame my mother for lots of things, I was actually strangely thankful for her having given up on me, for sending me here. After all, I had Henry now.

CHAPTER SEVEN

Henry had decided to lie. We had talked it over, wrapped around each other last night in the semi-darkness of the shed that felt more like home now than home ever had. As he swirled a finger up and down my collarbone and over my chin to my waiting parted lips he had asked how I would feel about him leaving. I had shuddered, involuntarily, at both the pleasure of his caress and the idea of being without it. Henry had confided in me that he had been thinking he would like to be a teacher, not in a school but a private piano tutor if he could, when he wasn't composing or playing. I knew that he could play but had still not had a chance to hear him perform. The tapping of his fingers on my back and the humming of slightly modulating refrains let me know where his thoughts went after we made love.

Henry's parents had planned on sending him to the Schulich in Montreal and even I had heard of it so I knew it was a big deal. That is, they had planned on him going there until he had his little 'mishap' as his mother insisted on calling his ordeal with Gregg. If he started telling the doctors and lawyers and his parents what they wanted to hear then there was still time for him to apply for a place at the school. His parents would call in some favours and Henry would slip back into the society he had fallen from so guilelessly.

Montreal is so very far away though and I cried silently at the thought of this place, of life without Henry, after we had returned to our separate beds in the dorm last night. At breakfast this morning I saw Henry talking to another boy on the table next to mine and I imagined all of the temptations of college, the freedom, the excitement of being around those who shared his musical talent. I saw Henry seated at a piano, another man next to him, pressed close as their hands danced over and under one another across the keys. How could anyone resist falling in love with him, how would he hold back given that I was all the way out here and probably just filling time during his incarceration? My mind raced as I tried to swallow the dry cold toast that stuck in my throat day after day.

On the way out of the dining hall I felt a hand on my waist, subtle but insistent, guiding me to the right and away from the stream of boys heading off to the dorms to wash up before class began. As the other boys disappeared into the distance I moved into the alcove between the chapel and the medical office. I turned to Henry, ready to taste his lips on mine but it was not Henry standing behind me.

"Jason. So... surprised?" Lewis, another boy from our dorm grinned at me, but his eyes were dead, his expression cold. He was standing far too close for this to be a friendly chat and so I tried to step back but felt the sharp edge of a statue base behind me. Lewis moved in even closer, leaning his right hand against the wall, palm flat and just above my head, framing me as he wanted. His eyes were locked on mine and they became fierce and bright as he grew bolder, the hazel flecked with yellow like tiny bursts of flame in the centre of his vision. Everything about Lewis seemed like it was on fire now he had me captive. It was almost like his whole body cracked and sparked as he looked at me. "I've heard some rumours about you Jason and I'm a little curious to see if the things they say are true."

"I, well, I'm not sure what you mean Lewis. Who? What rumours?" I stammered out the words and tried to shrink back into the wall wishing Henry was here.

"Oh, you know, just the usual stuff," he moved his left hand from his pocket down to the zipper on the bottom of my jacket, toying with it and then moving the jacket aside to put his fingers around my waist. He gripped me tight and carried on staring so intensely that I looked away. "Ah, Jason, you see, you don't disappoint. All coy and shy and demure. You know how that might make a man feel. What it might make a man feel like doing to tease a little shriek from such a boy." Lewis had slipped his hand beneath my shirt and his fingers into the waistband of my jeans letting him pull me closer to him as I turned my head away.

I could feel him stiffening against me, the urgency of his grip and his eyes boring into my face. I tried to move to my right, out of the alcove but Lewis just held me tighter, now moving his right hand to the back of my head, not as Henry did but so his grip on my hair hurt and forced my head back a little. "I wouldn't try to get away Jason. I mean, what would Henry's parents say if they knew what their darling little boy was up to in the work shed? And with a lowly peasant like you, someone they'd hire to clean their car, not fuck their son." As he spoke he swung me sideways and backed me through the chapel door. Inside it took a second or two to adjust to the lack of light but Lewis had already manoeuvred me into a pew at the back, hidden away in the darkness.

He must have seen us sneaking out at night, followed us even and seen our bodies tangled up, sweat shining on our skin from the moonlight coming through the window of the shed. Lewis could ruin everything for Henry and he knew it. This was his bargaining tool and as I slumped down in front of him, on my knees, he knew that I had resigned myself to keep quiet, for Henry. Lewis unzipped his pants and took hold of the back of my head, guiding me in towards him. I felt the first swell of tears, and my mouth went dry, my throat tight and I felt breathless, how could I do this, how would I breathe. I swallowed down the first sob, not wanting Lewis to have the satisfaction of hearing me cry, to add to whatever other victory he might have won. He leant forward over me, his forehead resting against the pew in front as if in prayer, and I moistened my lips and prepared to wrap my mouth around his erection.

A cry at the front of the chapel startled us both and Lewis yelped in pain at the touch of my teeth rather than my lips. I had pulled back and now he pushed my head down and moved to zip himself back up as the chaplain's voice grew closer. "Lewis? What a nice surprise to find you here, I hope everything's OK, this is not your usual haunt." The old man's laughter played around the walls of the chapel, a burble in the silence.

"Everything's fine, Sir. Just needed a bit of quiet time, Sir."

"Oh, Lewis, you don't need to call me Sir, but you do seem a little jumpy, are you sure there's nothing I can help you with, any relief that God can provide?"

I felt the tension as Lewis tried not to laugh. God would provide no relief today. That opportunity had passed and I started to shuffle slowly down onto all fours and crawl to the end of the pew and away from the approaching chaplain. The chapel door was closed but I could at least make my escape before Lewis when the chaplain left. He had sat down in front of Lewis and now rested his own elbows where Lewis had been pushing against the bench in front. I imagined that the sight and sound of the old man had quelled that rising pulse of blood and that he was no longer straining against the material of his pants but even my adrenaline was still coursing through me, setting every nerve alight. I was not surprised that Lewis walked a little stiffly to the door as he took his leave of the chaplain, and I tried to ignore the presence of my own excitement, rationalising it as a result of terror. The light-headedness was understandable but I couldn't help wonder where Lewis would go to finish what I'd started, and if he'd be thinking of me as he did. I had missed my opportunity to sneak out before Lewis and was now stuck beneath the back bench waiting for the chaplain to finish his prayers and head back to wherever he hid when he wasn't tending to the boys here.

The old man was mumbling into his folded hands but I couldn't make out any of the words and so I wiped the last few tears from my eyes and stared at the walls and the benches, avoiding looking at the front of the chapel and the statue of Jesus hanging from the far wall. Most of the light in the hall was coming from around this statue though so my eyes kept getting drawn back in to stare at this figure of a man, the torso well defined in cold hard plaster, naked but for a wrap of cotton, suffering for all of us.

My mother had taken me to church every Sunday when I was little, but I didn't really remember. Most families in the town went and just before I'd come here they had restarted a Sunday school for some of the younger children. My father had not gone with us most weeks, and my mother always had the same tight lipped expression on Sunday mornings as she bundled me out the door without a second glance at my dad. I wondered if his issue with the church was just that it meant he had to get up early on his one day off from the store. He was always reading the paper in his slippers in the sun room when we came home, which seemed like a much better way to spend a Sunday than trying to differentiate the echoing words of Father Langley who always talked of sins and devilish thoughts and not the grace or the love of Christ as my mother did. I hadn't been to the church for years now, except for special occasions like Easter and Christmas.

I had no intention of attending the campus chapel at college either although my mother had noted how it seemed like a lovely place to seek solace should I have 'difficulties' being alone in Calgary. She had never expressly said what such difficulties would be, or why I would require God's assistance with them, but now it seems ironic that my mother would think God could help cure me of my love for Henry. If my mother thought God would consider our love an act of the devil then her God was not for me, nor any god that saw it as evil. What Lewis had just made me do though, that surely was proof enough that God didn't exist, or didn't care like my mother thought he should. I turned my face away from the statue of Christ and thought of Henry instead.

The chaplain had shuffled to his feet and was heading back up to the door at the side of the altar. I waited until he had disappeared into the backroom and then eased open the chapel door and bounded out. After running down the corridor to the washrooms I squeezed soap into my hand and scraped it around the sides of my mouth. The bitter taste still did not rid me of the memory of Lewis and I stared at my face in the mirror, scared at how my mouth looked like a gaping wound, angry and red at the edges where I had rubbed it with the soap. I thought about Henry kissing me, kissing that mouth, those lips, and I wondered if he'd be able to taste the bitterness Lewis had left. I didn't want Henry to have to kiss these soiled lips, or have to use my tongue to tell him I loved him when it felt so alien now in my mouth. My body had deserted me, it felt strange to me now, just when I had begun to feel at home in it and happy to share my skin, my self with Henry.

Even if what I'd done had been for Henry, would he forgive me? Should I even tell him? He was so close to getting out of this place and I knew he would want some kind of justice for what Lewis had done. I would wait until he was safe and he'd understand, he'd have to understand that I had had no choice. Not really.

CHAPTER EIGHT

I was waiting for Henry at the art studio. He had his final meeting with Dr Laurence this morning and if everything had gone to plan he would be cleared to leave this weekend. His parents had already booked him a seat on the Greyhound to get him to Winnipeg where they would meet him. Three days of travelling. He gets his freedom and then he has to spend the first three days stuck on a bus with a bunch of strangers. He had talked about waiting until things calmed down at home and then, once he found a job, moving into his own place so I could come and join him when I was done here. Henry had not looked at me as he had said this and we both knew that it would be a long time before we could see each other again, perhaps too long.

I was also worried that, once he was free, Henry would realise that I meant nothing to him really. I was just some solace while in this place, and I would still be here waiting to get out but not wanted when I finally did get to leave. I didn't even know who I was in the real world now and maybe neither of us would be the same.

I had been working on a plan with Henry though, a way to try to find out what really happened to Sara so that my case would be reopened. Having Henry outside Arbutus Lodge was a part of that plan as he would be able to write to Rose without his letters being screened by the staff here at the lodge. Of everyone in Pitcher Creek I figured that Rose had to know what had really happened. She had always been friendly to me, that is until we were no longer allowed any contact. Henry and I had decided there was little point in writing to Sara. She had her own reasons for lying about what had happened and she would be busy getting ready for the baby's arrival now so I didn't want to upset her any more.

Rose would be fifteen now and I cannot imagine how her life must have changed with all the craziness of summer and the imminent arrival of a baby in the house. It was obvious that she and Sara had not been close but she must know something, she must have worked out what really happened, she'd been in the house after all.

I wondered if Rose had carried on learning programming and if her dad had come back from England. She had talked about him a lot during the hours we had spent in the study, even showing me some old TV programmes he watched. Like Rose, I found it hard to work out why they were funny but she assured me that they made her dad laugh in a way he never laughed at anything else. Something about a Flying Circus and a dead parrot. I didn't really like TV anyway so it was no great loss that I just didn't get it. I think it would be nice to have a dad around that laughed sometimes though, not that sneering begrudging laughter that tumbled out of my father's mouth, but a full-on belly laugh with tears streaming down your face like Rose described when her dad had a fit at some antics on TV. I hoped he had returned home, for Rose's sake. How could he not given what had happened to Sara and now he was going to be a grandfather?

Rose had to know what had really happened. She had been the one at the house before I arrived and if Sara had been attacked in the house then surely her sister had seen or heard something. What I didn't understand, now that Henry had helped me see that I was innocent, was how Rose could keep it quiet for so long, and not just her but Sara as well. Other people in the town I could understand believing I'd done such an awful thing. They didn't know me. I never went to their houses, never talked to them. To most people I was that weird guy that had flashed some kid in the locker rooms once and been beaten up for it. I was the weird guy who went to the school out of town and was too smart for his own good, proving everyone right now by having raped a girl. Sometimes I wished my mother had just let me get on with it at Pitcher Creek High, a few bruises and scrapes but the other kids would have left me alone eventually. Maybe they would've even forgotten the locker room misunderstanding and been able to see that I would never be capable of hurting Sara.

Henry arrived and, after quickly scanning the room, he placed one hand on my waist and took my other hand in his. Arms outstretched, he whirled me around and around the easels in the room. I had to add dancing to his list of talents it seemed.

We came to a halt and Henry touched my forehead with his, collapsing into me, relief flowing through him. "I can go home Jason. I leave tomorrow."

I had known this would happen eventually but I just wanted a little more time with him. I wanted to make sure things would stick, that he would still be mine when I got out and that he wouldn't be able to forget me. Henry stroked my cheek with the back of his hand and said 'Shhh,'' even though I had not made a sound. Perhaps I had sighed without realising. "Jason, my Jason, don't be scared. Everything will be fine, I'll make sure of it. I..." There was a crash at the front of the art room, an easel had toppled over and behind it was the tiny form of Janice. Frozen in place she had some folders under one arm and a mug of coffee in the other that was at a perilous angle. Henry and I had jumped away from each other and we weren't sure what she'd seen but the art therapist who was usually a whirlwind of energy had stopped dead so I was sure everything was ruined.

Janice righted her coffee cup and took a quick swig before setting the folders down on a nearby desk and saying "Well, look at the lovebirds, eh? No wonder you're all aglow in class these days Mr Forrest." I looked over at Henry, not sure what was going on but he had started smiling and then let out a relieved breath and took my hand in his. "Now, boys, you do know that I saw nothing, know nothing, and will admit to nothing, right? I presume no one else knows anything either? I just got word that you're leaving us tomorrow anyway Henry, is that right?" She had looked at me as she had said this, instead of Henry and I felt the heat rising in my cheeks and nausea growing in my stomach.

"Yes, I leave tomorrow to meet my parents in Winnipeg, then back home to Ottawa." Henry squeezed my hand a little as he spoke.

"Well then, Jason, don't you think that it's only fair that Henry gets to take a little memento of his time here?" I didn't know what she meant at first but then I remembered why we were in the art studio and Janice beat me to the easel where my painting remained for all to see. I had tugged Henry over with me and he looked back and forth between me and the canvas. Eyebrows raised, he looked at Janice and she laughed a little meandering laugh that led into "It's true, it's real, it's his!" She placed a hand on my shoulder and then swung her arm around my back and gave me a squeeze. I felt a knot in my throat, pressure in the back of my eyes as if a faucet were about to burst. "Quite something isn't it? You've got yourself a real artist on your hands here Henry, so you had better nurture that talent, even after you leave." Janice had said this in an odd way, almost as if she was angry with Henry but he looked back at me and nodded, his face so calm that I really believed he would be mine forever.

"Can I, is it OK if, can I take this with me Jason? When I go tomorrow? Then I can carry it with me and give it pride of place in my new apartment when I get set up. Ready for more of your masterpieces."

"Right above the piano?" I swallowed hard to be able to get the words out. I was already seeing the two of us side by side on a piano stool, Henry's fingers dancing over the keys and the painting of the old arbutus tree looking down over us.

"Exactly where I was thinking."

"Jeez, you two, what a pair of honeymooners. So what do you have planned to celebrate your last night here Henry? A rave? Or just a game of tiddlywinks and an extra therapy session?"

We hadn't really thought about this. The day had been so long coming and the focus had just been on making sure nothing went wrong to stop Henry getting out. There was surely nothing we could do, short of sneaking out to the groundskeeper's shed.

Suddenly Janice clapped her hands and almost gave us both a bear hug. "I've got it, the perfect thing! I'll have to clear it with the doc but there shouldn't be a problem. My most talented artist," Janice nodded at me, "and one last hurrah for Henry before he leaves."

Henry and I looked at each other quizzically. What was Janice planning? After the frog escapade it could be anything.

"Don't worry fellas, I'm not going to make you sit through a lecture on minimalism in therapeutic artistic practice... ich. There's an exhibition on in town, free wine, decent work from local artists, and the chance to see a bit of the town before you leave. I was thinking of rounding up some students to go anyway but it'll be lovely if it's just the two of you. We could even get dinner somewhere first. My treat, because god knows that the director won't reimburse me! C'mon, what do you think, are you game?"

I looked at Henry, not really believing our luck. This sounded amazing, especially given that a few minutes earlier I had been convinced that we'd been caught out. "Hell yeah!" the words came out of nowhere and surprised all of us but I just hugged Janice and then Henry hugged us both and then Janice left to get permission to take us to a serious evening of art and culture, no fun possible if she could help it.

CHAPTER NINE

Janice had reserved a table for us at an Italian-style restaurant in the centre of town, which was basically a dozen or so stores. There had really been no need to make a reservation but Janice was in the habit of doing such things. I say Italian-style as it seemed all the staff were either Russian, Canadian, or Ukrainian but the menu was teeming with serifs and swirls telling us about pizzas and pasta dishes, and some more unusual kinds of gnocchi. The moose meatball Bolognese was possibly the finest example of fusion food in Western Canada. Janice nearly choked on her glass of house red when she saw the menu listing. She apologised for the plastic tablecloths and slightly drab atmosphere but she had heard the food was good and plentiful and, most importantly, cheap considering her pretty poor art therapist salary.

Henry and I were still a bit stunned from being allowed out on this trip, having been whisked into Janice's battered old pickup and the genuine craziness of her driving into town. The three of us were smushed together in the front seat of the Ford and had bounced along hitting, or so it seemed, every pothole on the ten mile trip. Now Janice was drinking I thought I might suggest I drove us back to the lodge later.

"I'll have the margherita, thanks, and a small side salad." Henry and Janice had ordered while I had been staring at everyone else in the restaurant. Embarrassed, I quickly pointed at something on the extensive menu and the waitress raised an eyebrow.

"You sure?" She had a thick eastern European accent and her eyes bored into me as she asked again "You sure you want the Steakhouse Special?"

"I, well, perhaps I'll just have a margherita." The woman sighed and grabbed my menu then turned on her heel and marched into the kitchen.

"The Steakhouse Special Jason? Are you trying to bankrupt me?" Janice laughed and then swallowed some more of her Pinot Grigio.

"So, Henry, you're planning on getting your own place when you're back in Ottawa? I presume this will be news to your parents?"

"Ha, yeah. If I have to stay with them for very long then there might actually be a legitimate reason for me to be back at the lodge." Janice frowned and shook her head as Henry spoke.

"Surely your time here has been fruitful in some senses Henry?" She glanced at me, "and I don't just mean meeting Jason here. I don't really know your case but if Dr Laurence thinks you're well enough to leave then you've made progress I presume."

"Dr Laurence doesn't know a thing about me. He doesn't really know why I'm here and he certainly doesn't know how to 'fix' me like he wants to. The thing about it is that I was never ill, it's everyone else that's sick." Henry's face had grown red with anger, helped along by the fact that he too was drinking the house wine, despite still being underage. Janice was certainly not your average teacher or therapist and the two of them were making steady progress on the bottle already. I stayed silent, knowing Henry needed to say his piece, but I worried that he'd gone too far; Janice was still a therapist after all, even if she wasn't Henry's art therapist.

"Can I ask why you got sent to Arbutus? You don't have to say, I'm just curious who I'm having dinner with and, well," she reached out and squeezed my hand across the table and smiled. At that moment it was hard to tell if the glow in her eyes was due to the wine or something more maternal. Janice had been so supportive and encouraging of my painting and drawing and we'd had many walks around the grounds and outside on occasion but I had assumed that was all part of therapy. Now I realised she really cared and I felt guilty suddenly for not having confided in her earlier about Henry. Perhaps she had already guessed though. She saw so much in the work I did, helping me work out what I couldn't say in any way other than with the paintbrush. Even the Old Arbutus Tree, which I had felt powerful painting and which had left me breathless when finished, had not seemed quite so eloquent as when Janice had asked me about stripping away the bark and I had had to hold back my tears as I stepped out of my old skin.

"I had a... relationship with another boy, a younger boy. It ended badly, he said some things, told some lies. I tried to fix it and everyone decided I was a child molester. If that's what love got you then I didn't want to know." Henry had been staring at his napkin, twisting it in his hands as he spoke until he looked up at me and said "For a while at least."

"I see, and this other boy, are you in touch still?" I stared, open-mouthed at Janice but she was focused on Henry. I was thankful that she'd asked what I'd been too scared to ask, and I held my breath waiting for Henry to answer.

"No. He's in Ottawa still I think, but I won't be looking him up when I get home." I bit my lip and tried not to concentrate on the thought of Henry loving someone else, someone who would be in the same city as him, the same province even, while I was thousands of miles away and unreachable. The way his eyes glazed over, the way his breath came sharp and quick as he said Gregg's name made me doubt his ability to resist looking up this first, intense love, but then I felt ashamed of that doubt, after all it was I, not Henry, who had already messed up.

"Do you have other friends back in Ottawa who you're looking forward to seeing?" Janice sipped her wine without taking her eyes from Henry's face, scrutinising every twitch it seemed. Was she trying to catch him out?

"Not really. Something like that really makes you see how little some friendships mean and how little those closest to you really know you. Keeping quiet about Gregg," Henry swallowed, shook his head and went on, "keeping quiet meant that it was easier for everyone to think badly of me afterwards and that was..." He stopped, and then, after a few seconds, Janice spoke quietly, seemingly deciding that Henry was the good guy he appeared to be.

"I imagine it was pretty upsetting? For no one to know who you really are?"

"Well, he did, Gregg did, but I guess that wasn't enough in the end." Henry was worrying his napkin, the cheap paper starting to fray before our food had even arrived.

"OK, let's change the subject shall we? I drag you both into town and then act like it's a therapy session! I might as well have brought some paints and crayons to daub the walls with insightful murals while we wait for our food... where is our food anyway?" Janice craned her neck to peer over Henry's shoulder and then ducked back down quickly. "Shit. Shit. Ah, we might want to talk a little more quietly guys, one of the nurses is over there with her boyfriend." I swung around and saw Nurse Statton, holding hands across the table with some man in a mustard coloured tweed coat with brown leather elbow patches. It was strange to see the Nurse without her usual uniform. The blue dress she was wearing made her look gentler, calmer, not so likely to report you to Dr Laurence for taking too many bathroom breaks, not so angry as the usual furrows of her brow had smoothed out as she smiled at the man across from her.

"Maybe I should say hello, otherwise we might look a little suspicious. Though I really don't want to. I'll just leave it. She hasn't seen us. Your doc knows we're here anyway but you might want to watch your body language a little." Henry and I had been sitting elbow to elbow without realising it, our knees touching under the table. We slowly slid apart and Henry leaned away from me and tried to look casual. It was hard not to laugh, he was such a poor actor. Luckily the food arrived and we all had something else to concentrate on instead of being so conscious of our movements and chatter.

Janice had finished off the wine and ordered another bottle, but Henry declined another glass, "Better not". He nodded over his shoulder, "Plenty of time to raid my parents' wine cellar when I get back home. If there's one thing I can rely on them for it's having a nice bottle or twenty of some good plonk."

CHAPTER TEN

Henry left two weeks ago and I had heard nothing from him, I didn't even know if he had made it to Ottawa and I imagined all kinds of catastrophes befalling him on his trip. When my mind turned to abnormal tectonic plate shifts I knew I needed to give in and concede defeat if I was to save my sanity. Henry had simply returned to his old life, his old friends, and forgotten his brief dalliance with me.

Janice, however, had other ideas. After class today she held me back, waiting until the other boys had filed out. She handed me a letter from Henry. He had written to her, care of the Lodge so as to avoid his letter being checked. Inside the envelope was a separate letter addressed to me. Janice gave my hand a little squeeze and said she was there if I needed her. I didn't know what Henry had said to her so at first this alarmed me but I quickly realised she was just being supportive; this was still new territory for me but I liked the feeling that someone who seemed to know me actually continued to care.

I read Henry's letter, finding it full of desperation at being back in his parents' home. He wrote of the expectation that he would go to the school nearby so they could keep an eye on him, and curfews they imposed. He mentioned that they had hired a new doctor for him, deciding that he should keep up his work in therapy. To fight back, Henry said he had put the painting, still in its brown paper wrap, under his mattress. This was to keep it safe and from prying eyes, but most of all so that he slept every night with a little piece of me close by. He promised he was writing to Rose, and said that the letter would have been sent by the time Janice and I received this letter from him; he had wanted to be sure it was worded just right. I just hoped that the

Hollisters had not moved since I was last in Pitcher Creek. If Jim Hollister had not returned then his wife might have married Bill Tether by now and they could be living in town at his place, back in the centre of things. Or maybe the baby would force them to move out of the area to give Sara a fresh start where no one would know anything. My mind wandered and I thought that they might even try to raise the kid as Rose and Sara's younger brother or sister, or perhaps it would have to be taken into care. Even though I knew the child was not mine I still felt attached, responsible somehow, wanting to take care of him or her and make their life about more than just the fear and terror of their creation. Writing to Rose was a long shot but I had to know what she knew, even if I needed to find her myself once I got out.

I ran my fingers over Henry's words, the paper rough beneath my hand, heavy, lightly scented with something unfamiliar. I missed Henry's smell, the richness of him as he lay beneath me, the glisten of his skin, and the gentle caress as he'd hold my head to his chest or trace his hands down my spine as I stood against him. I had his words but I wanted his voice, his face, his body. Everything.

We had talked about the need to move quickly when he returned home. He knew that living in that house would drain him of life. He had already started looking for a job and was hopeful of finding something in the next few days, despite his inexperience. I knew he'd just charm some people and then muddle through until he got the hang of things. I wasn't really worried about him getting work. I was more concerned that he'd like it so much that he'd forget everything else and find a whole new life back in Ottawa. In his letter Henry said he'd arranged an interview with the owner of a jazz club, just to wait tables and serve drinks. This was the place he had loved sneaking into as a kid and he had told me how he had imagined one day being up on stage, fooling around with some of the other musicians. I hoped that he got the job so that even if he was just bringing people wine he would be surrounded by the thing he loved, music.

Janice had been pushing me in art therapy. Not that she thought I necessarily needed to make breakthroughs in my treatment but more because she had high hopes of exhibiting some of my work in the town art show in January. She said it would win both of us points with the Director of the programme at the lodge. Plus, we could have another night out in Fernley, perhaps without the watchful eyes of Nurse Statton this time. Without Henry either I had thought, but the night out would be fun anyway.

I had come to Arbutus Lodge with no concept of being artistically minded but I had found a new kind of pleasure in the touch of pencil to paper and brush to canvas. I even had a go at pottery last week but, although the sticky mess had been strangely fun, I think both Janice and I quickly realised that I should stick to the less physical forms of art. Janice had given me a book to borrow on impressionism and suggested I played around with the technique, just for fun. My eyes had complained at first, thinking I was tricking them perhaps to see a whole that simply was not there. Then, gradually, the pictures started coming together and the spaces in-between added depth and texture to my work that the solid colour failed to achieve.

I had begun to think about taking classes in art history and would have to ask Henry to look into the art department at McGill, if that was where he was still going. I had no qualifications so it was unlikely they'd just let me walk in and study with those who had been painting and drawing for years. I had been doing this, mostly badly, for just six months now and although Janice was insistent that I had real talent it still felt a little like she was being an indulgent parent.

If Janice was acting like a loving substitute mother then Dr Laurence was certainly playing the role of the stern father. My therapy sessions in the last week had been gruelling, drawn-out, almost angry on his part. It was as if he had simply determined that I was lying, that I knew I was lying, and that he felt the need to break me down in order to build me back up containing the truth he believed. I tried to stay strong but without Henry to talk to this was proving difficult. He still hadn't even mentioned Sara's pregnancy and, for all he knew, I was going to be a father in a week or two. I wondered if he had a legal requirement to tell me, but who could I ask without revealing my own espionage?

Instead of telling me directly about the baby he talked incessantly of consequences, the need for me to accept my actions had an effect on others, that my world was not everyone else's. I stood up to the questions, confident in my innocence, but the way he spoke about Sara, the fear, the pain she must have felt crumbled my resolve. I thought about how awful it must be for her, carrying that man's child and then seeing his face staring out at her as she held her baby for the first time.

Despite my sympathy for Sara it was hard spending all my days here perceived as a convalescing criminal, with no one, aside from Janice maybe, telling me otherwise. I didn't understand why Sara and Rose continued to lie, why this hadn't all been sorted out by now. Life without Henry was taking its toll. The nightmares had returned last night.

CHAPTER ELEVEN

I was in the groundskeeper's shed, wrapped in the picnic blanket that we had found in there, using the tiny glow from my flashlight to illuminate the paper in front of me. I had not been back to the shed since Henry had left, the risk hadn't seemed worth it without him. Tonight, though, I had woken up in terror, streaming with sweat, and I knew I had to get out of that dorm. I had grabbed my sketchpad and pencils and shuffled slowly out, shoes in hand.

At first I was just drawing circles, lines, practicing control, but then I flipped the page and the form of Henry took shape on the paper. I had drawn him looking away from me, out of the window, hands resting on its sill. I drew his long fingers, the smooth, flat fingernails with the large half-moons. His hands had grown calloused and hard while he had been here, unused at first to the abrasive cleaning fluids and the repetitive push and pull of the rakes, hoes, and shovels. For a boy who knew so much he had looked so lost given the simple addition of a trowel or a back hoe. But he had enjoyed the work once he understood it, the simple physical pleasure of turning hard earth into crumbly tilth ready for sowing the winter brassicas, garlic, and onion sets. In here, surrounded by the smell of damp earth, fertilisers, and chainsaw oil, we had talked about having our own garden, but Henry had said he'd be happy with just a window box to grow some tomatoes. He would have to wear gloves so as not to stain his piano-playing fingers green and yellow. Here, he had watched sadly as the dirt in the lodge's gardens became ingrained, wondering how long it would take to be clean again. I imagined his fingers splayed on the keys, sweeping across the notes, and me, standing next to him, turning the pages. I vowed to learn to read music so he had a reason to have me close at hand.

The drawing had lost its flow, Henry's face and torso slipped into the blank page and my pencil hovered, uncertain of where to go next. I heard a scrabbling noise at the far wall, too big for a mouse but it could easily be a raccoon or a coyote looking for a warmer place to hide. I didn't feel like sharing the blanket and so I stood up to scare it off, shining my torch in the direction of the door as it opened. Lewis covered his eyes but I could see it was him, pushing the door slowly and sidling in.

"Get that light out of my eyes damnit!" I lowered the torch and it took a moment or two for our eyes to adjust. My space, our space, had been invaded, and by Lewis of all people. He had no real hold over me now Henry had gone but he could still get me in trouble for sneaking out of the dorm at night. Lewis was wandering around the shed, picking things up here and there and then he opened up a garden chair and sat down, leaning back with his hands behind his head. "What you up to Jason, no more night time trysts so why sneak out again?"

"Bad dreams." I mumbled the words and then made for the door but Lewis jumped up and put a hand on my chest, lightly but insistently.

"Stay a while, please." He spoke softly, neediness in his voice rather than the fire and intensity of our last whispered conversation. "I don't want to go back just yet."

"Why did you follow me Lewis?"

"I was curious, that's all. Thought maybe I'd see how cosy it was in here." He gestured around the room and sat back down, pulling another chair out next to him and staring up at me, the whites of his eyes startlingly clear as they reflected the moonlight at the window.

I lowered myself into the garden chair, it was cold and hard and I pulled the sleeves of my sweater down to cover my hands under my coat. The metal pencil box was tucked along with my sketchpad into my jacket and I could feel the chill of it penetrating my chest. It was almost three so we couldn't stay here too long anyway, not before the second set of dorm checks took place. We sat in silence, Lewis gripping the arms of his chair and staring out of the window. I wrapped my arms tightly around myself, wishing I'd kept the blanket but not wanting to draw attention to it. The last thing I wanted was Lewis deciding he liked this place and me losing my one sanctuary at the lodge, other than the arbutus. "Why weren't you asleep?" I hoped I could make him feel tired and force him back to the warm bed in the dorm.

"Dreams Jason, same as you. The doc gives me Valium but only one and it doesn't do anything anymore. Maybe twenty would touch it. I'd give that a try."

"It doesn't work. They find you."

"Oh? Really? Is that why you're here then? I thought it was 'cause you raped some girl?" He spat the words out at me, but drawled the word 'girl.' He span round to face me and he looked furious suddenly. I wasn't really sure why but I knew enough to know he was unpredictable.

"That's what they think. I know different." We were both silent a second or two, staring at each other. I was curious about Lewis's history. I'd heard rumours but I really wanted to know what he'd done to be put here and why they thought he was worth saving so I asked, "Why are you here Lewis?"

"I told you, I wanted to check this place out."

"No, why are you *here*, here? At the lodge. What did you do?"

"I set fire to my school." He said it quickly, with pride, and a mean little sneer spread across his face. I had just been getting used to this quieter Lewis but now that calm had passed and his eyes searched my face for a sign of awe, fear, or something to make him feel strong I guess.

"Did anyone get hurt?"

"Nah! I only did it when I was sure no one would be there. It wasn't the other kids I was after, just a spectacle, a show, some excitement for once." I didn't think he'd meant to say so much, just getting carried away with the memory. I wondered if he had set fire to other things just to see them burn. I remembered the yellow flecks in his irises from that day outside the chapel. The heat, the intensity of the boy, wound so tightly, coiled and poised.

"But you must have had a better reason than that, right? You can't have just wanted to burn down the school for fun."

"It's surprising what people do for fun though, eh?" Lewis sprang up out of his chair, folded it up and then turned to me, a hand outstretched. I kept my arms wrapped tightly around myself and turned my head away from him. "Jeez, I was just going to help you up, we should get back before anyone misses us." He turned and headed to the door.

CHAPTER TWELVE

"Henry says he talked to Rose. Jason? Did you hear me? He's pretty sure she's holding back but he doesn't know why just yet. Jason?" Janice had brought me another letter, but Henry must have filled her in on the details so there seemed little point in opening it. "Jason? Are you listening?"

"Yes, sorry, yes. It's just, well, it's all so futile. She's never going to admit that her sister lied, that she lied, not now. Henry should just get on with his new life and forget I'm even here. It'll be easier."

"For you or for him? Why give up now Jason? Henry might be thousands of miles away but he's still in your corner isn't he? Is it fair to just tell him to let go? It seems pretty obvious to me that he really cares if you get out of this place."

Since Henry's last letter I hadn't been so sure. His job at the jazz bar let him get to know a few people and he'd even had a chance to play with some of them after hours. He wrote at length about the piano at the club and how full bodied it was when the club was empty, reverberating around the walls as he played to an audience of one or two only. He mentioned a drummer, Gary, a little too much to avoid suspicion. I was jealous of this man I'd never met - after all, he had heard Henry playing but every time I had asked Henry to play for me he had refused. I knew it was unfair to doubt him from afar, especially when he was, as Janice had said, still fighting for my exoneration.

Henry was always a little aloof though, thinking too much and saying too little. This was certainly not a fault I could find with Lewis who I seemed to keep bumping into and who insisted on talking at length every time. He talked about sports, movies, magazine articles he'd read, girls at his old school, the school he'd tried to burn down, and his brothers, both quite a bit older than him and already graduated, working, and married.

Lewis had showed me pictures of his family, dragging me over to his bed in the dorm and shuffling through the well-thumbed pile of holiday photos. He would tell stories about his family's stupidity, how hideous his brothers' wives were, how annoying his dad was, and how he hated them all, but I got the impression that he was talking too much and that he actually craved their love, their approval, whatever it took to get it. I knew he felt lost here, that no one understood him, but I didn't want to be the person to try as there was something just too desperate about him. Something so needy it felt like it would just sap all my energy, all my love, if I even tried a little.

I didn't dislike Lewis, or even hate him for taking advantage when he had. He'd been here a little longer than me but it would be two years until he would be moved to an adult facility or paroled, depending on his psych assessment. He had just become familiar somehow, part of the background noise at Arbutus Lodge that filled the days and nights, which had rolled into weeks, into autumn, and now winter. Lewis just had the squalid air of desperation all around him, like he would never really leave this place even if he moved to another centre.

Some of the boys had headed home for Christmas and New Year. There had been lots of special permissions granted, and lots of tears and shouting when others were denied. Parents arrived throughout the week, shepherding kids out to their cars, gloved hands clutching instructions about how not to break their child further over the holidays and emergency numbers to call, just in case.

An air of general anxiety filled the dorms and the corridors. There was a suspicion that some of the beds would be empty after the holidays, the bedside cabinets cleared quietly while we were in class. This way no one would see the sad packing up of combs and books, hockey cards, and family photos into anonymous boxes, sent back to bereft parents as a reminder of their apparent failure. Christmas was notorious in these kinds of places, Lewis said. Kids used the holidays to try to finish what they had started, what had landed them here in the first place in many cases.

I was not going home. Dr Laurence still deemed me a risk and my parents had told him that I would probably find it too stressful being back in Pitcher Creek. The truth was more likely that they'd decided Christmas would be easier without me around. I didn't mind. I preferred it this way as I'd get to spend Christmas alone, no need to smile at the receipt of tennis rackets I'd never use or the Calgary Flames jersey that only accentuated my scrawny frame.

Christmas was a time to highlight disappointments in my family. Everyone got a present or two that made them want to run off with the brandy and hide until it was all over. Last year my mother had bought my dad a cassette of popular hymns, and he had returned the insult with a book on common accountancy practice and tax tips. I had resorted to chocolates and socks, safe bets to apply only the expected amount of annoyance, no more, no less than any other year.

I wondered what Henry would be doing for Christmas. I worried about him, rattling around in that big house with his parents, cold and lonely, probably hiding out in the wine cellar. Even though I was jealous, I hoped Henry got to spend some time at the jazz club, with Gary even, so he had company and friends and warmth around him. He may act aloof but I know how sensitive he is to things.

I had arranged with Janice to send a Christmas present to Henry. It was just a little sketch I'd done that Janice had taken to get framed for me in town. The ink drawing was of the two of us sitting on a balcony, staring out at the mountains, drinking coffee, with planters of tomatoes tumbling all around. It was all in black aside from the vivid red and green of the fruit. I had done hundreds of versions of a different sketch; me and Henry sitting together at a grand piano. Each new version had seemed so lifeless, so contrived, though, and I had taken to burning them in a sad little ceremony in the groundskeeper's shed on my midnight forays. I told myself that each one brought me a little closer to the reality and that that was why it was never quite right because it would actually happen one day and everything else was just a rehearsal. The sketch I was sending had more warmth in it, hopefully brightening up Henry's cold Ottawa Christmas with the promise of summer and my release from this prison.

Janice wanted me to talk to Dr Laurence about my case. She said that it was possible that if I got him on my side he could talk to the police on my behalf, perhaps even provide professional testimony at a retrial. It was funny that Janice and Henry had just decided that I was innocent without having even met any of the people from Pitcher Creek and their faith in me made me feel strong but at the same time I knew that the police were just Pitcher Creek people and so their minds were already made up. Sara's real attacker would not come forward now, there was no reason to, especially with the baby and all. I thought about Rose and Mrs Hollister, how their Christmas would be, without Mr Hollister if he was back in England.

I wanted to know what Rose had said to Henry, how he had explained who he was and why he was calling. She hadn't replied to his first couple of letters so I'd dredged their number up from the recesses of memory and he had said he'd call before he next wrote. I realised I wasn't really angry at Henry, or at Janice. They were just trying to help but Janice had had enough of my pity party for now and she left, throwing the letter down on the table in the art room, shaking her head at me and telling me that she was there if I needed to talk.

I would apologise later. I shouldn't have let my bad mood affect her. I opened Henry's letter.

Part Three

CHAPTER ONE

The school bus pulled up at the end of the lane and Rose shuffled towards it slowly, her bag heavy and a bowl of porridge balanced in one hand. She took a final few mouthfuls before stashing the bowl and spoon in the bush where she would retrieve it on her way home. She did not eat breakfast in the house any more, not now that this meant staring across the table at her mom, quietly crunching granola, and Bill, slurping coffee, her coffee, from her dad's mug, conspicuously avoiding her gaze.

On the bus, Rose pulled out Henry's latest letter, hiding it behind her new copy of White Noise, which she was rereading, vaguely hoping there would be a toxic cloud passing over Pitcher Creek sometime soon. Something real on which she could hang the general gloom of the world.

The first letter from Henry just before Christmas had shocked her. She had tried so hard not to think about Jason, about what had happened to him after he was dragged away from Pitcher Creek. Now, here was somebody who had clearly grown to love him while everybody in town continued to hate the boy while he was conveniently absent and unable to defend himself.

Rose's surprise at receiving Henry's letter had quickly turned to shame and she had hidden it in her underwear drawer, stuffed inside the torn edge of the lavender-scented cushion her mother had given her from the boxes of Sara's things. When the second letter arrived in the New Year she had retrieved the first from its hiding place and reread Henry's questions. He was writing on behalf of his good friend he had said, who he could not believe capable of the things of which he had been accused. Rose had wondered if Jason's new friend was training to be a lawyer, his speech so formal and his tone cold and distant at first. After she had not replied to his second letter Henry had simply phoned instead, taking the chance that she would answer and not just hang-up when she realised who she was talking to. The phone call was the start of a much more friendly conversation and Rose almost felt now that she knew this man living all the way out in Ottawa, working at a jazz club and composing songs in his spare time.

Henry had asked outright if Rose knew who had raped her sister and the bluntness of the question had made her sit down quickly on the chair next to the hall table. In doing so she remembered the night that she had called her mother at the store, sobbing into the phone for her to come home, telling her that Jason was there. Rose knew that while she had been watching some stupid television show Sara had been in the next room being held down, shouting, screaming even but Rose had just turned up the sound of the show to drown out the noise. At first the shock and the confusion and the questions of the police about Jason had made her unsure of what had really happened, everyone had been so insistent that the signs had long been there, that Jason was deviant. Then Bill had started spending even more time over at the house, keeping an eye on his girls he had said, and although Rose still didn't see how Jason was capable of hurting anyone she just came to accept the truth she had been given. How else could she live with Bill and Darren?

A month later and Bill had moved in. Jane said that she didn't feel safe without a man in the house and her derisive snort made it patently clear to Rose that her suggestion of her dad being that man was no longer laudable. Jim had come back straight away after Andy had called him to tell him what had happened but Rose knew her dad had slept in his study and that he had packed up some things and moved them into the garage while he was home. Without meeting her gaze he'd said he was just moving things to make more space for her mom but Rose knew he was gradually removing himself from their lives. He was a coward, but she still loved him. She just didn't understand how he could leave them like this if he really cared.

Rose had tried to talk to Sara about their dad but Sara just ignored her and retreated to her room, shutting the door quietly behind her. Sara and Rose did not talk much after the assault and Rose found it hard to look at her older sister without feeling shame and guilt well up in her gut making her feel nauseous. If she'd just paid more attention she could have stopped it. She had seen Sara and Darren fighting so many times, maybe that time things just got out of hand. It seemed more likely than the idea of Jason suddenly attacking Sara, he was so meek, not like Darren. She didn't think anyone really knew what Darren was capable of though; Rose had always found him intriguing, there was something odd about the guy, a strange dark depth that drew her in. It scared her to think that she might be drawn to violence, to his anger, if that's what is was.

Jane Hollister had carried on with the flowers for her sister's wedding and together with Cassidy she had tried to convince Sara that being a bridesmaid would take her mind off things and make her feel better. Really, though, no one was in the mood for celebrating but this day had been planned for so long and if Cass postponed it she'd end up far too big to wear her dress. Bill had driven them all to the church and Jane had enjoyed showing him off in the new suit she had had made for him. Rose had stood silently next to Sara as her mom talked to Cass's friends, clutching Bill's arm the whole time and smiling and laughing like nothing was wrong, even when people looked past her at Sara and gave Jane a grim little smile.

Sara's bruises had turned from black to purple to a dirty yellow by the time Aunt Cassie's big day rolled around but in the purple dress the outward signs of the assault were still clear for all to see. A white shawl had covered Sara's shoulders but the marks at her neck were hard to disguise even under heavy layers of concealer, bronzer, and whatever else they had tried. Sara had left almost straight away after the ceremony, slinking off back to the house where Rose found her, curled up in her blanket on the sofa, the TV on and a half empty tub of Heavenly Hash ice cream oozing its contents onto the rug underneath the coffee table. Rose cleaned up while her sister slept, turning the TV off and pulling the blanket down a little to cover Sara's exposed feet. She remembered seeing the red shoes on Sara's bed, shoes that had now disappeared, along with the dress she'd been wearing that day, and the bed sheets themselves. Sara often fell asleep in the living room, or even in her dad's study now, avoiding her own room at night.

Sara had thrown lots of things away since the assault, piling box after box of skirts, shorts, dresses, and makeup in the hallway for her mom to take to the thrift store in town. Some things she had just thrown out, stuffing magazines, and loads of clothes into the trash. Rose had been tempted to rifle through as she was sure there were things that she could use but the closed-off expression on her sister's face as she disposed of these things made her see that reclaiming them was not a good idea. Sara had ditched her old clothes in favour of loose sweatshirts that came down almost to her knees. Her volleyball uniform had been returned to the school.

Rose knew Sara was excused from gym class, but it didn't really matter as she rarely went to school these days anyway. She had given up her place on the volleyball team, and Rose figured that her lack of exercise and heavy ice cream consumption explained her growing belly these past few months.

After her assault everyone treated Sara as if she'd just fracture and crumble at the slightest knock. This fragility was so stark a contrast to how Sara had been seen before that Rose struggled to remind herself that maybe Sara would never be the same outgoing, brash, and loud person she had been before. As much as she hated to admit it to herself, the old loud Sara who teased her and humiliated her was preferable to the hollowed out older sister she now had.

Sara spent more time than ever on her own, walking by the creek or sitting up in the tree house, smoking cigarettes. She sometimes barricaded herself in her room, using her dresser to stop anyone coming in. Rose had overheard her mother talking to Bill about how concerned she was about Sara, worrying that she had stopped seeing friends and hadn't really smiled for weeks. At first Bill had said it would be different once Jason, 'that boy,' had been found guilty and locked up. Things were different once Jason was sent away, but not like they hoped.

Bill's stuff had started taking over the house, the odd sweater here and there at first and then a parade of random tools, shoes, wires and gadgets that Rose kept falling over in the hallway. Rose was getting sick of tripping over this man who took up so much space and added to the general gloom of the house. When she fell over his checked slippers for the third time in a day she picked up the battered, smelly things and slammed them down on the kitchen counter in front of her mom, demanding that he either move out or be tidier.

"Rose, sweetheart, a pair of slippers isn't going to hurt you. You know the last few months have been tough on everyone and, well, with your dad not bothering to be here, I need a bit of support too."

"But... he's so... messy mom!" Rose spit out the words and a flash of anger crossed her mother's face.

"Messy? Really Rose? Because I haven't picked up after you for almost sixteen years now? You want messy? You can do your own laundry then, cook your own dinner and you can change the damn baby's nappy when it arrives!" Her mom turned away from her, her body wracking with her sobbing and Rose just stood there, her hand still on the slippers, as she stared at her mother's back.

She tried to say something but all that came out was a questioning exhalation, "Wha...?" Rose let her hand fall to her side and pulled her thoughts back together. "Mom? You and Bill are having a baby?"

Jane turned and looked wide-eyed at her daughter. "No, honey, Sara's pregnant. Your sister is the one having the baby, not me."

"When did... how long have you known?" Rose recalled so many visits to the doctor in recent weeks, for sleeping pills, to get Sara's iron levels checked again, even to have Rose's blood pressure checked as she'd fainted a couple of times and couldn't remember blacking out. Her mom and Sara had been at the doctor's office this morning, she must have found out today and now the five of them would all sit around the dinner table and pretend that Sara wasn't having Darren's baby.

"Is Darren moving in then, or are we moving in with them in town?"

"No one's moving anywhere yet, we need to work out what's going to happen." Jane grew even quieter and said slowly, "We'll see what the situation is once I tell Bill." Rose saw that her mom was scared, she was probably worried that Bill would abandon her. The shame of Sara having a baby and the unspoken origin of the child. Bill would be furious and Rose wondered how her mother could continue letting Darren sit at their table, eat their food, and drink their wine. She also noticed that her mother had said 'we' but that she did not mean herself, Rose, and Sara. She meant herself and Bill. Rose and Sara were pretty much stuck, then, waiting for others to decide their fate.

Could her mother really be so blind to what was going on? Rose knew her mom loved her and Sara so maybe it was her that was wrong. Perhaps Darren wasn't the baby's father, maybe it was Jason. But how had Sara managed to hide her pregnancy for that long if that were the case? She must still be sleeping with Darren, otherwise it made no sense, she never went out any more. Rose must be wrong, Darren could have been trying to comfort Sara, to stop her crying, to calm her down, but that was before Jason had arrived, before the noise of the truck on the gravel.

Everything was so jumbled and Rose felt dizzy trying to fit things together. Her mother wouldn't deliberately have Sara's attacker in the house, that would be madness.

CHAPTER TWO

"Rose, would you like to say grace?" Bill stared at her, his hands clasped in front of him over the dinner that her mother had prepared for 'all the family'.

"But, we don't..." she put down her fork, already loaded with food. "I don't know how." Bill snorted softly and raised his eyebrows and Rose's mother lowered her head as Bill got Darren to thank God for his three-cheese lasagne. Darren had raced over on his bike, arriving just a few minutes before dinner was served and he had said nothing prior to mumbling through grace. Opposite him at the table, Sara had not looked up from her plate since sitting down and Rose could see the tension in her jaw, the whites of her knuckles as she squeezed her hands together. She pushed the food around on her plate and sipped her water between each mouthful. She didn't take any bread or salad and seemed to be mashing up the food rather than really eating it. Bill was already onto second helpings of lasagne before anyone even talked about the real reason for the dinner.

"So, girls, your mom and I wanted to run an idea by you and we're really hopeful that you'll be receptive to it." He stared across the table, fixing his eyes on Rose. Sara did not raise her head or say anything. She had given up and this was Rose's fight now. Bill took a long breath and put down his knife and fork. Clasping his hands together he addressed Rose. "As you know, your mother and I have become very close this past year and we feel it best that we have the opportunity, all of us, to try to be a family. It makes sense for everyone you see, financially, in terms of time, it'll mean you all have someone around to fix those lights over the porch and to drive you to school if you need a lift. Basic stuff but the things that keep a family going and make a home a loving home." Rose thought she might be sick and she put down her fork, dinner was done.

A loving home? Had he really resorted to that? And, was he so desperate he'd appeal to finances and time constraints as genuine reasons to move in? Rose looked at her mom and at Sara and she wondered when they were going to tell Bill about the baby.

"Rose, Sara, did you hear what Bill said? We really want this to work but we need your support to give things a go, don't you think? We could have a real family Christmas this year." Rose thought it would be more like a real nativity if Sara was nearly eight months pregnant, although she certainly didn't look it.

Sara pushed her seat back and stood up to leave but Bill grabbed at her hand and told her to sit and respect her mother. Sara's whole body shook and Bill let go of her wrist, an angry red mark forming across her pale skin. She did not look at him, or anybody at the table, but turned and walked away upstairs. Rose thought about that mark and she felt herself tremble slightly. There was no use fighting this, her mother had not even questioned Bill's restraint of Sara, just sat there open-mouthed and then turned away. Why were they even bothering talking about this when Bill was living here already and had been for months. Rose thought that this must just be their way of claiming Christmas, letting them know that their dad wasn't coming back.

"Dad, maybe this isn't..."

"Darren, eat your dinner, it's not your place to decide anything here." Bill shot his son a glare across the table and then let his face soften and his shoulders fall a little as he looked over at Rose's mother. "She'll come round, maybe I should go and talk to her, or maybe you can help us out Rose, you've always been the more sensible one. Smart enough to see what's best for everyone in the long-run. Have a little talk with your sister won't you and make her see sense?"

"She doesn't talk to me anymore, not after..."

"Try." Bill picked up his fork again and the conversation was over. Everyone finished the meal in silence and Rose wondered what time it was in England and whether she could get away with calling her dad from the study, soon to be a nursery it seemed.

CHAPTER THREE

Rose arrived home, having retrieved her breakfast bowl, still full of porridge from the hedge. She rarely felt like eating any more in the mornings, always waking groggy and tired. Sick of the sight of Bill at the kitchen table. Sara must have felt the same as she was never there for breakfast these days, hiding up in her room. Sara was so pale now, and so thin except for her swollen belly. Rose worried about her, but what could she do when Sara wouldn't talk to her anymore?

Bill's truck was already in the driveway as she walked up to the front door. This was strange as he would usually work until seven and then arrive just in time to get washed up and change his clothes before dinner. Rose had skipped last period as her teacher knew she had a doctor's appointment to get the TB shot she'd missed earlier in the month. Her arm was still throbbing and she was annoyed that her mother had not bothered to meet her at the surgery as she'd said she would.

When Rose had walked past the flower shop afterwards she could see her mom hunched over the cash register, scissors in one hand and the accounts in the other. She didn't go in, no point causing a fuss now that the appointment had been missed anyway. She stood and watched for a while, leaning against the wall of the town's library. She saw Heather's mother enter the store and the brief conversation between the two women before her mom started crying and the other woman took her into the back of the store, away from prying eyes, including Rose's. She decided not to bother heading back for the school bus, if she walked now she'd get home faster anyway.

Opening the front door to the house Rose saw Sara's schoolbag slung under the telephone table, next to her shoes which were, again, unworn today. Rose hung up her coat, slipped off her gumboots, and started upstairs. She heard voices, quiet, coming from Sara's room which was odd as, these days, no one was usually allowed in there. The door was slightly ajar as Rose got to the top of the stairs and she could hear a knocking noise, over and over. Rose pushed the door open, slowly, quietly.

Sara was lying on her back in her bed, staring at the stars she had stuck to her ceiling when they had first moved into the house. Rose could just see her sister's face as Darren was on top of her, covered by the sheets, his head buried in her hair. The bed's headboard was knocking against the wall with every one of his thrusts and then Rose heard him say "Good girl, good girl" and she knew it was not Darren holding her sister down.

Her sharp intake of breath startled Sara who looked over at her but did not, could not, move. Her eyes were wide but Bill had not even noticed her flinch and he carried on and on, his hands in her hair, on her head, intent. Sara mouthed 'no' at Rose and her eyes filled with tears which she could not wipe away, pinned as she was. Rose retreated and quietly moved down the hall to her room, sitting on the edge of her bed, staring at the door until she heard Bill's footsteps heading down the stairs and the slam of the front door. She couldn't bring herself to go back into Sara's room, she knew everything now. She knew there was nothing she could do.

A knock at her door made Rose jump back onto the bed but it was Sara who crept in slowly and sat beside her, saying nothing. She took Rose's hand in hers and Rose felt an urge to pull her hand away but wasn't quite sure why. "It's not so bad, if you just..."

"No!" Rose jumped up and looked down at her sister in disbelief. How could she say this, how could she defend him.

"He loves mom. He means what he says about being a family, and to look after us."

"How is that, what he was doing to you, looking after us? Are you that stupid, do you have any idea what is really going on or are you just so completely dumb you don't understand? He raped you Sara, you're having his baby for god's sake!" Rose covered her mouth with her hands. She just couldn't stop herself, she didn't want to hurt her sister but it just poured out of her, she was so angry and felt so helpless, suddenly realising how wrong she'd been about it all. "Sara, he beat you, he's a monster, he's still raping you, I saw him grab your hand the other night and I knew then but I didn't really let myself think it. Sara? Sara? Look at me... why?" Rose had knelt in front of her sister who was crying into her hands, her head at her knees, her whole frame, shrunken, shrivelled from so much sobbing over these past weeks. "When did it start? Does Darren even know? Does... does he do it too?"

"No! No! Darren didn't know, until I told him about the baby. At least he said he didn't but he's so scared of his dad. Bill's just so jealous, he always has been, that's why I broke up with Darren, I had to. When he heard Matt say I'd slept with Darren that's when he, well, he wasn't so... gentle that day."

"Gentle? Sara, really? That's not being gentle, he was holding you down."

"You don't understand, he loves me, he says he loves me."

"I'm not stupid Sara, I know you know that's not love."

"It's close enough." Her sister's words just fell into the space between them and Rose let go of Sara's hands. What had happened to them both? How had she missed this, nearly a year now and it was still going on. Just a single wall separating their rooms. How had she been so oblivious? Rose's mind slowed down a second and a chill ran through her. Did her mother know? How could she not, after all Rose had just walked in at the wrong moment and caught him, her mother must have seen something in all these months, she must know the baby was Bill's not Darren's, certainly not Jason's.

Rose looked up at her sister and asked quietly, "Does mom know?"

"God, no! She'd be heartbroken. She loves Bill. She'd hate me. She'd think I'm a whore as well as being stupid."

"But Sara, it's his fault, it's not yours. Mom would throw him out, she'd call the police, she'd..." Sara cut her off, grabbing her hands and pulling her in so they were face to face.

"No. No one is going to call the police. No one. They'd find out I'd lied, the whole town would know. Mom would throw me out, I'd lose Bill. What would I do then? No one is telling, you have to promise. Promise?" Sara had hold of her sister's hands so tightly that Rose was squirming to free herself. "Besides, I can't get thrown out Rose, not now." Sara put a hand over her belly, protecting it.

Curious, Rose asked to see and so Sara lifted her sweatshirt to reveal her slightly swollen stomach, the soft blue lines of veins starting to spread out across the bulge which looked alien on Sara's tiny frame. Rose thought about the morning sickness, the lack of appetite, and the pallor of her sister's skin. "Shouldn't you be, well, bigger by now?" Rose was suddenly confused, she had, up until a few moments ago, just assumed that Sara's baby was a result of her attack but surely the bump was too small.

She didn't doubt though, however far along Sara was, that this was a child born of pain, born of struggle and fear, and a child who would be born without a father because to admit the truth would be impossible now. "Six months, but the doc says the baby's small and that the stress and things have affected stuff so it might be longer, they don't really know. I just thought I was sick at first."

"But how can they still think it was Jason, surely this proves it wasn't?"

"It doesn't prove anything Rose, I mean just because I'm pregnant now doesn't mean they don't think he was the one that hurt me in April. Anyway, once a slag always a slag, right. I'm fair game now so this is just how it goes." Sara was suddenly calmer and she brushed her hands down the fronts of her jeans then turned to leave the room.

"Sara?" Rose called out to her, "This is not love, whatever you think is going on and however much you think I'm too little and stupid to understand, I understand that much. Bill does not love you, he doesn't even love mom. He's not capable of it. You can't build a family like this, surely you know that? However much you want it, surely you know you can't have a family with him. It's not real and, what if he..." Rose stopped but she knew Sara must have thought about the safety of her child. She couldn't ignore it, however deluded she might be about Bill's love.

Sara didn't look at her but said "He wants to. He'll look after us. He just doesn't want anyone else to know yet. We told the police but only because we had to, and they just think the baby's small. It's not an exact science Rose so everyone will carry on thinking it's Jason's unless you say different. Bill checked into it and nobody tests for this stuff, it's too expensive and takes too long so there's no point if there's enough other evidence. Just keep quiet and be happy for me, for us. Otherwise it'll be your fault that the family breaks up, not mine." She stalked out strengthened by her anger and left Rose kneeling on the floor as if in silent prayer, but there was no one listening, there never had been.

CHAPTER FOUR

"No! Where is she? Where's Sara? Where did she go? You threw her out, you're just jealous! Where is she! Where is she?" Rose stood in the middle of her sister's room staring at the bare walls, the boxes stacked in the corner. She was clutching the letter addressed to her, her mother standing in front of her, crying and holding a similar letter that she thought she had hidden well enough from Rose.

"Rose, honey, she's gone, she's gone. It's been two weeks now." Her mother was staring at Rose glassy-eyed, terrified. She had just returned from the police station, she had been to sign out Sara's body, but, still, she hadn't dared to look at her dead daughter. It was Bill who had identified the body after they pulled Sara out of the water, and Bill who had had that final moment, seeing what he had done. Then Bill had brought Jane home and put her to bed and they had waited for Andy to fetch Rose from school. It was he who had called the doctor as they held Rose down while they tried to calm her screaming that pierced the falling fog of the Valium Jane had taken that afternoon. As she held her youngest daughter, Jane thought for a second about how it could have been her, not Sara who had walked out into the creek and just let go of herself. The temptation revisited her again and again over the coming weeks.

Rose tried to calm down but the noise in her head was just overwhelming. She felt like she might fall and so she sat down suddenly in the middle of the floor. Her mother knelt beside her and held her head to her chest as she sobbed for what seemed like hours. "Honey, I'm sorry. I'm so sorry for it all."

"Where is she? Did she really do this?" Rose waved the letter at her mom but she already knew. Sara had boxed things up, even labelling them to make things easier for her mom. She'd stripped the bed, put the sheets in the laundry, written the letters, sealed them and then walked to the creek, picking up stones to fill her pockets on the way. Sara had stripped her room of herself, and then washed herself away, but it was Rose that felt cold, surrounded by darkness, her breath held tight inside her.

Hours later, Rose lay in bed thinking about how it was her fault, how she should have said something, told someone. Her mom was lying next to her and Rose saw she was lost to sleep. Where was Bill? He had caused all of this and she had wanted to scream at him but she knew he'd just look through her, like he always did, not caring if she was hurt.

Had Bill known what Sara planned? Rose didn't know what had changed, why suddenly Sara couldn't go through with things like she'd said she would. She had been so adamant about them being a family. Bill had painted the nursery pink and purple because he was convinced the baby would be a girl. When he had finished he had stood in the doorway, a horribly smug smile on his face and his arms folded across the slight bulge of his belly. It almost looked like he was the one who was pregnant. Then he had made cocoa for everyone, with extra sugar in Rose's cup and he had watched her drink it, while Sara rested her cup on her belly, twisting the repaired heart pendant round and round in the same way her mom toyed with her daisy pendant.

As Rose's memory started to return she saw an image of Sara on that last night. Her sister's attention had switched between Rose and Bill, who was, as usual, contentedly sipping his drink without a word. There had been a strange intensity in her sister's eyes, like she wasn't just turning the necklace round and round, she was coiling up an immense anger, condensing it, keeping it from spilling out, from hurting Rose perhaps.

Rose had gone to bed that night and slept a dreamless sleep, woken covered in sweat, with horrible cramps and the shame of seeing the mess of her period, early again. She hadn't seen Sara as she showered and got ready for school but she had noticed that the sign for her sister's room had disappeared and Rose remembered thinking she had heard doors slamming in the night, perhaps Sara had had another fight with her mother. She had been more alive recently, more vivid and present than in these past few months. She had begun taking some new medication from the doctor, something to help her with her anxiety they had said.

Gradually growing used to the darkness, Rose made out the shape of her dresser and then the desk and chair by the open window. She thought back to the letter and she wondered what Sara had meant. Her last words to her sister and Rose didn't understand. "I'm sorry, I couldn't help. Be stronger than me Rosie."

What couldn't she help? Rose turned onto her back and looked up at the bedroom ceiling and then she saw the stars. The tiny stickers glowing on the ceiling. Rose felt a sudden weight on her chest, pain, and she couldn't breathe and there were hands in her hair, in Sara's hair, and all the painful fragments of memory in her mind suddenly came back together and she saw her sister's reflection turn into her own face, and she knew what Sara had done and she knew why.

CHAPTER FIVE

Henry's letter arrived the next morning and now that she had come out of her stupor Rose was the first to check the mail. She snatched up the envelope and hid it in the waistband of her jeans. It was the beginning of February. Sara had been gone for two weeks and Jane had discussed the on-going need for Rose's sedation with her doctor, deciding that it was time her daughter was given a chance to come to terms with Sara's death. Rose had little recollection of the time since she had been pulled out of school by Andy. She remembered sobbing in Sara's room, and then there were just fragments of conversations between her mom and Bill, standing over her as she fell in and out of consciousness.

Taking the letter up to her room, Rose looked at the large loopy handwriting and felt the familiar guilt snatching at her breath. She'd forgotten about Jason these past few weeks. Everything had been slow and hazy, even before Sara's suicide. Rose had found herself falling asleep at school and she had been dizzy, her heart palpitating at her ribcage like a plucked, sonorous cello. Afraid she was anaemic, her mom had made her an appointment to see the doctor but recent events had postponed any tests.

It seemed that Rose had missed Henry's phone calls and she felt like she'd betrayed Jason all over again. Although she knew he was innocent it had been a struggle just getting through each day as best she could, never saying anything. How could she tell Henry that it wasn't Darren, that she couldn't tell anyone what was really happening, that she couldn't help get Jason out.

Henry had told her how he had moved out of his parents' place and was living in a small apartment near the jazz club, just space enough for an upright piano which his parents were considering moving from their townhouse. He was hopeful that Jason would be out soon, with Rose's help, and that he'd join Henry in Ottawa. The excitement in his letters made Rose stop and think. Wouldn't Jason be going to school in Calgary? Perhaps he had changed his mind and found a course in Ottawa, staying with Henry while he got set up. Rose thought about how Jason would be sharing Henry's living room with a piano, squeezed in on the sofa, perhaps.

None of these things would happen, though, if Rose kept her promise to Sara about keeping quiet. She could hardly tell Henry the truth. She didn't even really know him and how would he be able to do anything from so far away when he wouldn't even be able to find Pitcher Creek on a map?

Rose knew that if she didn't answer the letter there was a chance Henry would just keep calling and she couldn't risk that. A strange man ringing the house for her would throw Bill into a frenzy, protecting his girls. Bill was insistent about them needing a strong man around the house. Even before Rose knew the truth her skin shrank hard and tight over her bones with every word.

Something else about Henry's letter suddenly struck her as strange and she ran upstairs to her room and rummaged through the dresser to find his other letters. She realised that this was the first time Henry had mentioned the baby, assuming Sara had given birth already because he didn't know any better. Did he also know about Sara's suicide? If he did then Jason must know now too. Everyone would blame Jason for Sara's death, Rose thought. She had to help set things right, she just hoped it wasn't too late.

CHAPTER SIX

Rose didn't go to school the next day, staying at home in her bedroom and only letting her mother in to bring her Tylenol. Rose said she had cramps and she deliberately left a box of tampons on the bathroom shelf just before Bill was due home. She knew that her mom would tidy them away if she had a chance, so as to spare Bill's blushes; he found such things distasteful and Rose was relying on his disgust.

The next morning she got dressed and she said she'd go to school, although her mom insisted she could take as long as she needed. Jane had not been back to work since Sara had died. She hadn't really left the house, just sitting, instead, in her robe, drinking tea and eating the warmed up soup Bill put in front of her with two slices of Wonder Bread perched precariously on the side of the bowl. She told Rose that she would make an appointment for her to see Sara's old therapist, so she had someone to talk to. Rose acquiesced but wondered what help it would be, after all, Sara hadn't been saved.

Instead of heading into school when her mom dropped her off, Rose waited and then walked through town to the bus station, devising a plan. She would check the bus schedules and use her saved allowance to buy a ticket to Calgary where she could get the Greyhound to Vancouver, and then hopefully hitch a ride to the address Henry had given her. Seeing that the bus left on Thursday, three days from now, Rose realised she would have to hide out somewhere. Thinking about who she could stay with, Rose realised that over the past few months she hadn't really spoken to anyone. Her friends were all busy with their boyfriends and thoughts of prom and so Rose had just stopped seeing people outside of school, unable, or unwilling to bring the requisite double date partner. She had been so tired, struggling to get schoolwork done and losing her evenings to a haze of somnolence. The fatigue of their house had become infectious it seemed and she hadn't spoken to anyone since Sara had died. She was glad she hadn't run into anyone at the school gates that morning but she would have to face them soon, unless she skipped school and hid somewhere for the rest of the day.

As she walked back from the bus station Rose passed the Tether house, where Darren was still living most of the time. Without really thinking, Rose opened the gate and walked up to the front porch. The door was open. Pitcher Creek was still a small enough town that people trusted each other, although God knows why, Rose thought.

Inside, the house was dark, the curtains all drawn and the blinds down at the back of the house so only small slivers of light spread across the front hallway. Rose walked quietly through into the living room and she saw pizza boxes and beer cans stacked on the coffee table, an ashtray overflowing along with a glass next to it. The smell was rank. Stale, old beer and cigarette smoke seemed soaked into the very woodwork of the house but Rose felt safe. Bill could not have been here for weeks if Darren felt comfortable enough to leave the house looking like this in the middle of the day.

Curious, Rose padded upstairs softly, noticing how her socks caught in the splinters of the worn wooden steps. She peered into Darren's room and was surprised at its neatness. He had library books piled on his desk, exercise books spilling pages covered in notes and sketches of animals, coyotes it seemed. The partying was clearly relegated to the lower half of the house as his room actually seemed fresh, clutter-free, inviting. Rose moved along the hallway, past a side table with a dusty, rust-stained crocheted doily, homemade and half covered by a random assortment of combs, matchboxes, medicine bottles and ointments. She picked up one of the now empty semi-transparent orange bottles and looked at the faded label. Rose could just make out the name, 'Andrea Tether,' but the name of the medication had faded under a sheen of grease from thumbprint after thumbprint as the bottle cap had been popped open.

Carrying on down the hall, Rose came to Bill's room. It was mostly empty as the bulk of his things littered her house now. There were twin beds in the room, one still with sheets on it, rumpled and ripe. On the nightstand was a broken lamp, the figure of a naked woman holding a white globe with a crack all down the side and cobwebs covering the lady's hands. The bottom of the white orb was thick with dead spiders, dead flies, drawn in by the promise of warmth and light. A similar lamp sat, without the globed shade, on the nightstand next to what must have been Andrea's bed. On the wall, between the two beds, was a simple wooden cross. It was the only decoration in the room besides a photograph on the large, cheap, and scratched dresser with a warped and mottled mirror.

The photograph was of the family outside the church. Bill had his arm awkwardly around Darren, who looked to be about three or four in the picture. A woman stood at a slight distance from them, her hand resting gently on the back of the little boy's head. This must be Andrea, Rose thought and she studied the thin smile of the petite blonde who looked eerily similar to Sara, and her mom. At about five three, with a perfectly neat waist-length plait, Andrea looked very young. A paisley dress hung over the woman's thin frame, shadows emphasised the collarbone, her visible breastbone. Rose was shocked at how thin and how sick Darren's mom looked.

She had never met Andrea, who had died a year or so after Rose had been born, but she had heard people in the town mention her a few times, mostly with hushed voices and in connection to Darren being in trouble. Bill was seen as something of a saint to raise his son alone after his wife's death, waiting until now to find himself someone new.

It seemed that people had little sympathy for Andrea herself, remembering her as a nervous woman, very house proud and highly strung. So much so that few had ever ventured into the Tether house, invites not often being tendered, due to Andrea's anxiety it was presumed. It was this tension in the woman that many blamed for the return of her cancer and, subsequently her quiet death when she refused treatment. Rose recalled overhearing a couple of teachers talking about Darren after a fight at school. They had been smoking outside the library as she had been fastening the pannier onto her bike. How a mother could leave her husband and son like that, without even fighting, they could never understand, but Rose understood alright. It was all too clear to her now.

Rose tried to recall Darren saying anything about his mom but she didn't think he'd mentioned her at all. Nor had Bill talked about his wife. Andrea could only be twenty or so in the picture, putting her at Sara's age when she got pregnant with Darren and married Bill. Rose thought about her sister's swelling belly and saw a familiar animal-like fear in the eyes of the woman in the photograph. She put it back in its place, marked by a clear, dust-free line on the dresser's top.

Rose looked around the rest of the room, seeing a pair of abandoned socks coated in dust in a corner, a couple of books on a chair next to the closet, the door slightly ajar. Bill had brought lots of his clothes over to their house so Rose was curious to see what was inside. Opening the closet door she half expected to be confronted with moth-eaten dresses left behind after Andrea's death but the rail was empty. A couple of white hat boxes were stacked on the floor at the back of the closet and Rose noticed that these were free from dust, reminding her that it was still possible that Bill might return to the house; she couldn't hide here until Thursday, that had been a foolish idea.

Feeling suddenly dizzy, Rose knelt on the closet floor, steadying herself as her heart slowed to a normal rhythm again. She reached out and quickly lifted the lid of the top box. Rose saw more of the orange bottles, many still full of pills, their labels intact. She lifted a couple out and saw Andrea's name again and recognised the same sleeping pills her mom now took. Another bottle read 'doxepin', and another 'dextromoramide.' There were small vials of morphine, some Numorphan, and Rose lifted box after box of more drugs, many untouched, the patient name always the same. Had Darren's mom taken all of these? Why had Bill kept them?

Rose replaced the lid and moved the box aside, lifting the lid on the second, smaller box. At first she thought that there was just leftover tissue paper inside, padding for a Sunday hat Andrea might have worn once. When Rose unfurled the paper she felt the cool metal underneath and quickly drew back her fingers. She replaced the tissue paper, closed the lid, stacked the boxes at they had been and left the room as quickly as she could.

Back in the hallway, Rose wondered if Darren knew about the gun, and the pills. Maybe he even used the pills to get high sometimes, maybe he hadn't been stoned in the woods that time, he'd been high on his mom's old pain medication. Thinking about all that had happened this last year, Rose could see how Darren might be tempted, assuming he knew his dad had kept all the pills. It seemed that Bill rarely spoke to Darren these days, she hardly ever saw them together except when they were all forced to have family dinners. Did they fight, she wondered? She couldn't recall hearing about anything like that and Darren never seemed to have fought with other boys at school, which seemed odd to her now considering his reputation for being tough. She guessed that his hardness was a result simply of Bill's neglect and suddenly Rose felt guilt wash over her.

She had hated Darren so fiercely for what she thought he had done to Sara but now she wondered if he had actually been trying to protect her. After all, Sara said she had broken things off with Darren, that Bill had been the jealous one. Could Darren really have done anything to help. It was his father after all, and he'd already lost his mom. Rose had her own shame, her own guilt now and any blame she placed on Darren was subsumed by those new feelings.

She had been there too long and there was always the chance that Bill would stop by. Rose crept back down the stairs and, after pausing for a second, went out of the front door, thinking about what she would need for her trip and how to avoid Bill until she left on Thursday.

That night, Darren was absent at dinner and Bill told Jane that he thought it about time to move Darren in with them so he could keep an eye on his son. "He's had too much freedom, that boy, I've been too lenient and he could use a good mother figure." Rose looked over at her mom who just nodded and said it was probably for the best, to have them all together now, for support. The room that had been her dad's study and which was being turned into a nursery would now become Darren's room and Bill said he'd head over to his place at the weekend and get Darren to pack up his stuff. Rose thought she should warn Darren; she would head back to the house tomorrow and then she could tell him that she was leaving, but she'd have to lie to him about going and seeing Jason, otherwise he might try to stop her. Rose quickly cleared her plate and excused herself so she could start washing the dishes. She wanted to get upstairs and start packing.

Rose's mom brought the rest of the plates into the kitchen and put a hand on Rose's shoulder. "I have to go to the store tonight, just for a bit. There's an order that I need to sort out and I've left Noreen to deal with things for too long. Bill will be here though and you can always call if you need anything." She kissed the back of Rose's head and patted her shoulders.

"Sure, it's fine." Rose smiled weakly at her mom and then watched her reflection in the kitchen window as she gathered her things up and left. Bill was still in the dining room, finishing his glass of wine, or pouring another. He used to give Sara a small glass with dinner, her mother finally stopping to bother arguing with him. "It'll do the girl good," he had always said, "build up a tolerance."

She finished the dishes and turned to go upstairs but then stopped and looked at the knife block, her breath slowing down as she tried to think but couldn't keep her thoughts still enough to make sense of them. She reached out and pulled one of the shorter, sharper knives from its slot, turning it around to sneak it up her sleeve.

Upstairs, Rose began packing a bag, listening out for sounds of footsteps in the hallway. She took Henry's letters and folded them into the side pocket of the hold-all, then she threw in a couple of changes of clothing and some meal-replacement bars she'd grabbed from her mom's stash in the kitchen cupboard. Her mom had started eating these in place of dinner some nights and Rose thought about the picture of Andrea.

This man just drained people, destroyed them, but it was her mom who had invited Bill into their home.

Rose tried to shake off the thought, she had to concentrate on herself now. Her mom could not protect her; she hadn't looked out for Sara and she wasn't looking after herself so Rose would have to do it. She put the knife in her bag but then changed her mind and moved it under her pillow instead. A quiet knock at the door made her jump but Bill couldn't push it open as Rose had lodged a chair under the handle. She heard him recoil in surprise, and frustration. Then he gathered himself together and called through the door. "Rose, everything OK in there? I just came up to talk and to see if you wanted this." Bill twisted the handle again and shoved at the door and Rose knew she had to open it or risk him getting angrier. He stood in front of her and smiled, one hand resting on his protruding belly and the other holding a small glass of red wine. He raised a finger to his lips and said "Shh. Don't tell your mom of course, but I think you're plenty old enough for a little drink, don't you? It helps."

Rose hesitated, not wanting to upset him but with no desire to accept this false gesture of affection. She took the glass. She had to act normally until she could get away. Tomorrow she would leave, perhaps sleep at the bus station and hope they didn't find her. Bill still stood in the doorway smiling and she took a mouthful of the wine, looking up to meet his eyes and wondering if the alcohol would make her braver. Her dad had always called it Dutch courage and so she took another mouthful and Bill gently shut the door saying he would leave her to her schoolwork but was downstairs if she needed him.

Rose flicked her tongue over her teeth, exploring the strange coating from the wine. She sat down on her bed and tried to push the image of Bill's leering smile from her mind. He generally paid her so little attention, but now Sara was gone he had finally noticed her. Or, perhaps, Rose thought, he saw she was dangerous, that she knew, that she might tell someone. Rose put the empty glass on her nightstand and felt for the knife under her pillow. Had she given herself away?

She thought about Jason, that she had to get out of Pitcher Creek, find him and help prove his innocence. Henry's letters were already packed, she needed a map, she should take a notebook, get her toothbrush. She didn't even really know where she was going but she had to leave.

Rose stood up to fetch things from the bathroom but now her head was spinning and as she tried to focus on her face in the mirror of her dresser her eyes kept shutting. She was suddenly exhausted, so tired, perhaps she could just sleep until Thursday morning, she could just fall into bed and ignore them all, forget everything.

Rose fell back against her pillows and looked through half-closed eyes at the wine glass Bill had brought her. It sparkled in the lamplight, the last few drops of wine thick and bloodlike. She reached out to touch the glass but couldn't judge the distance and swept it clumsily to the floor, the droplets spattering the cream coloured rug next to her bed. Her mom would be angry, the rug was new, her mom would be so mad with her, for everything, she had warned her and now Rose was drunk and alone and so so tired. She closed her eyes and the thoughts rushed away into nothingness, a deadness, she felt calm, just for an instant before she collapsed into unconsciousness.

The light had changed in the room, the darkness denser and Rose blinked, as if trying to squeeze more light into her eyes somehow. She tried to sit up but there was a weight on her chest, forcing her back down and she searched the darkness desperate and afraid. Controlling her own breathing she heard his, laboured, wheezing almost and she felt his hand move up to her shoulder and smelt his breath as he leaned in to her. How had he got into her room without her hearing anything? She shouldn't have drunk the wine, she couldn't take it and now he was here, again.

The many many things she had blocked out started crying out in her mind, everything had an intense clarity, seen through the lens of fear. Rose knew this wasn't the first time but she couldn't even remember when that was. Before Sara? Before the baby? Or maybe just last week while she was so drugged. How many times had he held her down like this, how many times had she just slept through it, or forced herself to think it had been a nightmare.

This time she was more awake than ever as he moved to cover her but still she couldn't get free, her arms outspread, like a snow angel fallen dead into soft powder and covered over with white cold, muffled, numb. Her feet were cold, her legs frozen without cover of the sheets or her tights and she felt his hands creeping up her belly lifting her dress and pushing it over her head but her arms still wouldn't move.

Why couldn't she feel her arms to move them, she was awake this time but it felt like her words were trapped under a thick layer of ice, her lips moving silently as she screamed at him to stop. He pushed the thick cotton of her dress into her mouth and held his hand over her face as he whispered "Good girl, good girl,' then sighing and grunting and the cold sweat and wetness and the rhythmic thump of flesh on flesh and the headboard against the wall. She couldn't breathe and she saw Sara in the darkness, her face amidst the cloud of blonde hair and her mouthing 'no, no' over and again and again, trapped like her.

Her body was waking up and she felt the stab and the contraction of her insides fighting against him. Her body was screaming at him, matching the intensity of her terror but still she couldn't seem to control her movements. Rose tried to clench her fists, to move her toes and finally she gripped the sheets with her fingers and managed to raise her arm in the darkness. Scrabbling up to the pillow, trying to reach under it, she felt for the cold metal of the knife. It wasn't there. She searched again, moving both arms up now beneath the pillows, her chest burning with the strain and the weight of Bill on top of her. She was breathing heavily, her lungs fighting against the pressure holding her down, and she was choking on the cotton in her mouth. Rose coughed and gagged and for a second Bill stopped, realising she was conscious this time, that she was moving.

Then he laughed, a hollow gloating sound in the silence and darkness of the room and he moved his hand from her face to pin her arms above her head instead.

She felt something cold against her cheek and Bill whispered "Looking for this?" He sighed, "Ah, Rose, you disappointed me. You were always so... good, so willing, where's my good girl gone, hey?" He laughed again and she could feel him shaking against her as he held her down, not waiting for an answer, just carrying on, the knife flat against her cheek until he stiffened and trembled, letting it fall, and climbed off her.

Rose lay in the damp sheets, her arms raised above her head, cold. She waited until she heard the sound of her bedroom door closing behind him, then the bathroom door being locked. She pulled the fabric from her mouth and her body broke into sobs as she scrambled out of the mess of sheets. Pulling her dress down to cover her wet thighs, she tried to wipe herself clean but her dress was already soaked with her tears, her saliva, her sweat, and his. The edges of her vision rushed inwards and she had to steady herself on the back of the chair at her desk. She felt like her legs were about to collapse beneath her. Her bones had turned to sand which was running out through her body like a broken hourglass.

She looked over at the half-packed bag and saw that the contents had been rummaged through, but when she checked she found that Henry's letters were still in the side-pocket, seemingly untouched. Perhaps Bill didn't know yet what she was planning, perhaps he had waited longer this time so she would remember, thinking that she'd be too scared to do anything. The harshness of his laugh came back to her as she thought about the knife. She had been stupid to think she could use it to protect herself but as she saw it lying on her pillow she felt an urge to run with it to her mom's room and to show him she wasn't afraid of him anymore.

Instead, she left the knife where it was, not wanting to go back over to the bed. Now Bill was down the hall in her mother's room she crept out to the bathroom, where she locked the door and turned on the water in the tub. The drumming sound drowned out her thoughts and Rose knew it wouldn't wake her mother from her own dead sleep. Bill was probably still laughing at her and her childish attempt to stop him, not caring now if she had a bath in the middle of the night, thinking he had complete control of her. That he had won.

Rose stepped into the bath and lowered herself into the water, her dress floating up around her as the water rose to cover her legs. She pulled the damp cotton over her head and threw it down onto the bathroom tiles. She didn't want to look at herself, at her body. She was angry that it had let itself be numbed, let itself be tricked into betraying her. She turned off the water and drew her knees into her chest, rocking back and forth slowly until she could feel the warm water bringing life back into her skin, her blood. Slowly, Rose came back to herself and realised that she needed a plan, and she needed help.

CHAPTER SEVEN

Rose woke to the tapping of crows on the bathroom skylight and she rubbed her arms and legs before sitting up, stiff from sleeping on the tiles all night. She refolded all of the towels that had served as her makeshift bed and put them back in place. The tiles were freezing and she pulled her mother's bathrobe tighter around her and wondered if it were possible to flush the dress, discarded in the bathtub, down the toilet. She decided not to risk it, she would only have to explain herself to her mother and risk Bill getting angry. Shoving her cold hands into the robe's pockets she scraped her fingers on something sharp and found a half-empty packet of Valium.

There were so many pills everywhere, so much to numb and block out. Rose wondered if it was Valium that the doctor had given her after Sara's suicide and, for a second or two she was tempted to swallow what remained of the packet but then she remembered the plan she had come up with the night before and tried to draw her strength from that instead.

Leaving the pills in the pocket of the robe, Rose stared at herself in the bathroom mirror. Her skin looked ashen, almost purple under the eyes and for the first time in her nearly sixteen years Rose felt the slow creep of age. How her body could, and would let her down, time and again. She saw how her face would carry the memory of everything that had happened to her. Every time she looked into herself she would see that little bit of darkness, its edges growing ever outwards day by day, spreading like black oil across the surface of her mind. She needed to contain it, to bring back the light.

Rose raised her hand to her face and poked a finger into her cheek, half expecting it to sink into the hollow space that she felt existed inside her now. This void, an abyss into which her former self had fallen. Rose had no pretensions about ever having been a giddily happy child but she knew now that she had been blind to the horror of life, blissfully unaware of the cruelty others could inflict. This aching expectation she now had of that cruel desperation and terror felt cold and heavy, even Sara's suffering had not weighed on her quite like this and that made Rose feel even worse, as if there were a part of her capable of its own shade of evil through neglect.

Still staring at herself in the mirror, Rose felt removed from the little girl staring back, copying her movements. What she saw was no longer who she was. This girl did not match the self she now felt moving through the world. Her long brown hair stuck out in tufts around her shoulders, and the static created a peculiar blonde halo at the crown of her head as her hair caught the sunlight. It made her look childlike, the serene image jarring with the thin, tight expression she now wore. She tried to dampen down her hair but that just made the static worse.

Rummaging in the bathroom cabinet she found some nail scissors, tiny but sufficient. Holding her hair in a bunch at the back she hacked away at the ponytail, close to where her hand was at the base of her skull. Small pieces of her hair fell into the neck of the robe but when she was done Rose was holding a shock of hair in her hand, years of growth, and she stared back at herself in the mirror. Her hair now sloped forward towards her chin, short at the back and long in front. She definitely looked older, more severe, more serious. She felt some of that darkness from inside taking hold of her outside. Perhaps this had been a mistake. Or, thought Rose, maybe this was a safety valve of sorts, a nod to her fear, her shame, her terror, the little bit of evil she felt lurking underneath her quietude. She threw the lock of hair into the waste bin and a little of it hung out the side when she let the lid fall. She was tempted to keep a piece, a memento of how things were, but she already felt different, and she didn't want to go back. For a second or two she felt lighter, her interiority let out for a brief moment to dissipate the darkness in the air around her. It was just hair but Rose actually did feel different, that she could change and that there was cause for hope.

It was still early, the sun not even fully up as she split the blinds with her fingers and looked out at the frost covered field behind the house. The sky was clear and it would be another cold day. She would need a scarf to cover her naked neck and as the veil of sleep lifted Rose remembered packing a bag. She remembered Henry's letters, and she grabbed her toothbrush and thought about what else she would need. She was going to see Jason, she was going to BC and she would try to fix things, at least, that is, what could be fixed now.

As she turned to unlock the bathroom door she grew faint, suddenly every thought felt like she was sieving it out of thick treacle, her mind trying to suck her back down into choking darkness. She felt the familiar tightness in her chest, the memory of Bill's body on hers, and she steadied herself on the towel rail until the moment of panic passed, taking deep breaths and staring at the lines of the floor tiles until they became solid once more. She could see herself lying there and the distance made her feel stronger, stable, she could see the things he was doing but she would not allow herself to feel it, this prone body was not hers. If all she could feel was helplessness then she would not feel at all.

After picking up the dress and wringing it out she returned to her room and stuffed the wet cloth behind her dresser. Rose dressed, retrieved the Valium from the robe pocket and put the pills in her bag, along with the knife.

Again the nausea and breathlessness made her stop for a minute or two as she tried not to think about how many times this had happened, how Bill's hands on her were so familiar with the terrain of her body, so practiced in keeping her still as he writhed above her. Rose felt that she had lost claim to the one thing that should be hers alone. She had no control of her body now. Those missing minutes, hours, weeks even, made her doubt more than just her body, though. He had stolen her mind too and it felt that no amount of rationalising could shake loose the fear that it was somehow her fault, something she had done, something Sara had done before her.

Finally, the nausea passed and Rose picked up the bag and crept downstairs. She left the house as quietly as she could and was relieved to see Sara's old bike was still under the porch at the front. Her own bike, too small for her now, had been abandoned in the field at the back, lying under a layer of snow for weeks. She dragged the bike out, checking for punctures, then she scooted off and swung her other leg over, feeling a sharp pain as she sat down and then more pain in her lungs from the intake of cold air. Riding was the only way she had to get to town before her mom and Bill woke but every jolt and slip on the icy road was a reminder of last night. She was awake to new parts of herself, but only through pain and fear. The wind whipped around her neck and Rose could feel the lightness of her hair as it blew out behind her. She thought about her mother finding the shank of hair in the bathroom and then wondered if she should have hidden it, that way they'd still be looking for a kid with long brown hair, not an older-looking girl with a sharp cropped bob. The cold air was making her eyes stream and she had an image of herself as she swept along the road into town, wild eyed. Her blood was racing, the grogginess wearing off as she rushed forward.

She hid the bike at the back of Bill's house, between the empty, lidless trash cans. Clearly Darren had not tidied anything, perhaps Bill hadn't told him yet about the plan to move him into her mom's place. She tried the back screen door and then snuck inside, hoping that Darren had stayed at a friend's place or had left already for school. She knew this was wishful thinking so when she saw the sleeping figure on the couch she wasn't too surprised. Sitting on the bottom step, quietly waiting for Darren to wake, she thought through what she would say to him.

He knew about Sara. Did he know about her too? Maybe it was better that he didn't, after all he might talk to Bill and then he'd know she was here. He'd been angry enough with Sara, and a vivid picture of her sister's red shoes and the finger marks at her neck flashed into Rose's mind. She should just pretend she was here to tell him about moving in and that she'd got an overnight bag because she was staying at a friend's. Darren didn't need to know. He couldn't help her. He hadn't helped Sara. Maybe she should just leave, she couldn't stay here until Thursday if Darren was here too, unless she told him why and she wasn't ready just yet to have that conversation.

"Spying on me?" Darren was perfectly still but his eyes were wide open and fixed on Rose. "I didn't recognise you. What happened to your hair?"

"I got sick of it."

"You look older, you look tired. Why are you here?" He swung his legs over the edge of the sofa and reached for a glass on the table but saw the cigarette butt just in time as he brought the water up to his mouth. Grimacing, Darren set the glass back down and rubbed his face with his hands, wiping the sleep from his eyes. "What's going on? You want tea?" He was playing house now, acting aloof, grown up but the mess of the place gave him away and he knew it. Rose wondered what state the kitchen was in but said yes to tea anyway, still thawing from her bike ride.

"Your dad wants you to move in, he's getting the nursery... the room ready for you today and wants you packed up and moved in by the weekend. You might want to..."

"Clean up a bit? Yeah, probably. Bill will kill me if he sees it like this but he hasn't been around much recently, too busy with your mom and things." Darren looked at her as she stood in the kitchen doorway, searching her face for answers to questions he hadn't asked but which hung heavy in the stale air of the room.

"Yeah, something like that." Rose looked down at the floor and followed the line of her wet footprints back to the door. Suddenly, Darren handed her the mug and she flinched, moving back into the hallway. Biting her lip she moved forward again to take the mug and Darren's eyes narrowed, his forehead wrinkled, and she thought she saw pity in his expression, pity she didn't want so she turned away.

Darren retreated to the kitchen counter, cleared a small space, and pulled himself up to sit on it. Staring down into the steam rising from the mug he asked gently, "What happened Rose?"

"Nothing." No, that wasn't quite right. She hesitated and then mumbled, "Well, nothing new, I guess."

He glanced quickly at her and then lowered his gaze back to his mug of tea. "You look like her you know. Right before she..." his words fell off into the murky liquid but Rose knew Darren had seen Sara the day she walked into the creek. She thought again of the image she had of herself, cycling into town, racing along, eyes bright and skin flushed. She wanted to keep that idea of herself, not the idea Darren had of her being just like her sister. She wanted to feel stronger but his pity brought back her helplessness and she was just a girl running away, thinking a haircut would change things.

She put the mug down on the counter, muttered thanks, and turned to leave but Darren put out a hand, gently holding her forearm. She didn't turn but she didn't pull away this time.

"Rose. Stay. I'm sorry I said that. Really. Let me find something for you to eat while I tidy up and then I'll pack some things and we can head back to yours together. Maybe if I'm there I can keep an eye on things, maybe I can help this time."

Rose stood still, this was the closest thing to an apology she had heard and she saw the flushing creep of shame across Darren's face and knew he had struggled with what he knew and what he could do about any of this. His hand was still on her arm and she tried not to be angry with him. He was her ally now, in his own way, and she knew that this was all he could really do. She realised that he was as scared of his dad as she was, as Sara had been.

She stayed and together they set to work on the house, the smell of stale beer and cigarettes kicking her in the gut, but providing a useful excuse for her waves of nausea. Darren kept stealing glances at her, as though he were about to say something and then changing his mind over and over. They worked in silence for nearly an hour until the living room was clear and clean, the trash outside, the kettle boiling to top up the hot water for the kitchen floor.

It was still only nine in the morning but Darren poured himself a shot of bourbon from a bottle that had been under the sink, hidden behind washing powder, a plunger, scrubbing brushes, and other dusty detritus. He offered Rose a drink and for a second she thought about taking it, wondering at how easy it would be to offer herself up to that foggy delirium, to forget everything that had happened just for a little while, but she needed to keep her head clear. She should go to school or at least hide for the day until her bus in the morning. She couldn't stay here, getting drunk with Darren, the risk of Bill walking in at any time.

She handed Darren the mop, retrieved her bag, and headed towards the back door to go and get the bike. Darren looked after her, holding his empty glass in one hand, the mop in the other and then he called out, asking her to wait.

"Where are you going? You can stay here if you like, you'll be safe. We'll work something out." He smiled at her gently, and she thought about how little he looked like Bill, how much like his mother, those same petite features but with the healthy weight to make them striking rather than sickly. She hesitated for a moment, wondering if she could just stay, hide from Bill and her mother, from everything, but she knew better.

"Thanks, but I'm leaving. I have to." When she had arrived at the house she hadn't intended on telling him of her plans but in the silence between them there had been an understanding of sorts.

"Where will you go?"

"I have a ticket on the Greyhound, tomorrow, to go and see Jason." Rose turned to look at Darren and saw the surprise in his face. "I'm going to tell him everything. Everything I remember anyway, and all the stuff Sara told me before she, before..."

It was all too much suddenly, the fear seeping from her skin, the icy terror of being held down, violated, and knowing that it had happened to Sara too. Knowing how it felt she could see why Sara had done what she did and now she spoke the words she felt for the first time that her sister was gone, and that she had done nothing to help. Darren folded her into him and she let herself go, she let Sara go, all the rage flooding from her, her body shaking against his.

He mumbled something to the top of her head and she pulled back, looking at him questioningly. "I said, I'll drive."

CHAPTER EIGHT

The pickup rattled over pothole after pothole as it bounced its way down the highway towards Crowsnest Pass, Darren studiously avoiding the snow that still covered parts of the road. Rose had thrown a couple of blankets in the Ford's cab before they left and she was grateful for them now as the passenger-side window no longer rolled all the way up, the chill air of the foothills whistling past her head.

They were three hours out of Pitcher Creek before she realised what she'd done, that she had escaped, that she was going to put things right. She looked over at Darren, a cigarette ponderous on his lower lip, having hung there for the last half hour. The lighter in the truck no longer worked and he had left his Zippo on the kitchen table as he'd thrown some stuff into a battered canvas backpack and whisked Rose out to the rusty blue relic sitting on the back lot. Bill's old truck had become Darren's pride and joy now that his dad had a shiny new Dodge bought with money borrowed against the flower shop.

They were taking highway three so that Darren could check something out on the way to Vancouver. Rose didn't ask what, she was just glad to be leaving early, with company, and not squashed into the Greyhound with the dust-filled heating and strange chatter of people she didn't know. Darren was, mercifully, a quiet driver. He had tuned the stereo to CJSW when they had hit Calgary but it had dropped out of range soon after and been replaced by static. Darren had carried on tapping his fingers on the steering wheel, still hearing some remnant of a song it seemed, happy enough to be putting more kilometres between them and Pitcher Creek. In escaping the town Rose felt a small sense of victory but at the same time she knew she could not go back without things changing. She imagined returning home to see Bill, with his arm around her mother, and she shivered again.

Rose pulled her legs up and tucked them beneath her, covering herself with the blanket. Darren dug out an old balaclava from the shelf in the door and an extra scarf. She took the scarf, laughing at the black balaclava, tempted by its promised warmth but worried she'd look completely ridiculous. Darren had raised an eyebrow and told her to suit herself. She hunkered down below the open window and looked over at Darren, his eyes now focused on the road ahead. Closing her eyes she let the grumble of the truck's engine wash over her. As she drifted into a dead sleep, she heard the radio being tuned and the voice of Dave Rutherford, discussing the metric system, accompanied by snorts of derision from Darren.

While she dozed, Rose dreamt of her house. She saw herself climbing the steps up to the front door. As she swung the door open a rush of sound hit her, her hair, long again in the dream, streaming back behind her as the screams forced their way into the open air. Rose stood facing the barrage of terror, closing her eyes but letting the awful howl wash over her, knowing it would stop soon, that she was setting it free. The house shuddered, the door trembling in her hand and then a brief silence before the walls collapsed inwards, the roof came crashing down and Rose was left standing on the porch staring into a hole where her home had been.

She woke with a start as Darren shook her and excitedly pointed out of the window. They had stopped at the side of the road, by a fruit stand abandoned for the winter, months to go before it reopened. To the right of the wooden shack was a coyote, small and scrawny, its white belly sagging with wet fur in the snow. Darren had found some matches in the glove compartment of the truck and he'd been lighting a cigarette as the coyote had wandered into view.

"Looks like just a lone female." Darren was holding the cigarette but not really smoking it now, just staring wide-eyed at the wandering animal about ten feet from the truck. "We'll wait 'til she's gone, don't want to startle her with the engine noise." He didn't look at Rose, his eyes fixed on the animal, and she sensed a degree of pride and awe in the way Darren was talking, his words hushed, reverent.

"It looks different to the coyotes I've seen. Is that just the winter coat or are they..."

"Shh. Look! She's not alone. He was in the shack." A larger animal had emerged from the fruit stand followed by six pups that yipped and fought each other as the family moved away, empty-handed it seemed. Darren pursed his lips and blew out, "Bit early for a litter, they won't survive. Must be hungry. They usually don't start having pups for a couple of months, May most often." Rose wondered how he knew this stuff. She couldn't believe that Bill had taught him anything on those hunting trips, but after Bill started seeing her mother Rose guessed Darren had spent a lot of time at the cabin by himself, happy not to be around when his dad got angry like he did. She remembered the sketches she had seen in Darren's room, the stack of books, and Rose realised that she really knew nothing about him.

She thought about the hungry coyote family and fought the urge to throw one of the energy bars to them as she imagined Darren would think it inappropriate. Instead, Rose breathed deeply, enjoying the mountain air, the slight tightness the cold produced in her lungs, knowing that it wasn't fear responsible for the sensation, that she was safe up here, with Darren, where everything was still, quiet.

Darren broke the silence as he started up the truck, the radio kicking back into life. He turned the volume dial and without looking at her he began telling Rose about the programme in Castlegar to which he was thinking of applying. His enthusiasm was overwhelming, and Rose laughed at him, amazed as he talked about wildlife fences and reintroduction schemes seemingly without taking a breath.

She wanted to ask how he'd afford school but knew it would kill the mood so she just listened, learning about the fervent debate over the sixteen subspecies of coyote, how they were more like dogs than wolves, and how a lone coyote lived around the cabin where Bill used to take Darren to stay when they went hunting. He told her of the times he had listened to the coyote howling, seen her stalking something in the long grass outside the cabin, and of the innocence of his childhood when he had hoped she would just walk into the cabin one day and sit by the fire with him. Now he was older he knew better than to welcome in the wildness he said, but he hadn't looked at Rose as he spoke and she wondered what he meant. Darren hadn't seen his coyote yet this year and he was afraid she'd not survived the early snow that had covered over the ground before Halloween.

Rose thought about this coyote. The way Darren talked it was almost as if she were his family dog, not some wild creature. Perhaps that was the closest he had come to family, given his mother's death and Bill being so distant and uninterested in the son he likely never wanted. She remembered what Sara had said about Bill's brutalising being 'close enough' when Rose had mentioned love and she wondered what had gone wrong in her own family for her sister to have thought that way.

Rose realised that she hadn't seen her dad for almost nine months, he hadn't even come back when Sara's body was found. Rose wondered if he even knew, he hadn't called for weeks. Her mom seemed to have forgotten he even existed, never mentioning him and gradually stacking stuff up in front of his boxes of stuff in the garage. If her dad had stayed then maybe Bill wouldn't have crept into their lives quite like he did, perhaps her mother wouldn't have let him. She had been so happy to have someone to sit next to in church again, to be able to go to the movies as a family and to have people over for dinner with an even number of place settings. Rose wondered if, one day, she would have similar priorities. It just didn't seem to matter all that much anymore.

She knew it was pointless to think about how things might have worked out differently, that what had happened couldn't be undone. Rose wondered, though, if Sara had blamed her dad for everything. Then she thought about how easily Sara could have blamed her too. After all, she had been right next door, drowning out her sister's screams with the canned laughter of the television. Bill had held Sara down, done those things to her, and all Rose had been thinking was how irritating Sara and Darren's fights were and how she had thought they were just teenage angst. The recollection left her feeling cold and ashamed. Sara must have felt so alone, carrying Bill's baby. No wonder she had rationalised everything, convinced herself that he loved her, in his own way.

Bill had a way of making her mom, and even herself, second-guess every thought, every belief. Her mom's voice had changed since Bill moved in, her inflection suddenly unsure, appeasing, her eyes darting to and from his face to check she hadn't slipped up and angered him. The house had become very quiet, constrained. Her dad had not been there to help them but at least he wasn't complicit. Rose thought of the coyotes again, the pups, and she wondered at how they'd survive the remainder of winter. When had her mother started needing Bill's approval and what had she sacrificed for it?

He was just a man, though. Rose could think that safely now she was out of his reach and the thought felt good, it made him answerable, it meant he could be fought against and that she could win somehow. She knew Darren was fighting his own battle with his dad and that, for him, their trip was also cathartic. Rose fiddled with the dial on the radio and she laughed as she heard Los Lobos singing "drifting by the roadside, climbs each storm and ageing face..." Darren sang along with her as the radio asked 'Will the wolf survive' and Rose looked ahead as the Rockies disappeared behind them and the sun sank lower over the horizon. They were in BC, with hours yet to go but they would make it, they would find Jason.

CHAPTER NINE

Lewis picked up a seed pod and split it in two, throwing both halves up in the air. "You'll be leaving soon then I guess?" It was more a statement than a question and he didn't dare look at me as he spoke. Turning onto my front, and propping myself up on my elbows, I thought about Henry's letter that I had received this morning. He had been in touch with a lawyer from Pitcher Creek, Robert MacGowan. I recognised the name because I think his mother used to teach piano in town. I never played but Rose had told me that she went to the old lady's funeral. Anyway, Henry had hired this guy to dig around and see what he could find on Darren Tether, to see if anyone else had been attacked by him as he had the impression from speaking to Rose that Sara and Darren's relationship wasn't quite what it seemed. Henry had decided it was time to step up his efforts and I was thankful that he still believed in me, even while I was here, painting pictures, lying in therapy about my guilt, and screwing around with Lewis.

Lewis knew Henry was using his money and his connections to arrange my acquittal, he even joked about Henry being my sugar-daddy. His jokes were always tainted with a faint desperation though, and sometimes I just couldn't look him in the eye. I was lying to everyone and I felt guilty, dirty and wrong. Some days I just couldn't fit all the pieces of myself together and I wanted to hide, but there was nowhere to hide here, where every part of you was supposed to be aired and analysed and fixed. I was disingenuous in almost everything and I wondered, if I was so good at lying to everyone else, how much I was lying to myself.

It didn't feel real being here, almost like you could do anything and not have it affect the outside world. In the weeks since Henry had left, Lewis had just become familiar, and useful. I knew he only pretended to care, that, really, he wasn't capable of loving me like Henry did.

Somehow I rationalised this, I made it out to myself as a good thing, that we knew our boundaries. I excused my behaviour by thinking that we had an understanding, knowing that this was just for now, that there was no 'us' outside the grounds of the lodge. I wasn't proud of how I was using him but I didn't think Lewis had any pretentions to be my great love for all time and it was actually this pragmatic streak, tinged with a little sad anger, that was alarmingly attractive after Henry's quiet solicitous courtship. I'm pretty sure Janice knows what's going on, she knows me too well after all these months. She won't tell Henry though, even though they write to each other. I feel ashamed to be putting her in that position but I'm lonely and Lewis, well, he's here.

We stood and dusted ourselves off, the dry ground under the old arbutus sticking to my elbows and the front of my jacket. It hadn't rained for weeks and, although it was still cold, the first tips of bluebells were scattered around the base of the tree. This ribboned trunk had become my haven with Henry, hidden just out of sight of the lodge behind the high perimeter hedge. It seemed that the staff were less inclined to follow us around these days, we weren't considered high risk any more, just long-term inmates finishing up our time. This was the first time I'd brought Lewis here and it seemed to make the betrayal worse as we lay staring up at the peeling red bark, the soft green emerging underneath. I wouldn't bring him here again, this should just be for me and Henry, our anchor, our safe place holding it all together.

"Will you go back to Pitcher Creek do you think?"

"I guess. I'll have to try to convince my parents to give me the money for college and I've still got all my stuff there, of course. You're going straight to work for your dad right?" Lewis's father had been to visit him a few times in recent weeks, making arrangements for him to come home and start learning the family textile business. Talking about this with Lewis was always strained as he knew without agreeing to the work he'd have to stay here for at least another year, instead of leaving in the summer to head back to Lethbridge. I recognised the look on Lewis's face when he talked about his father. It was the same expression as when he gripped me tight, pushing me against a wall, a desk, and turning my head back to face away from him whenever I tried to turn around. We didn't kiss, except for once. It had felt wrong, his teeth banging against mine. I had expected to taste blood on my lips when I pulled away but instead we shared a glance that seemed a silent agreement not to pretend this was something it wasn't. We were bodies, crazy, locked up, desperate flesh on flesh, nothing more. It was Henry I loved, and Lewis knew that. Once we left here we would not be in touch again.

Arriving back near the dorm, Lewis lagged behind and lit a cigarette. I carried on into the building and checked my watch again, I had a few minutes before I had to be in my session with Dr Laurence but I figured I'd go and sit outside his office and reread Henry's letter. When I got there, though, there was another boy waiting in the corridor. This was odd as Dr Laurence only ever saw one person at a time and seemed to schedule sessions so we could carry on if he felt good progress was being made. I nodded at the other boy who was new here, younger than me. I had no idea what his name was and didn't really care.

"Doc's got a laaaady in there." The boy wriggled and laughed girlishly, his hand to his mouth. I looked away, trying to act like I was above such idle gossip, but, really, I wanted to know who was in the room with my therapist.

"One of the nurses, or one of the teachers?"

"Nope. That lady from in town, the arty one, with the stupid skirts and the mad hair."

"Oh, Janice. They won't be long then." The kid laughed as I spoke.

"She's been in there nearly an hour, shows what you know."

"You saw her go in?"

"Yup. She looked mad as hell too, like someone stole her broomstick or something." Although I didn't like how this boy was talking about Janice, I knew what he meant. When she was caught up in something she did look like she was half-crazed, even from a different world where the sky was filled with pixie dust or something. She had once told Henry that just because he believed in math and science it didn't mean there wasn't room for the magical, after all neither of us should be arrogant enough to think that our creativity was solely our own doing or that we would have it forever. The genius was just on loan she had said and we had laughed later, wondering if Janice had been a good artist at some point and decided to be a therapist only when her genius had run off with someone else.

More recently it seemed Janice had been gaining her inspiration from the liquor store in town. I had seen her sitting in the art class late in the evenings, a glass of wine in her hand as she stared into space. I wondered what her husband thought, these late nights at work. Some of the boys had started some idle gossip about her having an affair with Dr Laurence but that seemed like the least likely thing as Janice had always been quite scathing about the psychologist and his pseudoscientific abuse as she called it.

No, the flushed look to her face was purely due to the wine she drank so desperately, not to any heated passion. I wasn't sure why she drank so much, perhaps to drown something out day after day, like I had tried that one time and had been tempted to do again.

There was a crash in the therapy room and then the door swung open violently and Janice tore out and down the corridor, her skirt flying behind her and for a second or two it did look like her feet were not touching the ground, even without a broomstick at her disposal. A minute or two later Dr Laurence walked out of his office. He calmly apologised for the disruption and called the giggling boy in, cancelling my session for today unless I wanted to discuss anything in particular. I shook my head and said it was fine, taking off down the corridor after Janice, but trying to walk at a normal pace so as not to raise suspicion.

I found her in the art room where she was throwing things into boxes rather haphazardly, tears trailing down her face. I knocked quietly and stood in the doorway, hesitant.

"Jason, Jason, oh, come in, don't mind me I'm just having a bit of a meltdown, nothing to worry about." She laughed and wiped her face with her cardigan sleeve, then she smiled at me, sat down and started sobbing into her hands, her hair falling in waves to her knees. "That man, that creep. What does he know about you kids, he's never even there for his own." She was gasping, words forcing their way out through the wracking wretched sobs. This was not a romance gone wrong, and I wondered if Janice had been fired. Everyone knew she'd been drinking a lot recently and there had been a couple of times I'd wondered if she was totally sober in class. It was hard to tell with Janice as her energy was so volatile anyway, great if you were on the happy side of it but quite unnerving in its unpredictability.

I pulled up a chair next to her, having shut the door to the art room and pulled down the blind to cover the glass pane in the door, contravening the lodge's open door policy when it was just teacher and student in a room alone. Janice might not care right now if someone walked past and saw her so broken up but I knew it would just add to her reputation for being a bit crazier than some of the inmates here.

"What's going on Janice? Can I do anything?" I put a hand softly on her shoulder, feeling the slight scratch of the wool. Janice was trying to get some words out in answer but they were swallowed along with half the air in the room it seemed. We just sat like this for a while and gradually the shuddering subsided and Janice raised her head, wiping her face and flicking her hair behind her ears before turning to face me.

"Totally professional, heh? Sorry Jason, it means a lot that you're here, were you just passing? Was I that loud?" She smiled a little and I realised that she hadn't seen me outside the therapy room.

"I was waiting for my therapy session. I saw you and thought you might need, or might want a friend."

"Oh? I guess I just rushed out of there without looking, did I make you miss your session?"

"It's fine, it was cancelled. Saves me the trouble of having to lie through my teeth for an hour. I should thank you really."

"So you're wondering what happened, well, no... Jason, I'm not sure I should really bother you with it, it's best if I just get on with things myself."

"I'm good with secrets Janice, remember?" I smiled and raised my eyebrows, hoping for a laugh but Janice just narrowed her eyes and searched my face for some kind of reassurance.

"Yes, I suppose you are, a little too good for your own sake, right? It's just that it's about another student, someone you know, and if I tell you what's going on then it puts you in a pretty awkward position. You're so close to leaving now. Henry's so confident that this lawyer will get the charges dropped before your birthday. I don't want this to jeopardise anything for you." Janice held my hands in hers and her face tightened, her lips a thin line, totally out of place in a face that was usually so expressive, so bursting with life and energy. I was beginning to think that maybe I didn't want to know whatever it was she was struggling with, if it did this to her then maybe she was right to keep it from me.

Curiosity got the better of me though so I asked and listened wide-eyed as Janice told me about her seeing Dr Laurence and Lewis's father in town. He was a well-dressed man, greying but he carried it well, a fine bone structure, beautifully tailored suit. It was hard not to notice the guy, Janice said, especially in contrast to the stuffily academic appearance of Dr Laurence. Janice had been having dinner with her husband and she overheard the men talking about Lewis being cleared, then she had seen the younger man take an envelope out of his jacket pocket and slide it across the table to the doctor. She was worried about Lewis, about him going home before he was really ready, and how she didn't trust that the doctor had his patient's best intentions in mind when there was clearly another incentive at play.

"And you told Dr Laurence you saw him? You saw him take... a bribe I guess to sign Lewis out early?"

"Yes, I can go over his head, to the trustees of the Lodge but I wanted to make sure that what I thought I saw was actually true. Stephen, Dr Laurence's response made it pretty clear. He really blew up at me but he didn't deny it, just talked about an invasion of privacy, ironic considering his job. Then he said he'd have to file his own report about my competence if I persisted."

I thought about her drinking and wondered if Dr Laurence knew what had made her so sad recently. "So, will you tell Lewis, or the board, or the police?" Lewis wanted to get out but was very resistant to working with his father, he always made out he hated him but I could see he secretly longed to be the good kid his dad had always wanted. I'd gotten good at spotting that in others in this place. I think he was also scared that he couldn't be that son, no matter how hard he tried.

"You can't tell Lewis, he mustn't know. How would it make you feel if the only reason you got certified as sane and able to rejoin society was because your dad paid for it? Jason, promise me not to tell Lewis. I'll sort it out my own way. Promise?" I nodded and squeezed her hand. I had my doubts about Lewis's sanity anyway; he had these fits of aggression where he'd hold me down and be too rough really. At first I thought it was just playful and I'd kind of liked it but recently he seemed to just enjoy the physical control rather than anything else. He'd been cutting himself too, using pieces of glass from a mirror he'd smashed in one of the bathrooms. I'd felt the rough ridges of skin and seen some of the older scars and the newer, angry red welts on the inside of his thighs where no one else would see them. Lewis had always been a little too intense but this had excited me at first. Recently that intensity had switched back to being threatening, menacing, and this last week I had become scared of him, again.

"He cuts himself you know?"

"What? Who? Lewis? How do you know? No, never mind. How long for?"

"Maybe a couple of months, it's worse though now. He, well, he scares me a bit." I wanted to say that I didn't think he should be allowed to leave here but at the same time I didn't think this place was really doing anyone any favours. Although Lewis's parents could afford to keep him here and, apparently, afford to arrange his release when they wanted, most of us were just here at the whim of charitable decisions by the board of trustees. Lewis made fun of Henry's money but he had the same privilege, he just wanted to pretend he was normal I guess, like me maybe.

The thing about being here based on charity was that no one was actively engaged in influencing the therapists on our behalf. It would certainly be cheaper in the short-term to have us passed as safe for release and back out in normal schools, and I had wondered how much that went on. Some of the younger boys might spend eight or nine years in prison, part of that here, and it seemed pretty likely that they'd become institutionalised as adults too. We were being trained, day by day, to sublimate everything just to get by. This was not life, this was limbo, but some of the younger kids hadn't been around long enough to tell the difference. At least, I didn't think so.

"Has Lewis ever threatened you Jason? With a knife, or in any other way?" Janice's question made me think about last time Lewis and I had sex; he had held his arm around the front of my neck, a little too tight and I had twisted and gasped. He had apologised afterwards, saying he wouldn't really do anything to hurt me, ever. That he wanted to protect me. He had started sobbing while he said this and the idea of him protecting me seemed like a desperate request somehow, more like he needed a job, or ownership of me more than anything else. I couldn't tell Janice this though, how could I explain the roughness of our encounters, how I liked it, but only to a point. She wouldn't understand, she was too gentle, she'd just think we were both mad so I said no, not directly.

"Lewis told you why he was here though, what he did to get locked up?"

"Yes, the fire, he set his school... what?" Janice was shaking her head in disbelief and now her fear soaked the air and as I breathed it in I started to tremble myself. Would Lewis hurt me, had he hurt others?

"No, Jason, Lewis shot a boy. I thought you knew. I shouldn't be telling you this but you need to know. You need to know what you're getting yourself into. They said it was an accident but there was enough confusion that his parents sent him here." I stood up, stunned. Lewis had killed someone and he had lied to me, and I had let him take Henry's place. Henry, who could never do anything like that, who loved me still even so many thousands of kilometres away. I walked over to the window and asked Janice who the boy was that Lewis shot.

"Jason, you need to be very careful. It seems like you and Lewis have been... close, since Henry left but I think you should try to put some distance between the two of you. I should've said something sooner but I assumed that it was a harmless crush on his part and that you knew why he was here."

"Were he and the boy involved?"

"The one that got shot? No. But there was another friend who was there and it may have been that Lewis and he were more than friends."

I could see it all now. Lewis had just been protecting what was his, the other boy had gotten in the way. I closed my eyes, Janice walked up behind me and span me around slowly.

"Jason, what's going on with you two? How worried should I be right now?"

I swallowed hard and smiled weakly at her. "So he was jealous?"

"It appears so. There were rumours and his parents were not happy and so, well they sent him here to try to cure him of being gay." As Janice spoke the word out loud I blushed and felt ridiculous for doing so.

Was that all I was? Did that tiny word really describe me, Henry, Lewis, the relationships we had, who we were and who we would always be no matter how much we changed in other ways. I felt tied up in those three letters, that simple utterance. Somehow I knew that they were the depth and breadth of me, at least to other people for whom the word was irrelevant.

Janice went on to say "Lewis's parents hoped that therapy would fix him and avoid the taint of prison, make this out to be a phase, a confusion. They cut him off you know, until he gets better, or until he at least pretends to be who they want him to be."

Lewis hadn't told me this and it struck me that both Henry and Lewis were fighting a similar battle, but for different reasons. "If you report Dr Laurence will Lewis stay here?"

"Most probably, yes. He'll have to serve the rest of his time, at least until he's eighteen next year, then he might be transferred to an adult facility if a judge thinks it necessary. Jason, I think we need to consider getting you moved to another centre, or maybe just really step up the efforts to get you released, your charges dropped. Henry got in touch with this lawyer so is anything happening?"

"No, not really, the lawyer's more a businessman, corporate law or something and nothing's going to happen unless Rose talks, or Darren confesses. She's too young, she probably doesn't understand what's going on and now her sister died and so she's the only one really."

"You might be surprised. Think about everything that's happened to you both in the past year and think about how much you've changed from who you were before. This girl might have grown up a lot too. If she knows what really happened then perhaps she'll see that telling the truth is all part of her own recovery, the best thing to do for her sister."

I thought about Rose, how keen she had been to talk to me about geeky things that no one else I knew cared about. We had a connection I thought but she must have lied for me to still be here and so I wasn't sure I'd ever forgive her for that. As for Darren, I hadn't known him too well but he had a reputation for being a bully. He wasn't one of the kids in the locker room that time, or the other times, but I'd seen him around town and knew to keep my distance. That Sara and him had been together had surprised me at first, but as I'd gotten to know Sara more I saw how she had enjoyed the excitement of being with someone risky, dangerous, someone who skipped class, got high and didn't give a crap, or so it seemed. I understood Sara's attraction to the darkness she probably saw in someone like Darren.

I had wanted to be that guy for a while, but I knew that would never happen. Had I, instead, decided to attract that guy? I realised that Janice was right about how much I'd changed this past year, how much more I knew about myself, my motivations. I was much more honest with myself than before, and a little more honest with others too, perhaps too much so at times. More than ever I understood that my actions, and those of others, were not necessarily premeditated. I could lose control and sometimes that meant good things, sometimes bad, but it was life either way and better than staying still in fear. If I strayed at least I had Henry to bring me back to the light.

Henry was confident Rose would talk. He said that she just needed to feel safe to do so, to get away from Darren for long enough. The Tethers had pretty much moved into Rose's house now Jane's divorce was settled and Bill and her were a proper couple. Henry said that Rose had missed his calls and that he'd written another letter, sending his condolences. When Henry found out that Sara had died he called Janice as he knew that Dr Laurence wouldn't tell me. Her suicide was so unexpected and I had asked about the baby, but there was no baby, even by then. She must have been terrified and I knew that I had to carry some of the blame for that, for not fighting earlier and helping her to fight too.

I wanted to speak to Rose, to see how she was but Henry couldn't get hold of her. He knew she was scared, after all the guy was sitting across from her at the breakfast table every day and no one knew but her. No wonder she was terrified and wouldn't talk.

I told Janice I'd talk to Henry straight away. There was a call-box at the gas station just outside the town so I could sneak out before dinner and get Henry to accept the reversed charges. Janice hugged me, told me to be careful and that she would try to work something out. I left her in the art studio, wondering if she'd be fired before she could talk to the trustees, wondering also if she always got so involved with her students. Did she have kids of her own? They were lucky if she did, to have such a great mom, but something told me she went home to an empty apartment each night, that the ring on her finger no longer meant anything and that the loud silence of her life was what she drowned out with her wine. There were no finger-painted pictures smeared onto her fridge, no wobbly pottery coffee cups with 'mom' painted onto them and presented with pride at Christmas. Janice was mothering me and I was thankful for it, but at the same time I knew it was tinged with sadness for her, I was using her too. In the end, did all my relationships rely on the desperate generosity of others?

CHAPTER TEN

Rose was thumbing through the college brochure, distracted by the grinning students and the ivy covered brick buildings and not paying too much attention to the descriptions of facilities and courses, research awards and societies. Darren had let her drive a little way earlier and she was tired now from concentrating and gripping the wheel so tightly. It had been nice of him to let her try but she was pretty sure her first car would be less grumpy, less idiosyncratic perhaps than this rusty bucket that seemed to be held together with string and tape. Darren had sat close by her ready to take the wheel if necessary or slam his foot down hard on the brake. They hadn't seen another car for what seemed like hours though, just mountain after mountain, tree after tree after tree. Not even any coyotes, just inconspicuous signs for private roads leading god knows where.

"Do they say if they have a Computing Science course?" Darren glanced over at her then back at the road before she had a chance to catch his eye.

"Er, I don't know, I didn't look. I guess they would but I was kind of thinking I'd go to Calgary, like Jason was planning."

"Oh. I guess that makes sense, then you'd have a friend around right. Someone smart like you."

"I guess. I hadn't thought about it much to be honest."

"Enough to think about Jason though, eh." Darren's voice had a hint of anger which made Rose feel the need to be defensive, even though she wasn't sure why he was angry at her.

"Only just now, and last year before all this happened." Rose waved her arms around in the car, knocking Darren's elbow and causing the truck to veer to the left a little.

"Jeez Rose! Be careful."

"Ha, I thought you liked living dangerously, Sara always thought you were such a bad boy. That's the attraction, right?"

"Hardly. We were just messing around. I'm not stupid, and I'm not dangerous, and you shouldn't distract me when I'm driving, alright?"

"OK, wow, sorry." Rose let out an exasperated breath, wondering when Darren became so serious.

"I just don't want you to get hurt, alright?" Darren's voice had dropped, it was almost husky and Rose saw him swallow hard and turn his head so she couldn't really see his face properly. He pretended to have something in his eye and she was confused.

"Darren?" Rose reached out her hand and placed it on his forearm. "You OK?"

"Fine. Let's just get there, yeah?" He put his hand over hers and squeezed it a little then lifted it off his arm and let it drop.

CHAPTER ELEVEN

The operator took a while to put the call through and I began to worry but then I heard the familiar and calming voice as Henry answered, breathless.

"It's me, are you OK?"

"Hey! Yeah, just got out of the tub and had to grab a towel and, oh, well there's now quite the puddle of water in my living room! How are you? I miss you." His voice softened and I could picture his smile, the lowering of his eyelids as his face relaxed.

"I miss you too, especially now I know you're just standing around in a towel." I tried to make it sound fun and light-hearted but Henry noticed the weariness in my voice.

"Hmm. Hang in there Jason. We'll get you home soon. That lawyer reckons he can get the police to reopen your case. He said that they only really have Rose's testimony to go on now and she was so confused that they can't really use that. She's obviously terrified of Darren but now she can't protect Sara any more it might be that she talks. Oh, and we're trying to get copies of the autopsy to see about the baby, we could even push for DNA testing, although that would take a while and it might cost quite a bit as there are only a few places doing it, even now."

Henry was so insistent on my innocence but sometimes I just felt guilty anyway, of nothing in particular just in general. Right now though, I knew I had to tell him about Lewis.

"Henry, I wanted to tell you something." I was scared that he would find out about Lewis if he got out soon and I knew it would be worse being told by someone else. I also knew that if I did get out soon any reunion would be ruined if I was still carrying this with me. "Since you left I've been sort of hanging out with... er, this other guy. It's not..."

"Are you sleeping with him? Who is it?" Henry sounded so broken, I leaned back against the phone box and closed my eyes.

"I'm sorry."

"Who? Do I know him?"

"It doesn't matter."

"Don't tell me what does and does not matter Jason. Is it serious? Do you..."

"I don't love him. It was just... company, I'm sorry, I'm so sorry I just needed something and..." I couldn't speak, Henry's anger was palpable and completely justified.

"So, it's over?" His voice shook, I could tell he was shivering and I thought about him standing in his towel, in his living room, shaking. Lewis and I were over, we had to be. Had we ever really been anything though? How can you end something unnamed? If I pretended it was not real then how could I say it was over.

"Yes. It was nothing really. I love you Henry. I'm sorry. I want to come to Ottawa and listen to you playing at the club and meet your friends and be with you, I just want to be with you Henry, I'm so sorry." I wiped my sleeve across my eyes and my nose and wanted to touch Henry's face and kiss him and tell him what a mistake it had all been and how I was scared and that Lewis was not who I thought he was. Or, perhaps I had known all along and that was what had excited me, the tingle of fear, the threat of violence, his intensity in comparison to Henry's calm and warmth.

"Jason, are you there still? Oh god I wish you were here, this is so damn hard, I just want you to come home. I just want you here." I imagined Henry's living room, the piano, my painting, perhaps a telephone table with Henry standing next to it, and wet footprints leading to the bathroom. I tried to picture myself in this apartment with Henry but it was so surreal to think beyond the lodge.

"I want to come home too. Henry, I have to get back, I'll ring tomorrow, you'll be home?"

"I'll be here. Jason, it's OK. We'll be OK." He hung up but I didn't start walking back to the lodge. Instead, I just leant against the call box, trying to think about what would happen if this lawyer succeeded.

Would I be taken back to my parents' place or would I just get a bus all the way to Ottawa instead. Henry had already offered to buy me a plane ticket and then maybe my parents would just have to come and visit and see how happy we were and how wrong they had been, about everything. They had only visited me here once, but I understood.

Finances were tight, the store not doing so well since I'd been charged. My mom and dad spent all their time in a town where everyone knew me only as a criminal, a rapist. Someone who had driven a girl to suicide. It was almost better that they hadn't been forced to pass Sara and the baby on the street, although I felt awful for thinking such a thing. My parents only knew someone who was not me and, as hard as it was to admit, I had played my part in that. I had hidden who I was for so long that they had nothing else to go on, no real idea of who their son was then or who I am now. This was as much my fault as theirs but if they could just see me happy with Henry it would be OK, things would work themselves out. I had to hold onto that idea. If not, then at least I had Henry, at least he knew everything now and still loved me.

I started slowly back along the road, away from the gas station, heading to the gap in the hedge that led to the fields at the side of the lodge. I had been out for too long but the cold had seeped into me as I'd stood talking to Henry and I couldn't face running back across the wet fields. I heard a car heading towards me from behind and turned towards the hedge to hide my face in case it was someone on the staff. The car slowed down as it passed and I saw it stop up ahead. The whites of the reverse lights cut through the gloom and I started running to the gap in the hedge, my calves cramping. Being caught outside grounds was a bad idea, especially when Henry was working so hard to get me released.

As the truck grew closer and stopped, I realised it wasn't one I recognised from the lodge car park. Then I saw the plates, Alberta, 'Wild Rose Country' and the passenger side door opened.

CHAPTER TWELVE

A figure emerged from the truck, holding onto the top of the door, shouting something at Jason. He carried on running along the hedge, the waterlogged ditch between him and where the pickup had pulled over. There was another shout, and another, both muffled by the wind whipping past his ears. The runner, a woman it seemed, was trying to head him off before the gap in the hedge, making her way through the ditch.

The ground was waterlogged and Rose's boots were sucked in as she ran making progress slow. On the other side of the ditch the ground was a little higher and so Jason got to the gap in the hedge before Rose made it across. He was about to duck into the shrubbery when he heard the woman shout again and something made him turn and look at her.

Rose carried on walking towards him, realising that Jason had recognised her. She chose her path more carefully, avoiding the deeper puddles but trying to keep her eyes on the running figure. She didn't want to lose him again. Back at the truck, Darren had shut off the engine and climbed out of the cab but he was still hidden from Jason's view.

"Hey" Rose was breathless as she stood just a few feet away from him, resisting the urge to hug him. Her face was flushed and the whipping wind kept blowing her hair into her eyes obscuring her vision of him. He couldn't think what to say, other than asking the obvious question of what she was doing here. "I thought we'd have to break into the jail, or hospital, or whatever this place is. What are you doing out on the road?"

"What am I doing? What are you doing here? And, who's 'we'?" He thought for a second she might mean Henry but then realised that was impossible and went back to being confused. "Who is that?" He pointed at the approaching figure. With the hat, scarf, and big jacket it was hard to make out a face but the man shouted across the ditch to Rose and Jason thought he recognised the voice. "Is that? No, Rose what the hell is going on?" He was angry now and scared, why had Rose brought Darren here? What were they planning to do to him?

"It's OK Jason."

"It's not OK. What's he doing here? Why did you bring him, of all people?" He felt like he might start crying again and he put his hands up to his face to rub his eyes and sweep his hair back. "Oh Christ, why is he here?"

"It's OK, it's fine, Darren drove me here, to find you, to try to sort everything out. I'm so so sorry, it's just all such a mess and my fault, but I promise Darren's here to help, he drove me here to help, he's a good guy really."

"But, he..." Jason lowered his voice, "he's the one who... Rose, you have to stop lying to yourself. There are too many lies, too much hurt. Whatever you told the police last year, you have to start telling the truth now. Why would you bring him here? Why would you even sit in the same car as him?"

"We were both wrong. Sara told me, just before she died, it was Bill. The whole time, it was Bill. Darren was trying to help her, trying to protect her, that's what happened that day when you came to the house. I saw Darren but it was after Bill had been in the house. After he had..." Rose trailed off, she didn't feel quite ready to tell Jason everything just yet, she hadn't really formed the words to explain things to herself. "Get in the truck, let's go into town and get coffee and talk properly. I'm freezing!" Rose laughed and reached out to him to take his hand but he just stood still, dumbfounded for a second or two. Then he followed her down the embankment and squeezed in beside her as Darren mumbled a hello and started up the engine again. Jason thought about how good a drink would be right about now, even gin would help take the edge off the painful tangle of emotions that was forming in his mind.

"Who else knows, Rose? About Bill I mean. Other than the two of you?"

"No one yet. That's why we're here, to work out what to do."

"Why haven't you just gone to the police? Why didn't you when you first realised?" He had raised his voice and was staring at her angrily.

"Hey! Don't shout at her, alright, she's been through enough without you yelling at her."

"Darren, it's fine, he's every right to be angry."

"Yeah, well, my dad's made a mess of everything hasn't he, Sara, your mom, you."

Jason wasn't sure what Darren had meant but the way he had said it had made Rose bow her head. He stared at the road in front and the three of them were quiet for a while before he asked quietly "Did he hurt you too?" and took Rose's silence as an answer in itself. He put his hand on top of hers and then reached his arm around her shoulder, pulling her into his embrace as her body trembled and then shook violently with her crying. Glancing at Darren over the top of Rose's head Jason saw a flash of anger in his direction, the younger boy's jaw set as he turned back to the road, his nostrils flaring and mouth tight. Darren may have driven for nearly fifteen hours to bring Rose here but he certainly wasn't happy to see Jason himself. There was something else going on and he wasn't sure yet if he could really trust either of them.

"We have to get in touch with your lawyer then. I'll make another statement and so will Darren and we'll stay here in town until they release you."

"I'm not sure it's that simple." Darren looked over at Rose and frowned, then smiled thinly as her face fell into a mask of despair once again. Her anger made her look young again, vital. The volatility usually hidden under a well-crafted veneer of intellect.

"Well, I can't go back until he's locked up. I won't."

"No, I know," he spoke softly, "but they won't just believe us now after we've been lying all along." Darren quickly added, "Even if it was for good reasons." Both Rose and Jason stared at him as they held their mugs of coffee, shoulders hunched over to conserve warmth, and Darren felt outside the loop again, like he wasn't really being heard, that Rose had no more need of him.

"Maybe not, so we need proof of some kind. But all Sara's things have been moved now Bill got rid of everything so even if there was evidence it's gone." She looked at Jason sitting next to her and took his hand. "We'll sort it though, don't worry." As she looked up she saw Darren turn away, whitewashing his expression like he had in the truck when she'd talked about college and Jason and Calgary.

Rose noticed a little scar beneath Darren's left earlobe, and she wanted to reach out and touch it and know where it had come from, if Bill had done it. What did he stand to gain from having his dad locked up? Surely he wasn't afraid of Bill any more, not if he was going to escape to college, get out of Pitcher Creek forever. Rose wanted to talk to him about his dad but he'd never open up in front of Jason, especially as Rose got the distinct impression that Darren was regretting ever agreeing to drive her, a deep loathing setting in for the boy whose hand she was still holding. She returned her hand to her mug of coffee and tried to think of ways to prove that Bill had attacked her sister.

Sara had kept a journal but she had been so much under Bill's control that Rose thought it unlikely that anything bad would be written in there. Besides, it was likely in a landfill now, or burnt by Bill in the garden along with some of the other things from Sara's room. Sara's clothes had been kept by the police but they had never had them tested. Even if they did find something, it wasn't like Bill was a stranger. He lived at the house, of course he would have touched her clothes, her shoes. Her.

Rose thought back to the day of Sara's attack, how she herself had helped Sara into the shower before the police came. Not knowing that they should wait, just wanting to help her sister feel clean and safe again. The more she thought back to that night in her sister's room the more she felt the cold creep of Bill's touch and she felt sick and lightheaded. Rose's first thought was to clean herself up too, to just sink into that warm bath even still wearing her dress.

"I've got it!" She pushed her coffee away from her and turned to Jason, bright-eyed. "When Bill, when," she fell quiet and then took a breath to calm herself. "I have evidence. I stashed my dress in my room, the dress I was wearing last time and the sheets, they won't have been changed yet, probably." Rose was thinking practically, she couldn't bear the nausea of really considering what she was saying and she turned away from Jason, not wanting to see anything like pity in his eyes. Now he knew what had prompted their trip, why Rose had run away now after all this time. "And there are the pills, your mother's pills at your house." She looked at Darren and he met her gaze, nodding at her with a grim little smile as he realised what she meant. She reached out to take his hand and Jason's too, her sleeves bunched up against the table's edge. They all saw the marks at her wrists, the bruises beginning to colour, but she didn't pull away and she was smiling, adding them to her arsenal against Bill.

CHAPTER THIRTEEN

I got Darren and Rose to drop me off by the lodge's entrance, there didn't seem much point in being stealthy as I'd already been gone for hours. As I walked through the lobby the nurse at the reception called after me and then a couple of orderlies ran through to stop me just walking back into the dorm. Someone had evidently called Dr Laurence as he appeared a few minutes later, thanked the nurse and the orderlies and led me off to his office.

"Jason, we were all rather concerned at your absence at dinner. Where were you?" He kept his voice level, inquisitive but not applying too much pressure.

"I bumped into a couple of friends, they bought me coffee, the time ran away with us."

"But... Jason, you do understand that you're supposed to stay within the lodge grounds? Who were these friends? How do you know anyone in town?" Jason couldn't help but laugh at his therapist's confusion but he knew that toying with Dr Laurence's pride was a bad idea.

"They came to see me, from back home, as a surprise."

"And, can I have their names Jason?" He picked up his pad of paper and flicked the top off his pen, getting ready to jot them down.

"No."

"Excuse me?"

"No. It's private. They came to see me. They didn't come to get grilled by a psychiatrist or hauled in for questioning, or to corrupt me, or to feed me drugs, or to help me kill myself, or to hurt anyone. They came to see me because they're my friends." I had gone too far, the doctor's face flushed with anger at my outburst.

"Jason. You seem a little on edge. Perhaps these friends of yours are not the positive influence you seem to think they are. Sometimes it's hard to recogn..." I stood up and he stopped abruptly.

"No. I have spent months in this place letting you convince me of all kinds of things about myself that are not true. You don't know me, you don't care, and I would like to leave now."

"But Jason..." The doctor also stood up and reached out to put his hand on my shoulder, "Listen son..." I shrugged him off and shouted at him to leave me alone, that I was sick of him, of this place, that there was nothing wrong with me, that I hadn't done anything wrong. "You need to calm down Jason, this could be a great opportunity for a breakthrough here, all this anger is a good sign, it means you're turning things outwards, maybe even getting ready to let someone in to help." We stood, facing each other and I saw the doctor's moustache twitch, a little tic he had at the corner of his top lip. It happened again.

"Tomorrow, you'll get a phone call. The police will tell you to release me, that the real criminal has been found and that this was all a mistake. I don't care what you think, this is not a delusion, you can't just give me some lithium and strap me to the bed again. I'm done with that." I turned to leave but when I opened the door there were the same two orderlies standing outside.

"Come back into my office Jason. The police already called. They said there had been a lawyer poking around, someone hired by Henry Hadley it seems. They also said he had been in touch with that young girl's sister and that now she's missing. You might think you've been very clever son but let me tell you this now... We're not finished."

CHAPTER FOURTEEN

The waitress at the Husky café came over to refill the coffees and asked if they wanted anything else.

"No, thanks. We're good." Darren smiled at her and she gave him a little wink and sauntered as she went back to the counter.

"I saw that." Rose laughed as Darren blushed. It was funny that she was seeing all these things about him that she'd never noticed before. How he locked the little finger on his right hand around each of the fingers of his left hand in turn, how women in cafés and gas bars seemed to stare at him an awful lot and how most of the time he paid no attention to them.

"What?" He looked at her, totally deadpan.

"She was flirting, she likes you, maybe you should go to college here, eh?"

"Really? I didn't notice. Anyway, what does it matter?" He sipped his coffee and looked away, out the window, craning to see if Jason was heading their way, he was an hour late, which they knew was a possibility given the sneaking out and all.

"It has to start mattering some time."

"Eh?"

"Dating, and all that stuff. Sara wouldn't want you to just, I don't know, carry a torch or whatever the phrase is. She'd want you to be happy, even if she couldn't be."

"I don't follow. I'm just not interested in that particular waitress is all."

"Not that particular one, or none?"

"Alright, no waitress that I have ever come across, who may or may not have winked at me is of interest to me. Happy?" He was hoping that

Jason would just arrive already, Rose was starting to annoy him with her teasing, she was so smart but so incredibly dumb sometimes.

"And no one else?"

"Look, Rose, just leave it. Yeah? We have other things to think about, more important things. If you want to get your precious Jason out of jail then we need to concentrate, alright?" He regretted snapping at her as soon as he finished and he saw her bite her lip and look away.

"Fine." She kept her head turned away from him and blinked, trying to keep any tears from falling. They sat in silence, watching the people coming and going in a slow wave for the next half hour. Everyone seemed to just be passing through, the waitresses not really doing anything but making small talk about the road conditions, the weather, how a hot summer was predicted.

The guy at the table by the door asked the waitress if she had a map he could borrow for a minute and she grabbed one from behind the counter, leaning forwards a little too much as she handed it to him over his shoulder. Darren saw the guy grimace as her breast touched the back of his neck. He turned to Rose, "Something's not right. He's too late."

"It's not like there's much we can do though right? They're not just going to release him and let him come with us, even if the police do reopen the case."

"But why? If they arrest your dad then surely they can just let Jason go. He'd tell them he was meeting us here, he'd be here now."

"Excuse me, are you Rose?" The guy who had asked for the map had wandered over and stood by the table looking down at them both.

"Ah, sorry, who are you?"

"Did Jason send you? Is he OK?" Rose jumped up, and Darren motioned at her to be quiet.

"Who are you?"

"I'm Jason's friend, he sent me to tell you he can't make it. He has to stay at the hospital for a bit longer, he's not well you see."

"But, we saw him yesterday, he's fine, he's supposed to be released and come home with us." Darren took hold of Rose's hand across the table. He might not be happy that Rose and Jason clearly had a connection but something wasn't right about what this kid was saying. Who was he anyway? He still hadn't even told them his name. Darren wondered if he was one of the other crazies from the hospital.

"Sorry, I should've introduce myself properly," the guy squeezed in beside Rose and took her hand. "Lewis, Jason's friend from the hospital. I work up there sometimes and I offered to help him out, he said to ask you what the story was as he couldn't really explain last night when I went to see him. I think he'd had another one of his 'turns' and the docs had to shoot him full of Dilaudid again." Lewis grinned at Darren and propped his elbows on the table, his chin on his hands. "So, what's going on, why'd Jason get himself so worked up?"

Rose started telling Lewis about how they were going to clear Jason's name, that they were from Pitcher Creek. Darren kept quiet but studied the other man's face, trying to work out why there was something off about him. He interrupted Rose.

"I'm sorry, what did you say you do up at the hospital?"

"I'm a medical assistant." Lewis looked from Rose to Darren and back again. "Problem?"

"Which school did you go to?"

"UVic, sorry, the University of Victoria. Out on the Island."

"And, when did you graduate?"

"Darren? What're you..."

"Jason sent you? While he was having a 'funny turn' he told you where to meet us, what we looked like, and to ask what we were up to? No, that's not right, something else is going on here." Darren nodded at Rose, "Let's go, I don't like this."

"Hey, Darren, what's wrong? I felt sorry for the guy is all, hell I didn't know his friends were crazy too!" Lewis followed Rose and Darren back out to the parking lot, and Darren opened the passenger door to the truck telling Rose to get in. She was shaking her head, not quite sure what was going on.

"Look, no offence, but you seem a little young to have even started college, let alone graduated from med school and started working in some offender's institution for crazy people."

"Well, hey, can I help it if I have good genes? I worked my ass off for years and you're not the first person to question me. Everyone assumes I'm only a kid, my friend, not just you. Alright? Now, I'm here to help Jason and, frankly, you have some anger management issues. Jason asked me to come and I said I would. Anyway, it sounds like you could do with my help, Rose over there is clearly depressed, maybe even bipolar, who knows, and do you know how to manage a psychotic episode? Hmm?"

"You leave her alone, and Jason. They're not crazy, none of us are crazy, you're the one pretending to be a doctor when you're only a teenager, I reckon you're just another loony from the lodge, cackling because you're off your meds, isn't it time you went back for afternoon tea and some shock therapy?"

Lewis lunged at Darren, almost as if a current had been sent through him and he slammed Darren against the side of the truck, then pounded his fist into the older boy's gut. Rose tried to open the door but the weight of both boys kept it firmly closed, she scrambled across the front seat to open the driver side door.

Darren straightened up and kneed Lewis in the groin, pushing him down by the shoulders. As Lewis was doubled over Darren punched him hard in the jaw, his knuckles scraping against the skin and stubble. Lewis staggered backwards and then he saw Rose coming round the side of the truck, the knife in her hand.

"Jesus Christ. You are a pair," he wheezed and raised his hands a little as he backed away, "a regular Bonnie and Clyde, eh?" They watched him skulk off into the trees behind the Husky and when he had gone Darren heard Rose drop the knife.

He ran over to her as she fell to her knees. "I can't... Darren, what did he want? What did he want with us?" Darren held her head against his chest, stroking her hair. She felt so small, so birdlike, the clawing hands at his back, clutching at his jacket, clinging to him. He wanted to tell her he loved her but he knew it was stupid, that all she thought about now was Jason, that they would head off to college together, get married, have super-smart kids, be happy, while he just stayed in Pitcher Creek, drinking and dealing pot, but she had said his name, she was clinging to him and he held onto her, and onto hope. He had to. Even if she didn't love him back, even if she never would, he would still help her.

"Let's go to the hospital, they'll probably not let us in but we can try." Darren helped Rose into the car, wrapped the blanket around her and used the edge of it to wipe her face gently. She was so pale, her lips just a thin line, almost purple, so cold it scared him. He stashed the knife in the glove compartment but she didn't see. Rose just stared out at nothing, lost to him.

They passed their motel on the way back to Arbutus Lodge and Darren gathered Rose's things from her room, leaving the key on top of the television. He had lied, telling her he had paid for two rooms when he had actually just slept in the truck. He was used to it, old potato-sacking stuffed into the window to keep out most of the cold air. Rose didn't seem to notice him as he brought her bag back and placed it between them on the seat of the cab. She hadn't spoken since the parking lot and neither had Darren, not really knowing if there was anything he could say to make her feel better. He swung the truck around and headed back onto the road and in the direction of the hospital where there were ostentatious gate posts but no actual gate. Darren just rolled past, crunching the gravel under the truck's wheels. He noticed the giant arbutus trees perfectly spaced in front of the brick building. The neatness of everything troubled him.

"Rose, I'm going to see if I can find Jason, OK? Stay here, and keep down, you'll look suspicious but I might be able to just sneak in if I pretend I'm one of them." She glanced at him wide-eyed, as if she were about to speak but then she just bit her lip and slid down in the seat.

Darren turned to open the door but then looked back at Rose, pausing long enough that she raised her head to meet his gaze. Embarrassed now, he lowered his eyes and said "I love you, you know, even if it means nothing to you, I love you, and I just want you to be happy. If it's with Jason then OK. I'll still love you."

He jumped out and walked off into the building before Rose could respond and she sat in the cab, stunned, she wanted to follow him, wanted to tell him that as confused as she was about everything she had realised back in the parking lot as she scrabbled for that knife and ran out to help him that she felt the same, that the thought of him being hurt was as horrific as everything else that had happened to her. She had realised so much in just the last half hour, as she stole glances at him, his brow furrowed as he gripped the wheel. She knew she felt safe with him and that she had been so wrong about him for so long.

Picking up that knife again, in anger, but fully prepared to use it this time, she had shucked off one skin and felt cold and exposed but also alive to sensation. She felt ready and it was all she could do to stay down in the truck while she imagined Darren wandering the halls of this prison, searching for Jason, all for her.

CHAPTER FIFTEEN

Darren kept his head down as he walked through the lobby. The nurse at reception glanced up but then went back to her paperwork. They all looked the same to her, these dirty-handed boys. Molesters, thieves, liars, and rapists the lot of them. What was the point in trying to fix them when they were all the same underneath? Except for Dr Laurence of course, he was such a fine man, so intelligent, with all his books and those conferences he went to. She conjured up an image of the psychiatrist, with his debonair moustache and silver hair, and she stared off into the middle distance with a smile. Allowing herself a little daydream she imagined sneaking into the doctor's office and lying in wait on the couch for him, and she had to loosen the neck of her tunic and use some boy's file to fan herself, hoping no one had seen her flush at the thought.

Lewis Barker ran into the lobby and she shook her head, that boy was trouble, even more than the others. She could spot a con artist a mile off, after all she'd married one and learnt her lesson the hard way. She buzzed through to summon a couple of orderlies to grab Lewis, having received a note an hour ago to get the boy to go to Dr Laurence's office. She hoped it meant he was leaving like he was supposed to, some rich parents paying off some judge somewhere. She'd seen it all before. The kid was trouble, even if he wormed his way into everyone else's good favour with his money and charm, she could see through him. She had a knack for that kind of thing without needing all that fancy college education.

The nurse watched the two orderlies saunter through the inner corridor, one of them, a new guy, waved at her through the glass and she threw him a stern look. They were always trouble at first, these men who thought they could just roll in and swagger around, not realising that the nurses ran this place, that it was their hard work that kept things going around here, kept the boys in line.

The phone rang. It was that damn art therapist again, calling from her studio for the third time in an hour. Janice asked once more if Lewis was back yet. "Not seen him, sorry." She hung up. No amount of crayoning was going to sort that kid out so why should she bother telling her the truth. If he was leaving then what difference did it make if he painted a pretty picture first?

A few minutes later Janice called Ellen Carter, the person she knew best on the board of trustees for the lodge. She told her about the situation with Lewis, how she didn't feel, in her professional opinion, that he was ready to be released. Ellen, very politely but firmly noted that Janice was really just there to help to get the kids to open up. It was not her responsibility to assess them, she said, and any decisions about fitness were for Dr Laurence's to make. Janice had not wanted to mention what she'd seen in the café that day but she was worried about both Jason and Lewis. She told Ellen her suspicions and, a few minutes later, Ellen had promised to call the other board members and assured her that they would work something out.

"He's going to be released today though, whenever he gets back."

"I'll call Dr Laurence myself and ask him to delay things, tell him there's a mix-up with paperwork or something and you keep an eye out for the boy if you can."

Janice rang off and picked up her glass, ready to drain the last few mouthfuls. She stopped. She needed to get a grip on herself. How could she help these kids if she was a mess most of the time. She stared out of the window and saw the old arbutus tree waving the tips of its branches just above the perimeter hedge. There was new growth this year. Perhaps she should take Jason out one day with an easel and see how his self-portrait looked now.

This place was a real maze. Darren had already ended up wandering into the dining hall by mistake and had tried to open several doors that were apparently off-limits. He was thankful that many of the other kids here looked so lost, sad as it was. Finally he ended up back outside, near some fountain where he sat on the low wall trying to work out what to do. He couldn't just go back in. He'd end up going mad just trying to find Jason and they were sure to lock him up. He imagined that the place was closed down pretty strictly each night anyway and it was already going dark. Some of the lights had begun to be turned on and Darren realised that he could see into a few of the rooms at the lodge.

He scanned his eyes over the exterior of the building, working his way down from the third floor where it seemed there were lots of orderlies going around closing blinds. The second floor looked like it housed the dorms, bunks up against some of the window. On the lower level several of the windows were already dark, the blinds closed but the one right in front of him was brightly lit and Darren could see a woman sitting at a desk, a glass of wine in her hand. He saw her stand and empty it into the sink, following it with the remaining contents of the bottle nearby. Her shoulders slumped for a second and then she put her palms over her eyes for a moment.

The woman turned suddenly and looked out of the window as if she knew he was out there staring. Darren was unnerved but he knew he was safe from view. The lights in the room would make sure that all Janice saw was her own reflection. He was pretty much invisible as he sat here in the diminishing light of the day.

She walked over to the window, touching her cheek to the cold glass. Then she ducked down out of view for a moment and when she stood back up she was holding something but Darren couldn't quite make it out. As she fiddled around with the object he saw it take shape as an easel and a few moments later, paintbrush in hand, she was back staring into the glass. She couldn't be painting the view outside but it was disconcerting for Darren as she was looking right at him without seeing him. He sat and watched as she moved her eyes back and forth between window and canvas and although he couldn't see the painting take shape he imagined the sketching in of her hair, her oval eyes and the faint lines of her mouth. Darren stood up and moved closer, feeling like a voyeur but wanting to see Janice's impromptu self-portrait.

As he approached the window he saw the door open to the art room and watched with apprehension as Lewis walked in. The woman's body froze, her hand still halfway to the canvas with the brush as she'd seen Lewis enter the room in the reflection. She turned and stared at Lewis who started shouting something at her, each word hitting her almost physically as she moved back against the window. Darren watched for another second or two as Lewis walked closer towards the woman. Then, not quite knowing where he was going, Darren ran back into the lodge and tried to find the art room.

The door was closed and the blind pulled down but he had heard shouting and a quick glance at the nameplate told him he was in the right place. 'Janice Toews - Art Therapy.' Darren shoved the door open and saw Lewis and the woman over at the window. He had his hand at her throat but span around at the sound of the door and Janice took her opportunity, hitting him over the head with her water jar, splashing pale red liquid over everything. Lewis was stunned for a second and staggered to the left, allowing Janice to run over to Darren at the door.

"You should leave. I'll keep him here. Go and call the police."

"Who are you? You're not one of my students."

"Does it matter?" Darren looked her in the eye and she ran past him to summon help. Lewis had righted himself and was now leaning on a desk in the middle of the room glaring at Darren.

Enunciating each word carefully, his top lip pulled back and teeth showing, Lewis snarled at Darren. "What the hell are you doing here?" There was no response, Darren just stared back at him trying to stay calm and keep the boy contained until help came. He had no idea if Lewis was armed with anything but his fists and a palpable rage.

Lewis surveyed the room, looking for a weapon maybe, or perhaps just a way out other than through the door that Darren was currently blocking. There were sounds of running and shouting heading their way down the corridor and Lewis began backing into a corner of the room, ducking behind some easels as he went. Darren could just see glimpses of him as he retreated but he didn't want to follow the boy and leave the door accessible. Then, Lewis flung open a fire exit at the back of the studio and ran out. Giving chase Darren saw him scramble through the hedge just as the art teacher returned along with several orderlies. They followed Darren's directions and crashed into the shrubbery themselves, luckily not stopping to question who Darren was.

Janice moved back into the studio and called him inside, shutting the door after him. "Thank you. I know what he's capable of." She rubbed her neck and looked distractedly at Darren, trying to work out who he was. "You're not in art therapy with me, are you?" Janice was well aware that her drinking had started affecting her memory and so she had the awful feeling that this boy was in one of her classes but was unrecognisable to her. Darren shook his head though and she felt relieved but still curious. "So why did you just happen to be passing and rush in to help?"

"I'm looking for someone. I saw you from outside. I'm not one of the... inmates here, or whatever you call them. We were supposed to be meeting someone and he didn't show so I came looking for him and that guy, Lewis, right, well we had our own, ah, encounter with him earlier today."

"Here?"

"No, just down the road, we were waiting for Ja... er, someone, but he arrived instead. He said that he worked here." As Darren spoke he remembered Rose, waiting in the car, in the dark and cold and he knew he should get back to her. He wasn't going to find Jason in this place, everything was locked down.

"Who are you looking for? Can I help?" Janice blinked at Darren and frowned, wondering if he'd meant to say Jason. She had just been attacked and yet here she was offering to help them. Darren wondered if she was drunk but then he felt he was being unfair, and more than a little hypocritical considering his own behaviour in recent weeks. Maybe she could help. He needed to find Jason quickly so he could get back to Rose.

"We were supposed to meet a friend a few hours ago. Jason Forrest. He's here for something he didn't do and we just want to take him home."

"Jason?" Janice scanned Darren's face in surprise, was this another boy from Jason's past, someone before Henry? Somehow he just didn't fit, his paint-flecked pants and thick overshirt. But then, what did Janice really know about any of her students. "Jason's not well I'm afraid. Dr Laurence put him in the isolation ward after he started suffering delusions yesterday. He wouldn't let me see him today. He's been under a lot of pressure lately so perhaps it's true, perhaps not. To be honest, I was quite relieved to get him away from Lewis."

"He was fine yesterday, he was with us." Again, Darren thought about Rose. "Where's this ward? I'll go and find him, check on him."

"You can't just walk in there!"

"No? I just walked in here didn't I?" Janice said she'd go with him, maybe they could just get in or perhaps she could pretend to be delivering Darren to the ward himself. He laughed when she said he might need to look lost and depressed. "I've been practicing that for years."

CHAPTER SIXTEEN

My heart was bouncing in my chest, a crimson balloon careering against my ribcage, rapidly deflating, and wheezing all the way. I might die in here, this cell, so bright and white it made me see things that I knew were not really there, couldn't be there. I was trying to hold onto the idea that my mind was just filling the vacuum with noise, that I hadn't actually gone mad.

I tried to sit still but my body was on fire. I needed to move. The anxiety was making me twitch, making my skin crawl. That last injection had cut through my skin and filled me with boiling rage. I couldn't breathe. There was no air in here, no way out. They thought I was lying, they had locked me in to hide the truth, they knew the truth, maybe they knew I wasn't lying, I didn't know what was real any more.

I tried counting to ten, breathing deeply, trying to calm my racing heart but the sound of my own thoughts turned into a dull drone in my head and everything slowed down. The floor was soft. I lay down and hugged my knees to my chest. I would die in here, and everyone would think good riddance to another bad kid. I felt my body sinking into the floor, my nose and mouth covered over. I screamed but I heard no noise and then the whiteness turned black and I stopped struggling.

"Did you hear that?" Janice grabbed Darren's arm and rushed him forward, past the ward nurse who shouted after them and then ran out from behind her desk, her plimsolls flapping against the lino. Her modest calf-length skirt slowed her progress as she chased them. She had just come on shift and had been checking for an admission call for this boy the teacher was bringing in when some screaming had made them all jump. She hated being on the isolation ward. The rooms were still not sound-proofed enough for her liking. Screams and shouts all day, like an animal shelter where they all set each other off but none of them could just be taken out back and shot to shut them up. She thought back to her old job in the maternity ward in Hope Hospital. All the little screams and shouts there were happy, for the most part. She hated being here in Fernley, in this god awful place.

Janice and Darren were way in front of her and had already found the room with Jason's name scribbled on the white patient card outside. Darren was trying the door but she knew it was locked, they all were. As she caught up with them Janice demanded she unlock it.

"I can't just do that! That kid's in there for a reason, he might kill us all if I open that door." The boy glared at her and she took a step back.

"That's my friend in there and I want you to let him out. Now." He had spoken in a low voice, firm, on the edge of threatening.

The nurse folded her arms across her chest and pouted a little to one side, then she shook her head. "Not unless Dr Laurence tells me to."

"Fine. I'll open it myself." Darren walked down the corridor to where there was a fire extinguisher attached to the wall and he started yelling to Jason that it was OK, that he'd be out soon and it would all be over.

"Stop it! Stop! What are you, you can't do that!" The nurse tried to move in front of Darren as he raised the fire extinguisher to smash it into the door. She was shaking as she handed him the keys and then she ran off back to the desk, "I'm calling the doctor, you should all be locked up! Loons, the lot of you - no wonder society's gone to hell like it has."

Janice and Darren ignored the muttering of the woman as she scurried away and Janice stepped into the room first, looking down at Jason, curled into the corner, his back to them, his face tucked out of view. "Jason? It's Janice." She padded across to the prone figure slowly, talking quietly. "Jason, it's OK, we're going to get you out alright." She put a hand out to touch his shoulder but she could hear him mumbling and so she stopped and listened.

"I didn't, I didn't do it, I wouldn't, please, please, I'll die in here, there's no air, it's all gone, it's all gone."

"Jason, can you hear me? We have to leave now. Can you stand?" She called Darren over and together they rolled Jason into an upright position then lifted him and started back out of the room. As they carried him, one arm over Janice's shoulder, one over Darren's, Jason carried on mumbling.

"Henry, where's Henry, where's my Henry..." Darren looked over the top of Jason's slumped head at Janice, confused and she looked back at him. They were both trying to work out what the other knew.

"His boyfriend. You knew?"

Darren smiled to himself, a weight added and lifted all at once. "Well, that explains things." Janice wasn't quite sure why he was laughing, this whole thing made no sense any more. They carried Jason down the stairs at the back of the ward, out onto a fire escape and down to ground level.

Once outside they half carried half dragged Jason to the car park and Darren left him there with Janice while he went to get the truck and Rose. When he got back to the front of the building, though, the truck wasn't there and he span around frantically trying to trace tracks in the gravel but it was impossible. Had Rose taken the truck somewhere, where would she go? Perhaps someone had seen her and she had jumped into the driver's seat and reversed out, scared to be asked why she was there. Darren thought about her clutching the wheel and knew she couldn't have gone far. Did she even know how to put the truck in reverse, smart as she was? That truck had a mind of its own and even to start it needed some feel for the spirit of the thing. He turned to run back to the staff parking lot when a green pickup skidded through the front gates and stopped near to him. Janice opened the door and called to him to get in.

"Rose has gone! She can't have taken the truck, I only taught her to drive for two minutes and she was terrified, there's no way she drove off in that thing." He looked over Jason at Janice and she nodded.

"Lewis has her. Jerry, one of the orderlies looking for him, said that he saw Lewis drive off in a blue pickup, Alberta plates. I figured it must be yours. God knows where he's going."

Jason was propped up between them as Janice looked over her shoulder and span the truck around to get them back out of the lodge's grounds. There were boys rushing in from all over to head to the dining hall and Janice was terrified she'd hit one of them but she steered them clear of the gates and shot out onto the road again.

Darren thought about Rose, how he'd told her to wait in the cab, that she'd be safer there. He wondered if she'd remember the knife in the glove compartment, if she'd use it. He knew Lewis would, recalling the feral look in his eyes as he'd lunged at Darren, the wildness of his fists. Jason's head had flopped onto Darren's shoulder and he tried to prop him back up but then just held him there to stop him rolling forward.

"What did they do to him?"

"Some kind of sedative I guess, I'd rather they didn't give them such things. He's just drifting in and out. Not making much sense really."

"Lewis said he was having an episode and you said he was delusional, how would he know that unless he'd seen him yesterday before he came to see us at the gas station?"

"Lewis is a devious boy, lots of the staff here love him because he can be a real charmer when he wants. He probably did get to see Jason yesterday. Maybe that's what made Jason have a fit, who knows. Anyway, we have to find Lewis before he does something awful, he's quite obsessed with Jason."

"And he has Rose."

Jason was whimpering slightly and he tried to raise his head, the cold air from the dash firing towards him and waking him from the stupor.

"Where do you think they'll go?" Darren asked.

"I've no idea. Lewis has been in detention for years; he's nowhere to go other than home."

"He talked about med school in Victoria, he pretended to be a doctor and was talking about drugs. Would he hurt Rose?"

"It's... it's possible. I'm sorry. He's just a kid who... We need to find them before anything happens. We'll head south and see if we can catch up with them."

"He'll go home." Jason's words were slurred and Darren held up his head to try to get him to focus.

"What did you say Jason?"

"He'll take her home, he wants to make things better, for everyone. He's looking after me. Putting things right."

Darren and Janice both stared at Jason who was still drifting in and out of consciousness as the effects of the sedatives wore off. His heart had stopped racing, if anything it felt like it had slowed so much that his blood was not even moving through him, he was just running on fear, struggling to pull the thoughts out of his mind, to form sentences.

"Jason, what is Lewis going to do?" Janice asked him quietly, her eyes still fixed on the road ahead as the truck rattled along well over the speed limit. "What did he say to you?"

There was no answer and so Darren turned and slapped Jason across the face. The boy was startled and suddenly awake and Darren took hold of his shoulders and shook him, his head flopping back and forth. "Where is he taking Rose?" he screamed at him and Janice put out a hand to stop Darren.

"Don't! He's terrified, let him come to."

"We don't have time, if he hurts Rose, if he does anything to her I swear I'll kill him."

"Pitcher Creek," Jason whispered the words without opening his eyes and Darren tried to help him hold his head up. "He said he'd fix it. He thinks he's protecting me, making it better."

Janice spoke to Darren, calmly and quietly. "Look out for a payphone and then start explaining. The whole story Darren. Everything, and I mean everything. If I'm driving all the way to Alberta I have time to hear it."

Part Four

CHAPTER ONE

The blue Ford was parked on a logging road just off highway one, two people inside, a man and a woman. There was shouting coming from the cab as the truck driver approached to see if they needed help. He had been following the pickup for about five kilometres, had seen them hit the faun and swerve off momentarily. The front of the truck kept swinging back out, little shards of rubber flicking out across Wilf's windscreen up into the mountain air. It was sad about the faun, especially as these kids had just left it by the roadside to suffer. Wilf had taken care of it though, but he sure as hell wasn't taking it home for the boys to laugh at. He could hear their jeers now 'Another big buck Wilf!?' Bastards. He'd stick to the fishing this season he thought as he walked up to the parked truck.

"You folks alright in there? Looked like a bit of a nasty blow, you got a spare?" He presumed that the couple were having some kind of fight about safe driving or some such thing. They looked young, probably not married long, but long enough to realise their mistake he reckoned. They hadn't opened the doors yet but the passenger side window was down a little and the man heard Lewis tell Rose not to say anything. Ah, he thought, they were likely drug-runners from Grand Forks, heading up to one of the ski villages to sell their haul to the yuppies on vacation. Damn hippies. "If you're alright I'll just be heading on my way, but I'll give you a hand changing that wheel if you need it." Wilf might not like these young wasters but he sure as heck wasn't going to leave them in the mountains to freeze to death. It was a good forty clicks to the next town. The man stepped out of the cab and walked round the front of the truck.

"That's kind of you. I'm afraid we've no jack and, huh, the, er, little lady there won't lift a finger to help. You know how it is, eh?" There was something off about this kid, he looked about twelve but then they all did to Wilf, even with the shadow of stubble on the boy's face. He knew when he was being mocked too, this guy didn't talk like this back home. He was putting it on but Wilf could tell Lewis was educated, moneyed. He was just playing at being the outdoorsman, his wife the same no doubt. He hadn't really seen her face, the poor girl looked pretty shaken, but she was probably the same age as his eldest girl, maybe nineteen, twenty, one of those city haircuts to be sure, all uneven, like his Gracie's was now. A damn mess if you asked him.

"There's a jack in the truck, I'll go grab it." He turned round and walked back to his truck. He was always spotting folks at the side of the road, too stupid to prepare for things like this. He fished out his tools and turned, surprised to see the kid right behind him, like a damn cougar. "Hey, what the hell you doin'? Sneaking up on me."

"Just seeing if I could help." Lewis was looking into the truck's cab, he saw the man's lunch sitting on the dash; what looked like thick sandwiches wrapped in waxed paper, and a thermos. Then his eyes wandered over to the passenger's seat and he saw the rifle, propped in the foot well but poking its head out into view, a real relic but no doubt still serviceable. He'd let the man help him change the tire but the knife in his jacket pocket would come into play afterwards. He hoped the gun had rounds in it as Rose's money was running out, what with gas and food. Besides, he didn't have time to stop and find somewhere to buy ammunition. He just wanted to track down those on his list and get revenge for Jason. Then he'd show him who loved him more. What had Henry done, with all his money and privilege, his lawyers and silly letters. He'd just left Jason to rot at the lodge while he screwed some drummer at his precious jazz club. Lewis would make things safe for Jason, he'd make those people who had hurt him pay.

CHAPTER TWO

Cassidy Winlaw pushed the stroller into the West Shore Credit Union and thanked Bill for holding the door for her. They both joined the line, Cassidy asking Bill how her sister was, if they'd heard anything yet about Rose? Matt McReedy, the creepy kid who worked at the movie palace, walked in, stinking the place up with popcorn. Rebecca blew bubbles with her own spit and Cassidy hoped she would stay quiet while she talked to John about giving her an extension on their loan.

McReedy had passed Bill's truck outside in the parking lot, but didn't think too much about it until he overheard Darren's dad talking about how both kids were still missing and that Jane had just taken to her bed, disconsolate. Matt's dad had asked him about Darren and then smacked him round the head for being cheeky when he said that he had no comment and declined to be interviewed. Julian McReedy, editor of the Pitcher Creek Journal, had found out that Rose's house had been searched yesterday, though his source at the station didn't know what they found. His source also told him that Andy had been making some calls to the school. Something was afoot in Pitcher Creek and Julian wanted to be the first to know. However, everyone in town knew that his secret source was just Dave who'd tell you anything if you spent long enough at the police station's front desk plying him with coffee and Reese's Pieces. Dave was partial to the orange ones. Whatever the news, McReedy figured everyone would know soon enough. After all it wasn't like anything exciting ever happened in Pitcher Creek, aside from that whole thing with Sara and the Forrest kid, and everyone had seen something was up with that boy long before that mess.

Rob MacGowan was at the counter, flirting with the union clerk, Mel as she tried to concentrate on counting out hundred dollar bills. She kept being blinded by the union's strip lights bouncing off Rob's shiny cufflinks, little golf tees, expensive no doubt. Mel remembered when she had piano lessons at his house and he used to try to put her off by making fart noises with his hand at his armpit. It had been pretty sad that he hadn't even come back for Judy's funeral and Mel wondered why he was here now, what could be more important. She saw his posture stiffen as Bill walked in with Cassidy and Rebecca. Did Rob even know them? The dark look he gave Bill suggested there was some history there but he didn't say anything, just turned back to her, a dopey grin on his face which he clearly thought was charming.

When the woman walked in, sporting oversized sunglasses against the low winter sun, her short brown hair sticking out from underneath her hat, no one in the bank really took a second look. She walked over to the empty customer service desk and propped herself against it, her arms wrapped tight around her. Mel figured she was some tourist passing through, maybe going home after ski season and wanting some cash for gas. Or a student on some field trip, researching boredom in a small town. Rose stared across at the line of people she knew, penned in by the chrome markers and ropes.

Moments earlier, Rose had watched Bill and Cassidy walk past the truck. Lewis had parked outside her mum's store but she hadn't told him that, not knowing if her mom was inside there or not. Deep in conversation, Bill had touched Cassidy's arm lightly, playfully, oblivious to the presence of his son's truck and the two watchful pairs of eyes staring out from it. She had flinched as they approached and walked past and Lewis had asked, "That him then?"

He checked the knife in his pocket, fiddled with the rifle he had stolen from Wilf and turned to Rose. "Who else? That your mom?"

"No! God no!" Rose had been trying to stay calm, collected, but everything suddenly became very real and she mumbled quietly, without making eye contact. "Lewis, you don't have to do this. It doesn't help anyone, it doesn't help Jason." She thought she'd cry again but their road-trip had drained her of tears, of energy for anything it seemed. It was all pointless now.

"It does help him! It's all for him! I explained already, why don't you get it, you stupid stupid bitch!" His voice had started out quiet but rose to a yell. "He needs to know someone loves him, really loves him and will help, not just pretend to like Henry does. Now, who else?"

"No one." She folded her arms but Lewis carried on staring at her.

"Fine, they all go. No one in this town deserves to live after what they've done to my Jason. We'll get Bill first though, just to make sure."

Lewis laughed and Rose closed her eyes as he said "You should be thanking me, not trying to stop me."

She risked a glance at Lewis who was breathing deeply and methodically, gathering himself together. She whispered "Jason wouldn't want this you know." Lewis whipped around to face her, his breathing fast again now and his nostrils flared and mouth set so his lips turned pale before he spat the words out at her.

"What do you know about what he wants! You had months to help him, you and your disgusting sister but you just lied, all of you, so now you're going to make things better, you're going to help him by helping me, alright? I'll protect him, I will make things safe for him. Then he'll see who loves him more." Lewis looked down at the gun, resting between his knees, and he went over the plan again. "We'll pretend it's a robbery, then there'll be no connection to Jason. You just keep quiet until I need you. Then you'll show me where his parents live. Let's go."

Mel saw him first. She was staring over Rob's shoulder as Lewis walked through the door, seconds after Rose. He pulled the mask down on his face and raised the gun. She scrambled for the alarm button but having never used it she panicked and just screamed. Everyone turned at that point and some people instinctively fell to the ground, huddling together in fear.

Rose crept behind the desk and slumped down. What could she do? He had been watching from the truck. There'd been no time to warn anyone. She heard Lewis yell at Mel to start pulling money out of the drawers and bag it up, then she heard Rob MacGowan shouting and the first shot, then another and another and soon, silence and she still couldn't move. Then Rebecca began wailing.

A hand reached out to grab Rose and Lewis yanked her onto her feet, dragging her towards the door. She tried not to look to her right at the huddle of people, bewildered, unable to move even to help one another, as well as those that would never move again.

Lewis pushed her in front of him, telling her to open the door. He tried to keep his eyes on everyone, the gun shaking in his hands as he reloaded. The bag of cash was lying untouched on the counter, sprayed with blood. Mel had crawled into the back room out of sight and was wiping her face, her hair. Rob had been just in front of her, and Bill, and Cassidy, and the kid from the high-school. Why hadn't the guy just taken the money? Why shoot at people? This was Pitcher Creek, this did not happen here, it was a safe town. She picked up the phone to call the station, then heard another shot but it was muffled somehow, not like the others, then another followed and her hand trembled as she heard

Dave answer, his voice calm, steady. "We know Mel It'll be OK. Andy's on his way. Just stay where you are out of sight."

FALL

Rose held Darren's hand as they stood by the side of the grave. She remembered her sister's coffin being lowered into the ground nearby, Darren bending to pick up some dirt, throwing it over the plate. She had not been here when he had done the same for his dad, and her mom had not done the wreath that time.

"You didn't have to come."

"I know, but it's important. He was still your dad, whatever else." She stood up on her toes and kissed him just below his ear, on the little scar he got when trying to clean rust from under the truck. This was the first time she had accompanied him but the warm summer sun seemed to make it easier to forgive Bill, or perhaps just harder to imagine the darkness of last winter.

"Have you heard from Jason and Henry?"

"Yeah, Jason sent me a birthday card, sixteen little roses he had painted. It's cute. He got a job at the club, serving drinks, can you imagine?" She laughed, thinking about Jason leaning across a bar, hearing tales of woe, trying to keep a straight face.

"It's nice they're together, Jason's probably filling the apartment with paintings and Henry with concertos." He looked at Rose as she smiled, seeing the grazing that had turned to a constellation of tiny white scars at her temple. He brushed back her hair and kissed her. He still felt like this wasn't really happening, waking beside her some mornings now, seeing her dark hair spread out across the pillow, hearing the soft sound of her breathing as she shuffled out of sleep and into the day. She nudged him and his thoughts returned to Henry and Jason. "We should visit. Have a road trip, what do you think? Now your exams are done you're free right?"

"Not really, I have to stay and look after mom and Rebecca. It's weird having the nursery in use now and mom's definitely finding things hard going. Rebecca looks more and more like Aunt Cass every day. Oh, and anyway... Andy wants to see me." Rose tried to sound nonchalant but Darren looked concerned.

"Oh? I thought that was all sorted." Darren tried not to think about Lewis pointing the rifle at Rose. He couldn't bear to consider her terror in that moment, realising Lewis had no need of her anymore and that as he aimed the gun that last time he had not hesitated in firing, only to have the rifle explode in his hand. Darren squeezed Rose's hand a little tighter. She knew what was going through his mind so she smiled reassuringly and pushed the thought of the explosion and the piercing shards of metal from her mind. She had been so lucky that Wilf never cleaned that old gun.

"It's not that. No, all that stuff's fine. It's just, well, Andy was wondering about me replacing Dave at the front desk when he retires. He says it would be nice to have someone who'll spend less of the department's budget on coffee and maybe be able to keep a secret or two."

"And, what, you're thinking about it, but what about college?"

"Well, I might have to re-do some exams and I can start training for desk stuff and work while I wait for colleges to get back to me. I could be in Castlegar next year, assuming that's where we're still headed?" She smiled at Darren and pulled an envelope out of her pocket. She'd seen him put it in the glove compartment a few days ago, where it had remained, unopened, the university crest looming large in the upper right corner. That Darren was so studiously ignoring the letter meant that Rose hadn't pushed him at first, but she couldn't wait any longer and she knew it would be good news, it had to be, he'd worked so hard. She unfolded his hands and placed the envelope in them, moving her hands to his waist and gazing up at him, her eyes wide and her voice soft. "C'mon Darren, open it. Maybe your coyote's in there."

www.ingramcontent.com/pod-product-compliance
Lightning Source LLC
Chambersburg PA
CBHW060421130626
46555CB00005B/2164